Risky WHISKEY

Bohemia Bartenders Mysteries
Book One

LUCY LAKESTONE

Velvet Petal Press
Florida

Copyright © 2020 by Lucy Lakestone

All rights reserved.

No part of this book may be reproduced in any form or by any electronic or mechanical means, including information storage and retrieval systems, without written permission from the author, except for the use of brief quotations in a book review.

Any references to historical events, real people or real places are used fictitiously. Other names, characters and places are products of the author's imagination, and any resemblance they may have to actual events or places or persons, living or dead, is entirely coincidental.

Cover design: Sky Diary Productions

Print ISBN: 978-1-943134-23-6

First edition

Velvet Petal Press, P.O. Box 922, Cocoa, Florida 32923

Learn more about the author at LucyLakestone.com

About the Book

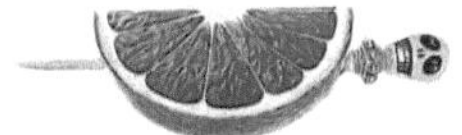

STIRRING UP TROUBLE IN NEW ORLEANS...

Eager to shake up her drinks and her life, mixologist Pepper Revelle jumps at an invitation to join the elite Bohemia Bartenders. Leader Neil thinks she'll be the perfect advance gal for his team at a colorful cocktail convention in her hometown of New Orleans, but the job turns out to be more bananas than a drunk monkey. Setting up the key tasting for their distiller client, she and Neil discover their whiskey has gone dangerously bad. But how? And was this shocking poisoning more than an accident?

As Pepper and Neil try to figure out what happened, keep the drinks flowing and help distiller Dash Reynolds survive the weekend, they find themselves the target of increasingly scary attacks. Maybe it's the danger, or maybe it's the drinks, but Pepper also can't help an inconvenient attraction to cocktail nerd Neil as they stir up trouble and try to figure out who's out to get them — before they're sliced and squeezed like a lemon twist in a Sazerac.

Risky Whiskey is the first book in the Bohemia Bartenders Mysteries, funny whodunits with a dash of romance set in a convivial collective of cocktail lovers, eccentrics and mixologists. These cozy culinary comedies contain a splash of cursing, a hint of heat and shots of laughter, served over hand-carved ice.

For George...
my favorite mixologist,
master of the Manhattan,
and the real storyteller in the family

Chapter One

The hotel was everything I loved about New Orleans: old, beautiful, decadent, redolent of whiskey, hushed in the hallways, and almost loud enough in the lobby to drown out the tuba player who'd been honking in the street for the last thirteen hours.

His jazzy oompahs pumped up my hangover. I hadn't drunk that much, only a Sazerac or three in the Carousel Bar, but the oompahs had kept me up until almost four. Plus, I was short. The cocktails had more of an effect on me.

Worse, I had to get up at eight this morning to meet Dash and Travis Reynolds in the lobby at Dash's request.

Travis was Dash's cousin and the marketing guy for Dash's distillery back in Bohemia, where I co-owned a bar. Dash was the stickler who wanted to go over everything one more time for the whiskey tasting this afternoon. He wanted the event to be perfect. Mostly, I just wanted to go back to bed.

Mr. Tuba made sleep impossible, and my romantic illusions of New Orleans were sorely tested at this time of day. Though spring was warm and soft outside, it was the hour when New Orleans smelled more like wet drunk dog than wine and roses, when weary workers hosed yesterday's effluvia off the streets, and when you weren't sure if the barflies holding down the stools on Bourbon Street were morning-fresh or left over from the night before.

They had classier barflies here at the Hotel Lebeau, especially during the Cocktailia convention. These were professional drinkers: mixologists, distributors, raconteurs. The courtly Dash Reynolds seemed oblivious to them, but the more boisterous Travis let his gaze linger on the women in their short, silky dresses. The gals joined guys in hipster hats who streamed to the portable Bloody Mary bar in the lobby, sponsored by whatever vodka had the biggest marketing budget this year.

"You look nice this morning, Kayanne," Dash said.

"It's Pepper," Travis said.

Dash looked puzzled.

"That's her nickname." Travis shot me a warm smile with enough charm to melt the cheese on a cracker. "Kayanne Pepper. Get it?"

"Well, isn't that cute," Dash replied. I wasn't sure if he was being sarcastic. He obviously hadn't been paying attention last night when I'd given Travis my nickname, but Dash struck me as an absent-minded-professor type.

Nervous, too. Dash's smooth, golden bangs flopped over his forehead, and he pushed them back. He did that a lot, when he wasn't wearing the straw hat he now turned over and over in his hands. He was slender but wiry under his white shirt and tan linen suit, white carnation in the buttonhole.

Dash was a refined kind of handsome, with distracted pale blue eyes and narrow features, more refined than Travis, whose unruly, not-quite-collar-length brown hair complemented broad shoulders, loose clothes, a scruffy chin, sparkling brown eyes, dimples and an easygoing manner.

"OK, Pepper," Dash said. "It sounds like you have everything you need. You sure they'll be here in time?"

"Neil and the rest of the bartenders will be here by one," I told them. "The tasting isn't until four. Plenty of time. I'll have everything set up and ready to go."

"I told you, cuz," Travis said to Dash. "They've got this. All we have to do is show up and let the whiskey talk for itself."

"The whiskey can't do all the talking. *We* have to talk it up. The idea is to get *everyone* talking. Everything rides on this." Dash pushed back his hair again, then put his hat on and stood up straighter, every bit the dashing distiller.

"No worries." Travis grinned and placed a hand on his cousin's shoulder. "I've memorized the name of every blogger and cocktail reporter here. None will escape me."

"That's what I'm afraid of," Dash said dryly, but he appeared mollified, and his smile returned. I got the idea that Travis built all of their sales on charisma while Dash worked his ass off on the technical side.

"Travis is right. We've totally got this," I echoed. "And Neil's cocktails are fantastic."

I tried to sound authoritative, but here was the truth: I was the newest Bohemia Bartender, and I hadn't even met Neil Rockaway in person. I mean, not really. I'd had drinks twice at his bar, The Junction Box, but never when he was there, because my day off from my bar was probably his day off from his. I'd read his kick-ass new cocktail book. But Neil had only just recruited me this past week to join the team.

He'd called me Friday afternoon during a slow shift at Nola, my bar in Bohemia, on Florida's east coast. He'd been in the Caribbean for a meeting at some high-end rum distillery, so we did the deal over the phone. He thought my insider knowledge of New Orleans and Cocktailia would make it easier for me to get some of the ingredients on site that his planner was having trouble ordering.

So maybe I didn't tell him that I hadn't lived in NOLA since I was fourteen. That's when my parents sent me to stay with my aunt in Bohemia Beach, just after Hurricane Katrina rearranged our house. I didn't think that was pertinent information, especially if it might change Neil's mind about hiring me.

I'd heard too much about the Bohemia Bartenders to pass up the chance to join them. A collection of smart mixologists from my Florida town, they traveled to high-end cocktail events to help clients—in this case, Dash and his distillery— and to spread the joy of a well-made drink. They offered just the kind of adventure I desperately needed to up my game.

I wanted to impress Neil. I wanted in. I was good. It's just that nobody knew it yet.

So I'd agreed to be the advance gal in New Orleans, lined up everything we needed and had the booth almost ready to go by one. And then I tried not to barf when I got the call from the team's Girl Friday, Millie, telling me the bartenders' flight was two hours late. Storms in Orlando were the culprit, not unusual for April, but a real pain in the patootie for me.

I was no faker with a shaker, but I couldn't do this whole thing myself, not with the ambitious cocktail menu Neil had designed to show off Dash's new rye and bourbon. And there was no way I could handle solo the thirsty hordes that would descend on the tasting room, which featured dozens of boutique distillers.

I was within a smidgen of freaking out. By the time three o'clock rolled around, the bartenders still weren't here, and we had another problem: The whiskey was missing.

Barnie, who'd been assigned to keep an eye on the stash of

cases in the Reynoldses' storage suite and bring it down for the tasting, hadn't shown up at the ballroom. While Dash and Travis did an interview with a couple of bloggers, I was tasked with finding their employee and getting him and the whiskey downstairs *tout-suite.*

If anything, the lobby was ten times as crowded as it had been this morning, and the scent of liquor seemed to saturate every carpet fiber and ooze out of every pore. These border-line flammable vapors were a signature of Cocktailia, which followed up the Bloody Mary bar with historic cocktails at midmorning workshops, snooty samples at high-end liquor seminars, besotted lunches, the first round of afternoon tastings, and the event I was desperate not to screw up: the boutique distillers' showcase.

As one of my old bartender friends said, you had to "find your level" of inebriation and maintain it, or you'd never survive the week.

Sober and stressed, I did my best to jog through the thronged lobby, jostled by elbows and big purses amid the kaleidoscope of fedoras and tattoos and retro clothes and loud, tipsy laughter.

My phone buzzed against my hip. My own big purse, really an upcycled gray canvas messenger bag that held more stuff than Dr. Who's time machine, guarded my flank like a shield. I stopped so I could dig my phone out of it.

"Crap!" *Where did I put my damn phone?* Then I realized the buzzing against my hip had come from my pocket, not the bag. I fished the phone out—not easily, because the pocket was squeezed into a tight, short, black denim skirt. It went nicely with my scoop-neck white T-shirt and black pinstripe vest, what the Brits called a waistcoat. Which also complemented my black-rimmed cat's-eye glasses and gray-green eyes, which a biology teacher once compared to lichen. You know, that mossy stuff pronounced LIKE-IN? There's nothing *lichen* the moment when someone compares your eyes to a symbiotic organism.

My hair was natural, more caramel than chocolate after going through a brief dark goth phase. It was just long enough that I could pin up most of it if I had to. Today, it was up, with several misbehaving tendrils. I liked to think of my look as "hot professional nerd." Well, pro nerd, anyway.

I checked out the phone message. "They're en route. 10 minutes out," Millie had texted me from back in Bohemia.

"Thank Dionysus." My confidence rebounded as I texted Millie a thumbs-up, stuffed the phone into my bag and began the trot up the wide back stairs of the Hotel Lebeau. My boots echoed on the marble. It was hell trying to get an elevator during the convention, so stairs were optimal. But it was a long way to the third floor.

I gulped air as I finally reached the quiet maze of third-floor hallways. I tried to remember where I was going, wondering if maybe I'd run faster if my curves were a little less curvy. Screw it. I might be short at five-four, but I was proportional, and running sucked. And there were always elevators.

I'd helped the Reynolds boys and Barnie load in last night after the liquor had arrived late. We'd filled the suite with boxes of whiskey and swag, stacks and stacks. Dash and Travis had opted not to store their stuff in one of the spaces offered by the convention for security reasons. It wasn't like anybody here was hurting for booze, but it was a known fact that drunk cocktail people would spirit away anything that wasn't nailed down. I'd been to Cocktailia a couple of times, and I'd seen swag-crazed tourists take a loaded picnic basket off a fanciful display and a feathered showgirl headdress right off a model's head and sprint out the door with it.

"Finally," I murmured as I rounded a corner and found the suite. The gin-branded *do not disturb* sign hung on the door handle.

I knocked to no avail. My key cards were stowed in the badge holder slung around my neck, so I held it out and touched it to the lock. A *snick* and it was open. I bent down the handle, pushed the door and felt the rush of cool hotel-room air whoosh out of the darkness and kiss my face.

"Barnie?" The room was weirdly quiet and dusky and crowded with piles of boxes stacked around the bed, some of them already loaded on a heavy-duty flatbed cart. The shades were drawn, and the TV exuded an eerie flicker.

"Barnie?" I called more loudly. The air-conditioning hummed, and distantly, I heard the tuba mooing. Had Dash's paunchy assistant fallen asleep?

I found the light switch, flipped it and gasped.

Barnie hadn't just fallen asleep. He was asleep on the floor, between the bed and the credenza that held the TV, which was flashing photos of elaborate entrees on the "what's awesome at this hotel" channel. An empty bottle lay next to him.

What the hell?

"Barnie!" OK, this time I might have shouted. We were on the brink of disaster, and he was drunker than a jilted groom.

He didn't stir.

Just then my phone rang, and I jumped about three feet straight up. I yanked it out of my bag and answered it while staring at Barnie.

"Yeah?" My voice cracked.

"Pepper? Is everything OK?"

"Neil?" I knelt next to Barnie and laid a hand on his forehead. He was cold. Still. His Hawaiian shirt seemed to glow, but his face was ghastly pale.

I touched his arm. Zero response. "Damn it." I grabbed his beefy shoulder and shook him. Still no response. A frisson of apprehension ran down my spine.

"Pepper? What's going on? We're on our way from the airport. We'll be there any minute. Is everything ready?"

"Neil, I—I have to hang up. I've gotta call 9-1-1. Suite 318. Hurry."

Chapter Two

My first call was to 9-1-1. The next was to Dash, who didn't answer. "Barnie's sick," I said in a message. "Come to the suite, please." I realized after I hung up that I hadn't identified myself. I had a feeling he'd figure it out. Next I called the front desk to let them know we had a problem, then turned my attention back to Barnie.

I was pretty sure he was breathing. That was something.

"Wake up, Barnie." I shook his shoulder again. "Shit. I mean shoot. Aw, shit." This was probably the wrong time to implement my campaign to cut down on my cursing.

A hotel manager opened the door a few minutes later without knocking, accompanied by a pair of paramedics. The manager wore a suit and a neutral expression of forbearance until he saw that Barnie wasn't waking up. Then his eyes widened into O's of real alarm.

The uniformed man and woman chattered in rapid-fire medicalese, checked Barnie out, fixed him up with oxygen, lifted and strapped him to a stretcher and were rolling him out by the time Dash and Travis ran into the room.

"What happened?" Dash croaked, almost as pale as Barnie.

I crossed my arms against the room's chill and shook my

head. "I don't know. I guess he's drunk, but I couldn't wake him up."

The elevator dinged, signaling the crew's departure.

"I should cancel this," Dash said to himself. "Go with him to the hospital."

"Absolutely not," Travis said, just before another man walked through the open door.

The newcomer wore a white shirt, red bow tie and black suspenders and had a close-cropped beard and mustache that matched his thick rusty hair. Well, brown with hints of red. Sharp cheekbones. Gray eyes rimmed in navy blue. They caught mine, and I caught my breath.

"Pepper?"

"Neil?"

"Are you OK?" He came over to me and put a hand on my shoulder. His confident presence and warm touch suffused me with calm, and I nodded as my heartbeat slowed. Neil squeezed my shoulder, then turned to the men with an outstretched hand. "We're a hundred percent ready to work if you want to proceed, but I understand if you don't."

So he'd seen Barnie, assessed the situation, maybe even heard the cousins talking as he entered the room.

Travis took Neil's hand first with a firm handshake. "Good to see you again."

Dash shook Neil's hand, too, and his expression of anxiety eased. Somehow, Neil had changed the temperature in the room, the emotional temperature, and the cousins looked more ready to deal with the situation.

"That was Barnard, right?" Neil asked. "I remember meeting him when I toured the distillery."

"Barnie, yeah. He's been with us since the beginning," Dash said.

"He'd want us to go forward," Travis said. "There's nothing we can do for him right now. Let's go downstairs to the event and make this thing happen. The cart's already loaded—where are your bartenders?"

"Most of them I sent to the ballroom with their kits to squeeze lemons, craft garnishes and do anything Pepper hasn't gotten to yet," Neil said, those cool eyes scanning the room, spotting the bottle on the floor. He picked it up and sniffed it. "Luke's dealing with the check-in and luggage, but he'll be ready to help in a few minutes."

Dash seemed to shake himself. "OK. Yes. Let's do this. Barnie would want us to."

Travis nodded at seeing his cousin take his words to heart and maneuvered himself behind the cart, pushing it toward the door.

"Wait a minute." Neil put up a hand to stop him.

"You just said you were ready," Dash snapped at Neil. "And we don't have a minute."

"Exactly." Travis starting pushing again, but Neil stepped in front of the cart, calmly flipping open the box labeled Beach-side Bourbon on top of the stack as the Reynolds cousins looked on in disbelief.

Neil pulled a wine key from his pocket and snapped open the blade, lifted out one of the squat bottles, and made quick work of cutting through the black wax and popping off the top. He looked at me. "Cup?"

I nodded and looked around, grabbed a clean foam cup from the stack by the coffee maker, and handed it to him.

"What the hell?" Travis asked as Neil poured a little brown liquid into the cup. Neil sniffed it, wrinkled his nose and took a sip. He lifted an eyebrow, ignored Travis and handed the cup to Dash.

Dash appeared as puzzled as Travis but took a sniff, then a healthy sip.

He immediately spit it back into the cup. "Something's not right."

"My thoughts exactly," Neil said. "Pepper?"

I held out a fresh cup for his pour. I had a superhero sense of smell, and one whiff revealed the whiskey's usually pleasant odor had a pungent undertone. I gingerly sipped it. I'd had the Beachside Bourbon before, and it had been rich and delicious, tinged in caramel. This was—off. Metallic? I shook my head. "What's wrong with it?"

"I don't know, but we have a problem," Neil said. "If this is what made Barnie sick, this could make everyone sick."

"Travis and I shared a bottle last night, and it was fine," Dash said.

"Perfect," Travis agreed.

"From this stash?" I asked.

"Of course," Travis said. "What are you saying?"

"Are you saying someone tampered with my whiskey?" Dash seemed truly angry now.

Neil shook his head. "I don't know. Worse would be methanol."

"A bad batch?" Incredulity raised Dash's voice. "Impossible. Our methods are perfect. Every process is controlled. Every stage is sampled, tested."

"And they're sealed, so tampering is out," Travis said impatiently. "Look, we have about thirty-five minutes, and then the door is going to open on that ballroom, and we have to be there with whiskey in hand. Bourbon and rye. Cocktails. This is why we hired you guys."

"I'm well aware of that," Neil said. "But I personally don't want a hotel full of sick drinkers."

"Dead drinkers," I said, then sort of wished I'd shut my mouth when Dash's jaw dropped.

But Neil nodded in agreement. "Worst case."

"I know a liquor store a few blocks away," I said.

"That was my next question," Neil said, then turned to Dash. "Your stuff is distributed here, right?"

"Yeah," Dash said. "My God, you can't be serious."

"I can't be more serious," Neil said, and I almost smiled.

"Travis and I can go," I said, thinking he had the muscle to haul the cases. "We'll be back before the event."

"There won't be enough!" Dash said.

"Trust me," Neil said. "Pepper, call them. Ask what they have."

A few minutes later I was off the phone. "Two cases of the bourbon, one of the rye," I said.

"More than enough," Neil said. "We're not doing full pours here. Half-ounce samples, four-ounce cocktails. A little shortage never hurts demand. And the people who get them will be talking about the drinks, and that will make the people who didn't get them want your whiskey even more. Can you do it?" he asked me as Dash mulled Neil's words.

"With Travis's help, yes." My adrenaline had kicked in. The room was quiet. The tuba player had stopped. A good sign.

Travis sighed and looked at Dash. "I have a friend who can go to the hospital with Barnie until we can get away. You OK with us buying the whiskey?"

Dash looked around at all the boxes, at his babies, pain in his expression. "Better to be safe," he finally said. "Yes. Buy it. I will taste it to be sure. All of it."

"Of course," Neil said, then shot me a look that said, *Get moving.*

Chapter Three

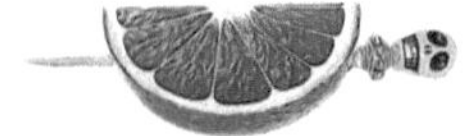

We worked together quickly to unload the cart and took it to the service elevator. Neil and Dash went to the ballroom while Travis and I rolled out of the building and to the closest liquor store to clean them out of Bohemia whiskeys.

Travis made a monosyllabic call on the way, presumably to his friend. Other than that, he said little, if you didn't count muttering under his breath.

We were back at three fifty-five, pushing into the first-floor ballroom via the catering door. There was a buzz as the distillers got ready. The walls were lined with temporary bars, tables and a few exceptionally elaborate setups; one even had neon lights and Vegas-style signage. We aimed for the one with the beach umbrella and whiskey barrels.

The five people behind the Bohemia Distillery tableau in one corner saw us coming. The bartenders were easy to spot. When they saw us, they lit up like a bunch of kids who'd just discovered the veggie drawer was full of cupcakes.

The two guys leapt out from behind the props and rushed over to speed the cart to the bar, cutting open boxes and pulling out bottles.

Melody beckoned me and gave me a quick hug. A girl-next-door blue-eyed blonde, she worked at a lame hotel bar in Bohemia Beach. She was my movie date when both of us were between guys. Tattoos of music notes and flowers danced up her arms in pretty colors.

"Just a second," Neil called out. As he'd done before, he popped the top off a bourbon, poured a small sample and handed it to Dash.

Dash, his face creased with tension, sipped it. Then he downed the whole thing and smiled. "That's my whiskey. How about the rye?"

Neil smiled, too, a lovely thing to behold, and went through the same ritual with the rye. Dash was satisfied, and Neil tried it, too.

"I think we're OK," Neil told the bartenders, "but Dash is going to sample every bottle we open. Got it?"

"Yes!" we answered, and the two other mixologists and Melody started mixing and pouring just as the double doors were thrown open and ticket-holders streamed in like fish thrown wide of a busted dam. I ran to the restroom to wash my hands, fought the crowd to get back to our booth with the others, and asked Neil what I should do.

"Help Melody," he said, shaking a drink with ice in two shiny metal shakers at once. *Shaka-shaka-shaka.* God, I loved that sound. He saw my expression of bliss and winked. "And thank you." I nodded, and my face heated a little. Geez, and I hadn't even had anything to drink yet.

"Pepper!" Melody added bourbon to the batch cocktail she'd made in a pitcher and stirred. One of Neil's creations. "We'd have been screwed without you." She handed me the pitcher. "Fill those little cups and add the lemon spirals and Bohemia swizzles, OK?"

"OK." As soon as I garnished a row of cocktails and pushed them to the edge of the bar, they were gone, snatched up by thirsty browsers. The same was happening with the tiny liquor samples one of our guys was pouring at the table. I didn't know him, but his looks were arresting—gold-streaked brown hair that just touched his shoulders, intense brown eyes, an inviting mouth pursed in concentration. A swirl of tattoos of monkeys and parrots and tropical foliage sneaked up his arms and under his rolled-up sleeves, suggesting more ink under the fabric. With his good looks, he might've escaped one of those TV shows about vampires in high school.

"That's Luke," Melody said, catching me watching. "He's working at The Junction Box with Neil now. And this is Barclay. He just moved to Bohemia from South Florida two months ago."

Hearing their names, the guys looked up and nodded and smiled at me briefly, and I waved. "Hi. I'm Pepper."

"We know," Luke said, and Barclay barked out a laugh. Probably at my name. It did that to people. Anybody named Barclay—pronounced *Bark-lee*—didn't have much room to talk.

I'd seen Barclay behind the bar at one of the newer clubs in downtown Bohemia. He was striking in a different way from Luke, taller, with tightly cropped wavy black hair, a hint of scruff around his mouth and chin, and light brown skin. His narrow eyes were a beautiful swirl of amber and green. He also had tattoos—a dragon curling around one arm and characters written on the other—Korean, maybe? I'd have to ask him what they meant. Barclay muddled a few raspberries in the bottom of each small, clear plastic cup, then topped them with sprigs of mint after Neil filled them with the rye mixture.

Together, they were damned efficient. I tried to up my game and match their pace.

When we had a brief pause in the traffic to the table, Neil passed me one of the rye drinks. "You're the only one who didn't get to try it."

"Thanks." The others watched as I took a healthy sip. A burst of lemon and raspberry popped through the peppery sweetness of the rye—and something else. "Wow. What is that? Lemongrass?"

"And I thought I was being obscure." Neil grinned. "Lemongrass simple syrup. This is my variation on a whiskey smash. We muddle the fruit first, and then I shake the rest."

"Delicious," I said.

"*Smashing,*" Barclay intoned, and the others chortled as the next wave of drinkers crowded our corner.

Dash seemed more relaxed once he saw the drinks and samples going out, and he and Travis shared enthusiastic tales of their origin story with visitors. Dash and Travis's fathers were brothers and owned an old factory building together in downtown Bohemia. The older men had a paint business, and when Travis's father died when Travis was in high school, Dash's dad took over. He retired from the paint business and, before he died, helped Dash and Travis launch the distillery.

It was a great family story, and the added allure of nearby Bohemia Beach gave them a unique image in this big room of small distillers. Travis was especially good at telling it, which was probably a good thing, because the more Dash tested the whiskey—and then tasted some of the cocktails just for fun— he became happier and less coherent. As his eyes drooped, our bartenders all exchanged glances, made sure Neil was tasting the last bottles for purity, and breathed a collective sigh of relief when we finally ran out of booze.

A toasted forty-something woman in bare feet and disheveled hair ran off with our beach umbrella thirty seconds before the doors closed.

"Did you see that?" Melody asked.

I shrugged as we started the cleanup. "What happens at Cocktailia, stays at Cocktailia. But nothing stays at Cocktailia if it's not nailed down."

"Neil, you bastard, what happened to your bloody mustache?" boomed a voice in a cut-glass English accent. We all looked up to see an angular guy who looked to be about thirty approach the booth. He wore tweed trousers and vest and a cream button-up shirt, and his straw-colored hair, cut short on the sides, seemed to overflow on top and curl out over his forehead. He looked like a model who'd fallen off the runway after one too many glasses of champagne.

"Alastair," Neil said evenly, but his usual cool tone sounded a bit edgy to me.

"Your mustache was *everything!*" Alastair bellowed, coming up close to Neil and reaching out for a pinch of our leader's tightly trimmed facial hair.

Neil slapped his hand away. "Back off, man. It was time."

"But the handlebars. The handlebars! You must be saving considerably on wax."

"This from the guy who spends the budget of a small country on hair products. How many chickens you have nesting in there?"

"Chickens, nah," said the dapper Brit, his cheeks glowing with drink, "but the chicks, as you call them—they love running their fingers through it." He looked around and grinned at Melody and me. "Wouldn't you, love?"

"Which one of us is he talking to?" I whispered to Melody.

"Beats me," she murmured back.

Luke had moved around us and now stood in front of the table, arms crossed. "Get out of here, Alastair. We've got work to do."

"Don't we all?" he said. "Did you try the Frilly Fairy? Delicate. Delightful."

"Yeah," Neil said. "Mark sent me a bottle."

"Oh." Alastair sounded disappointed.

"It's a really nice gin," Neil acknowledged. "What'd you make with it?"

"Only the best bloody gin and tonic you've ever had, but this was amateur night," Alastair said, dismissing our whole team with a sniff. "There will be *more to come.* Trade secrets. You'll just have to wait for the contest, won't you? I have my eye on you, Neil Rockaway, and I'll make you sorry you ever decided to leave your galaxies behind." He pulled down on one eye with his middle finger, shooting drunken malice at Neil, then bounded off laughing.

"Who was that asshole?" Travis asked. "And what was he talking about?"

Neil shook his head as he methodically stacked shakers and stowed bar tools in his bag. "Someone I knew in school. He's a bartender now. Toast of London, at least in his own mind."

"Good riddance." Dash took a deep breath. He'd recovered a bit from his round of quality samplings and was only partly cloudy now. At least he wasn't passing out cold.

Travis's phone rang. "How is he?" he asked first thing. "OK. We'll be right there." He looked up at us. "Barnie's in a coma. He might not make it."

A collective gasp escaped us.

Dash blanched and turned to Neil. "Can you clean up here? Pepper has the key to the suite so you can stow the props and swag and whatever else you need."

"No problem," Neil said. "We'll catch up with you shortly. Text us the hospital room number." He caught my gaze, and I got the feeling I was included in the "us." Which was good. Because I wanted to see Barnie in the hospital, too—and find out what sent him there before it was too late.

Chapter Four

Neil left the other bartenders to settle into their rooms and get some rest—or more likely to go out and sample the pleasures of the Quarter's better bars and restaurants—while we took an Uber to the medical center. The streets were crowded as evening settled in and the lights came on, and the young guy behind the wheel of the Toyota drove at a leisurely pace to match the incongruous new-age music blaring from the stereo.

"So how do you know Alastair?" I asked Neil over the din of dreamy piano arpeggios. "Is he your frenemy?"

Neil grimaced. "That's one way to put it. We knew each other at Oxford."

"Oxford?" I was pretty sure my eyes bugged out behind my glasses. "You went to Oxford?"

He smiled at my expression. "Only for a couple of years, until I realized my true calling was cocktails."

"That's funny. Most people start out as bartenders, then get serious about something else."

"Yeah, well. My other calling was astronomy. I'm still fascinated by it, but a well-made drink can be as beautiful as a nebula."

"Plus you get to drink it."

He laughed. "That too. Though I'm not into drinking *per se*. I'm into drinking *well*."

"That's what separates a great bartender from any old drink slinger. I mean, look at that. That's not pretty at all."

Our eyes followed a group of half a dozen tourists staggering in front of our car, toting bright plastic drink cups a yard long.

"That's a shitty hangover right there," Neil said.

"When I think of how many great places there are in this city to get a really good hangover, that just makes me sad."

Neil chuckled. "You'll have to show me some of your favorites."

"Um." I swallowed. "I have a confession. I don't know much more than you do about what's hot in NOLA. I visit occasionally, but I've lived in Bohemia for thirteen years."

"What? How come I never see you in my bar?"

"Probably because I'm always working in *my* bar. I've been to The Junction Box, but you weren't working."

He nodded. "Touché. But I've been to yours when *you* were working."

"No, you haven't! I would've remembered." *Whoops.* Did I just confess that I found him—memorable?

"You were busy, and we ordered drinks from our table. Very nice."

"What'd you have?"

"A Sazerac, of course, since it's a New Orleans-themed bar." He caught my frown. "What is it?"

"I may have had an excess of Sazeracs last night at the Carousel Bar. Don't get me wrong. They're delicious—in small doses." And it was easier to maintain one's equilibrium if the bar wasn't a rotating one like the Carousel.

"I prefer their Vieux Carré."

"They *did* invent it there."

He looked at me for a few seconds as if gauging whether he wanted to ask his next question. "So why did you leave New Orleans when you were—how old were you?"

"Fourteen. My parents shipped me off to my aunt in Bohemia Beach after Katrina."

"Why didn't you go back?"

I looked out the window for a minute, trying to find a way to say it. The elegant buildings of the Quarter slid by, lovely brick facades and wrought-iron balconies. This part of town was barely touched by the hurricane all those years ago. "First, the house was trashed, plus the city was trashed, so my parents thought it would be better if I stayed in Bohemia."

"And then?"

I turned to face him. "My dad was a pastor at a storefront church. My mom was devoted to making it bigger and better, though she had a secretary job to help pay the bills. We had a pretty normal home life before the storm, except for extended trips they took in the summer to Central America or whatever. I'd usually stay with friends or my aunt. But after Katrina, they became all about hurricane recovery—helping parishioners, building up the church. They became a funnel for donations. The hurricane was basically one big membership drive for them. With the money coming in, they doubled the mission work they did abroad. They were always traveling, running some fundraising program, whatever. They always had a reason why I shouldn't come back."

Neil's face didn't change, but I saw a flicker in his eyes, a warm light that drew me in, calming and sure, the same feeling he'd exuded earlier during the crisis in the hotel room. I just looked at him for a moment and breathed and didn't think of anything at all.

"We're here," our driver said, pulling up to a modern brown-brick high-rise.

I tore my gaze away from Neil's and got out of the car. I hadn't meant to tell him so much. Or maybe he just heard more than I was telling.

We checked in at the front desk, then boarded the elevator.

"So what's the deal with your mustache?" I asked after the doors closed, mostly to hide my awkwardness. "I mean, what was Alastair talking about?"

Neil let out a small chuckle. "It used to look different."

"Mixologist special?"

He smiled. "Yeah. Handlebar. Some of my regulars told me I might look better without it."

"*Women* regulars?"

"Sure. I wouldn't take that kind of advice from a man. Were they right?" His smile broadened as he rubbed a hand over his closely trimmed beard and 'stache.

"I wouldn't know. I didn't see you with the handlebars."

"Ah." The smile faded.

"But I'm really not a fan of facial hair that you can hang a coat on. You—it looks good." I smiled shyly, and his grin returned.

This was ridiculous. We were in a hospital elevator going to see a very sick man. Not the place for nerd-on-nerd coquetry or whatever this was.

The elevator dinged. Third floor. Our stop.

Barnie had a room to himself—well, himself and his visitors and the hissing and beeping machines that loomed over the bed. Dash, his hat tilted back on his head, stood next to the bed, staring at Barnie's unconscious form. Travis leaned against a row of cabinets, looking grim. Barnie was connected to oxygen, had an IV dripping something into his arm, and was hooked up to the monitors. At least beeping was a good thing, based on my limited television-based medical knowledge.

Neil and I stood at the end of the bed and exchanged nods with the Reynolds cousins.

"How's he doing?" I asked softly.

Dash sighed. "He's out of the coma for now, but he's still unconscious."

"Holy crap," I whispered.

"Yeah. They're treating him with ethanol."

I raised my eyebrows. "Ethanol? Isn't that like giving him more alcohol?"

"It counteracts the effects of methanol, if that's what the problem is," Neil said.

"That's what they suspect," Dash said. "I just don't understand it. There's nothing wrong with my whiskey."

"There was something wrong with this whiskey," Travis said.

"Maybe he got sick some other way," Dash said. "Maybe he drank something else. There are always people at Cocktailia with all kinds of concoctions in their pockets. Some hipster moonshiner might have dosed him up in the elevator."

"There was that empty bottle next to him," I said. "Plus you tasted one of the bottles yourself."

Dash nodded. "I know. You're right about that. I just can't believe it."

"We're going to throw all of it away. Pour it down the drain so no one else touches it," Travis said. "And we'll run more tests at home, make sure everything is good there."

I shifted from foot to foot and tried to think. A wave of fatigue washed over me. The craziness of the day was starting to hit me. "I hate to ask this, but suppose this was deliberate?"

Dash's eyes widened in shock. "Poisoning Barnie?"

"Or contaminating the bottles," I said. "Maybe Barnie wasn't the target."

"Then who?" Dash asked. "Me? Travis?"

"Worse," Neil said. "Everybody at the convention."

"Like ... like *terrorism* or something?" Dash asked in disbelief.

"Shit," Travis said. "If that's true, we should contact the cops. Hotel security. Everybody."

"I can't do that," Dash said hoarsely. "This will ruin me. This will end Bohemia Distillery. And we're just getting to where I want to be. Everything I have is invested in this."

"Same here," said Travis, "but we can't let anybody else get sick."

"They won't," his cousin said. "Look, I refuse to believe this is terrorism or some nut job trying to poison the convention."

"That leaves one possibility. A bad batch," I said.

Dash straightened. "I refuse to believe that either."

Neil held up a hand. "Let me talk to some of the other distillers and bartenders. See if they've noticed anything unusual. I'll have a word with hotel and convention security, too. We'll make sure everything's covered. I'll try to keep it quiet, but you have to prepare yourself for the idea of going to the police about this."

"Even if we don't, word's going to get out." Dash closed his eyes, then opened them and glanced at poor, pale Barnie. "You're right. We can't let anyone else get sick. See what you can find out. If nobody else has a problem, then maybe we can deal with this ourselves."

A nurse came in. "We have to get him ready," she said to all of us.

"Ready?" I asked.

"They're going to prepare him for emergency hemodialysis to clean up his blood," Travis said.

"Damn," I said.

"I know," he replied.

"Hey," I said, "where's your friend?"

Travis raised his eyebrows. "Friend?"

"You said a friend was coming to the hospital with Barnie."

"She went home." Travis looked again at Barnie. "I told her to go. She'd seen enough."

Awkward pause. I was good at generating those.

"We'll get going, then." Neil to the rescue. "Let's touch base first thing in the morning. I'll have answers by then, before the next round of tastings. Our next event with you is your Distiller Dinner tomorrow night. We'll make sure we have enough stock."

"Oh, yeah." Dash shook his head. "Wait. I'll give you a credit card."

"No worries. Catch me later," Neil said.

Geez, that was right. Travis paid for the emergency whiskey earlier, but Neil would be fronting these guys a lot by buying more cases for the dinner. Assuming we could *find* more cases and they weren't tainted.

"I hope he feels better," I said to the cousins. I stood there for another awkward moment, then followed Neil out the door.

He didn't say anything until we got into the elevator, after I pressed the button and the door closed.

"You have a key to their suite?" he asked.

I nodded. "Uh-huh."

"I'd like to know what was in those bottles. Know for sure."

"You mean before Travis makes good on his promise to dump them all out? I'll drop by and grab a couple."

"Good. Make sure you mark the bottles and put them aside so they don't get mixed up with all the booze we'll be handling this week."

"For sure." The image of a passed-out maid or bellhop crossed my mind. What if all the bottles really were tainted? What if the booze had gotten out into the wild? I shuddered. "How are we going to test the whiskey? If Dash doesn't want the cops involved, it's not like we can turn the whiskey over to CSI or whatever the nonfiction version of it is here."

"The cops are probably going to be involved no matter what, though I didn't want to lay that on him in there. But it could be weeks before they do a proper test. That's OK. I have a guy."

"I have another thought," I said as we stepped out of the elevator and made our way outside. "Let's have another few cases of the bourbon and the rye shipped here from Bohemia by courier."

"Sounds expensive," Neil said, but he was smiling.

"But worth it. First, we can test the stuff right from the plant, make sure everything is good there. Second, if it's OK, we won't be running all over NOLA trying to find bottles of the stuff."

"I like it." Neil hailed a cab, a regular cab this time, and we got in, heading back to the Hotel Lebeau. "I'll talk to their warehouse manager, have him get the cases ready and tell him not to ship out anything else this week until we know what's going on. Probably the Reynoldses are too distraught right now to think about that."

"Is he going to freak out? What if the warehouse guy is responsible?"

"I've known Tim for a long time. We used to bartend together, before I bought The Junction Box, and I trust him implicitly. Can you call Millie and have her arrange a courier for, say, 5 a.m.? Then we can have the booze in hand by tomorrow evening."

"That's cutting it close."

"That's why I'm counting on you to scrape together a few more cases before the dinner."

I narrowed my eyes. "Great."

Neil laughed. I liked his laugh. It was rich, deep and sweet, like a barrel-aged Manhattan with a hint of chocolate bitters. I had a thing for chocolate bitters.

We both watched the revelers roaming the streets as the cab navigated the maze and brought us back to our home for the next few days.

"I guess our exploration of the Quarter's cocktail haunts will have to wait until another night," Neil said as we stepped out onto the busy sidewalk in front of the hotel. "I'm dying to visit the French 75 Bar, but I've got a lot of people to talk to before morning." He stood there staring at me, and I started to wonder if I had lemon seeds in my hair or something before he spoke again. "You did a great job today under rough circumstances. Hang in there, and we'll get on track by tomorrow. Want to meet me for breakfast at nine in the hotel restaurant? We can go over everything then."

"Um, sure, but—why me?"

"Because I told the others they could party tonight, and they'll want to sleep in. And they don't know as much as you do about what's happening here. I'll update them tomorrow, but it's probably better I keep this on the QT tonight."

"That sounds reasonable."

"I'm nothing if not reasonable. It's one of my faults. Everyone finds me too reasonable."

It was my turn to laugh. "Like that's a thing."

"You have no idea."

A noise somewhere between a bellow and a honk made me jump. I turned around. The tuba player had set up directly across the street and had launched into a jaunty rendition of "Basin Street Blues."

I shook my head. "That guy must have lips made of platinum. He plays around the clock."

"Maybe he has a twin," Neil said.

"God, I hope there's not another one."

He chuckled. "Get some dinner and some sleep. The drugstore on the corner should have earplugs."

"Maybe later. I'm ordering room service right after I acquire a few bottles of whiskey."

Neil's eyes seemed to darken in the glow of the streetlights. "Acquire evidence, you mean. That sounds pretty grim, doesn't it?"

"Evidence of what? Tampering? Terrorism? Bad practices? I just hope Barnie gets better, or it's going to be evidence of something I don't want to think about."

Manslaughter. Or murder.

Chapter Five

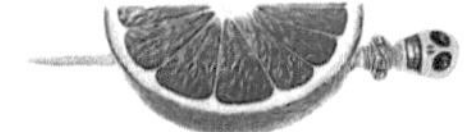

When I woke up the next morning, the first thing I heard when I popped out the earplugs was— nothing. Well, no, not nothing. There were city sounds: beeping, honking, trucks, construction, a hell of a lot more than I heard back at home in Bohemia Beach. But there was no tuba. It had stopped about three in the morning. Unfortunately, I knew that because my earplugs were no defense against Tuba Guy.

The first thing I *saw* was the whiskey sitting on the credenza under the television. Two bottles of bourbon. Two bottles of rye. This would look like breakfast to some of the people at Cocktailia, except for the fact that I'd used paper and markers and tape from the drugstore to wrap them up and label each *CONTAMINATED! TOXIC! DO NOT DRINK!* With a skull and crossbones just for good measure.

I took my phone off mute and glanced at the screen.

There was a text from Millie: "Whiskey on its way."

And a text from Neil: "I thought you were coming to breakfast?"

"Shit!" I threw off the covers and looked at the clock. Nine twenty. Could be worse. I pulled off my nightshirt, yanked on jeans and fresh undies and a black T-shirt, ran a brush through my hair and threw on some dangly silver earrings and my glasses. I grabbed my badge and was out the door.

Three minutes later, I strolled into the hotel restaurant. Pleasant natural light from the historic floor-to-ceiling windows spilled into the traditional-meets-modern sage and cream décor. The eatery had a literary theme, with typewriters, books and other props in niches and a few well-placed quotes in script on the walls. The biggest was attributed to Faulkner: "Everyone in the South has no time for reading because they are all too busy writing."

"Or they're too busy drinking," came a mellow voice in my ear, and I jumped and turned around. Neil looked fresh in a sapphire-blue button-up shirt, sleeves rolled up, and jeans.

"You scared me to death."

"I can see why you might be jumpy given what happened yesterday," he said, leading me to sit at a table by a window. "I know I'll be jumpy because I've already had two cups of coffee."

"I'm sorry I'm late. I meant to set my alarm, but I just passed out instead."

"Sazeracs?"

"Exhaustion." A dapper man in a sage-green bow tie came over, filled my coffee cup and handed me a menu before scooting to another table. "But Millie says the booze is on the way."

He nodded. "She texted me, too."

"What did you find out last night?" I poured a packet of raw sugar into my cup and stirred.

"Nobody has seen anything unusual. Mark at Fairyland—they make the gin Alastair is helping push this weekend—said their shipment got put in the wrong room. Something about someone else storing their booze in the Fairyland Distillery room. But it was intact and fine. Just the kind of mixup that happens here. I talked to security and the coordinators, and everyone is on hyper-alert for weirdness."

"And I guess no one has been hauled off by an ambulance?"

"There was one drunk girl who slipped on the stairs and broke her arm." Neil sipped his coffee. "Other than that, nothing, according to the manager."

"And the Bloody Mary bar is doing even more business today," I said.

"Cocktailia as usual. It will get busier as we get closer to the weekend. It's only Thursday."

I tried my coffee. Still a little too hot, but nice. "So you've been to this event before?"

"A couple of times."

"So have I. And I never saw you here."

"It's a big convention. Plus I had that handlebar mustache."

I chuckled. "Right. No wonder I didn't recognize you. Speaking of which, you grew up in Bohemia?"

"Bohemia Beach. Yeah."

"How did I miss you there? I went to Bohemia High once I got shipped off to Florida."

Neil looked uncomfortable for the first time since I'd met him. "I went to private school."

"Well, la-di-da. Private school *and* Oxford."

He quirked his mouth into a funny expression. "My parents don't have a ton of money, but my grandfather does. He wanted me and my brother to have the best. He's kind of a character."

"I envy you. My grandparents are gone." I looked up as the server approached. "Crab Cakes Benedict, please," I told him.

"I'll have the NOLA Breakfast," Neil said.

"Sure thing," our guy said, and he was off.

"So you have a brother?" I asked.

Neil's features assumed that cool, still look he so often had. "I did. He died."

"Oh, no. I'm sorry. Damn it. I always say the wrong thing."

"It's OK. So do you know where you're getting those cases today?"

I didn't blame him for changing the subject. "I called a few stores last night and had them put some aside. It should be enough for the dinner if the courier doesn't get here in time." Movement caught my eye, and I turned to see the other Bohemia Bartenders, all of them in T-shirts and jeans, heading our way.

"Excellent! Neil's buying us breakfast!" said Luke, pushing his fingers through that enviable longish hair. His T-shirt said, "VODKA PAYS THE BILLS."

"Awesome!" Barclay grinned. His plain rust-colored T-shirt appeared to be painted on his pecs, and I tried not to stare.

Melody, her long, blond hair in a ponytail, just rolled her eyes and grabbed a chair from a nearby table so we could seat five. Her T-shirt had a small Bohemia Bartenders logo on the front and "Shaken *and* Stirred" on the back.

They settled in with greetings and calls for coffee. Our server obliged, filling our cups with a fresh pot, and took the rest of the orders. Barclay just got water, bacon and fruit. There were weirder diets, right?

"I didn't expect to see you so early," Neil said drolly after the waiter left. "And yes, I'll buy you breakfast."

Luke looked around, then leaned in. "We thought maybe we should talk to you early before you heard it from someone else."

"Finally," Neil said. "You lost your virginity."

Barclay spewed the water he'd been sipping and Melody burst out laughing.

"No, I'm saving myself," Luke said with a sexy grin that suggested that ship had sailed a long time ago.

Now Barclay lowered his voice. "Word is getting around that somebody might be trying to poison the well."

"The liquor," Melody said. "Like a saboteur."

Neil groaned. "That's probably my fault."

"Dash will *not* be happy," I said.

"What did you do?" Luke asked Neil.

"Only what I had to. I told you we had a problem with the shipment yesterday, but I didn't tell you what it was." Neil explained about the bad whiskey and talking to security and the distillers and how Barnie ended up in the hospital.

"Hell," Barclay said. "I know that guy. He comes into the club all the time back home."

"Is he going to be OK?" Melody asked.

"I just don't know," Neil said. "I didn't want to bug the Reynoldses this morning. I know they must have had a late night."

"I did grab a couple of bottles of each label from their storage suite last night," I said. "It was eerie in there. I kind of looked around but didn't see anything that struck me as odd. I left the 'do not disturb' on the door so no one is tempted."

"Good thinking," Neil said. "Barclay, can you take these two out after breakfast and pick up our order of fruit and stuff for tonight from the restaurant supply store? I had a rental SUV delivered here this morning to make it easier. And Pepper will give you the names of the liquor stores we need to get cases from. What name are they under?" he asked me.

"Bohemia Bartenders."

"Easy enough," Luke said. "Can we just take everything to the restaurant?"

"Yes, they're expecting us," Neil said. He and I spent a few minutes giving the other three the information they needed, and Neil handed them a company credit card, all while I wondered what he had in mind for me.

My curiosity was shunted aside by the arrival of the crab cakes. It had been a long time since last night's room service, and this was no average hotel breakfast. New Orleans had great cocktails, but its food—it was better than sex. Well, almost, depending on the restaurant. And the sex.

I'd been thinking about serving more serious food at my bar back home, Nola. I'd already worked up ideas for a menu and was courting a chef who was looking for a change. And my business partner, Jorge, was totally on board. He was ten years older than me, spent his days working at the space center and let me steer the ship most of the time, though he and our staff were covering for me this week. And he loved food, too.

I just had to get through this weekend first. After I got through this divine dish. A tiny sound of pleasure escaped me as the savory crab and hollandaise sauce mixed in my mouth, and I shut myself up with a sip of coffee.

I glanced up to see Neil watching me with intense interest. He dropped his gaze when I caught him, picked up a piece of his maple-glazed bacon and glanced out the window, gnawing on it as the others chatted and laughed.

He'd caught me in a foodgasm. That was awkward.

I tried not to stare at the way the light outlined his cheekbones and set fire to the red highlights in his chestnut hair. And then it was my turn to drop my eyes and concentrate on my dish when he turned back to the table.

When I joined the Bohemia Bartenders, I wasn't counting

on this. On him. I was kind of over bartenders. I mean, not as friends or as people who were totally my tribe, because they were. I loved them, the way you love a great movie or a puppy or anyone who geeked out over the same stuff you did. But as romantic interests? Forget it. I loved creating and serving cocktails, but I'd lost interest in the party scene. I was an aberration already, since I only had one tattoo. And that might be one more than Neil had, judging from what I could see, not that I'd ever get to find out for sure.

Yeah, I'd had some flings. I'd been briefly drawn to shiny objects—a surfer dude or two, a quick wit, a Scottish accent. But I was getting closer to thirty than I was to twenty, and I was tired of the passing fancy. And there was no use in pursuing intimacy with another flaky, cocktail-shaking nomad.

Then why did this one intrigue me so much? I'd known him for less than a day, but I'd seen his confidence, his cool in a crisis, his sense of humor, and his incredible touch with a cocktail. He had a nerdy, quiet way about him that seemed at odds with being a leader, but there it was. Somehow he was both. Maybe it wasn't attraction. Hell, I wasn't sure *what* it was. Maybe he was just the friend I needed.

I focused on scraping up the last of the hollandaise sauce with my fork and chalked up my goofiness to sleep deprivation and stress.

"So when do we meet at the restaurant?" Luke asked.

"No later than four," Neil said. "I want to get all the prep done early. The doors open at seven."

"No problem," Barclay said. "That'll give us time to get the shopping done, and you can even buy us lunch."

Neil snorted. "You're on your own for lunch."

"What are you doing, then?" Melody asked.

"Pepper and I are going to see a mad scientist."

Barclay's pale amber-green eyes popped. "Not Cray?"

Neil nodded, and the others murmured.

"Cray?" I asked. "Like cray-cray?"

Melody laughed. "That, too. But that's his name. Conan Cray. Chemist. Mixologist."

"Nutcase," Luke said.

"Bitchin' rum collection," Barclay added. "He wrote the definitive book on the evolution of rum."

"You would know that." Luke looked at me to explain. "Barclay has a thing for rum."

"Doesn't everyone?" Barclay asked. "You sure I can't go?"

"Another time," Neil said. "I need Pepper for this one."

Barclay shot me a glower. I'd have to do something nice for him later. Maybe in the form of rum. In the meantime, I tried not to think about why Neil needed me.

"Meet me at eleven in the lobby with one each of the rye and bourbon, OK?" Neil was saying to me.

Oh, yeah. That's why. Work.

That's all this is, Kayanne Pepper.

Then why did the room seem so warm all of a sudden?

Chapter Six

I had just enough time for a shower and a proper reboot of the day. This time I donned my black leather zip-up vest over a cleavage-enhancing scoop-neck white T-shirt, along with a swirly above-the-knee gray skirt, mostly hidden pettipants and my trusty short boots. Comfortable with a dose of saucy. A touch of eye makeup behind my hot nerd glasses, complemented by red lipstick, and I was ready to meet Cray Cray. I mean, Conan Cray.

I put the bottles, a bourbon and a rye, in my messenger bag and took the stairs this time. They were crowded, but nothing like the elevators. The seminars had cranked up in earnest. Neil had one tomorrow that we were all making drinks for, based on his new cocktail book, *Cutting-Edge Classics: Cocktails With a Twist*. I'd made a bunch of the recipes in it, and they were great. He paired classics with exotic, delicious updates. It was the perfect book for new home bartenders or more experienced mixologists. I doubted I'd get around to writing my own book, but it was fun to know someone who had.

There he was, now dressed in a button-down white shirt with red suspenders and retro-looking black pants that emphasized his lean figure. Pretty much standard garb in the midst of the crowded lobby. He was talking to a couple of clean-shaven guys in fedoras and aloha shirts, one elegantly thin, one impressively muscular, both cute. They all laughed and shook hands, and the pair departed as I approached. Neil spotted me, and his eyes went cartoon wide for a second.

I smiled. "Bartenders?"

"Enthusiasts. Dick and Dale from Cocoa Beach," Neil said. I wasn't sure, but I think he stole a glance at my cleavage. "We'll be seeing them in Fort Lauderdale in a couple of months."

I liked the "we" part of that sentence. Not a "you and I" *we* but a "you are now in the Bohemia Bartenders" *we*.

"Where does Mr. Cray live?"

"Mr. Cray. He'll like that." Neil grinned. "He's in the Garden District."

Fifteen minutes and a cab ride later, we were dropped off in front of a mansion right out of *The Munsters.* From what I could see through the big oaks dripping Spanish moss in the unkempt front yard, the exterior was gray-green like the moss, with black shutters. It had multiple peaks and gothic spires, a balcony that was more *Hamlet* than *Romeo and Juliet,* excessive black, gray and white gingerbread trim, and lots of wrought iron.

"So this guy is a vampire, right?" I asked.

"He usually prefers rum to blood." Neil opened the gate in the black cast-iron fence and led me up the sidewalk and the stairs to the weathered gray wooden porch. It was crowded with terra cotta pots that had all kinds of plants growing out of them. I recognized some of the herbs, but most of them were mysteries to me.

There was no doorbell in evidence. Neil grabbed the hoop of the iron knocker, held in the teeth of a grumpy gargoyle face affixed to the dark green door, and rapped three times.

It took a few minutes. A crashing sound came from within,

and we exchanged glances. And then the door swept open, revealing a tall older man with flyaway white hair. He wore a tattered sweater over a collared shirt and slouchy khakis that looked a size too big.

"Neil, my son, come in! I was so intrigued by your call this morning. And this is?" He looked at me.

"I'm Kayanne Revelle, but they call me Pepper," I said, reaching out a hand.

He shook it vigorously and replied in run-on Southern, an accent that indicated he probably wasn't from New Orleans at all. "Conan Cray, but *they* call me Cray, so I expect you to do the same. Come in, darlings. Oh, yes. Are you married now, then?" he asked Neil.

Neil made a sound somewhere between a cough and a laugh as we entered the spacious front hall, dominated by a curving staircase and a terrifyingly large chandelier. "Um, no, Pepper is with the Bohemia Bartenders, my company. We do events like Cocktailia."

"Of course! My bad. I should know that, but it's been so long since I've visited your little bar in Bohemia." Despite his words, Cray had a grin on his face that revealed his delight in stirring trouble. "Do y'all want a drink?"

I was about to say no, but Neil asked, "What did you have in mind?"

"Well, it just so happens I have this particular new acquisition that I think you'll appreciate. And it's so hard to find an appreciative audience these days, isn't it?"

I caught Neil's look. Apparently this was part of the ritual.

"Sounds nice," I replied.

"Nice. Isn't that cute. Heh heh. Excellent. Go ahead and sit in the parlor there, and I'll be right back."

The parlor was a room off the central hall that held Victorian furniture, bookcases, a fireplace and an air of musty gloom. One sunbeam from a tall window pierced the dimness, revealing a colony of swirling dust that was just a few motes shy of settling into actual piles of dirt.

Neil gestured to the settee. Cradling my bag, I eased into the creaky seat with a wince. It was ornately carved with a tall padded back under peachy brocade upholstery, and the cushion was shot. Neil joined me, and we waited amid the distant sounds of clinking glass.

Finally Cray reappeared with a tray and set it on a side table. It held three round-bottomed glasses with flared rims. Each cradled a fat, square chunk of ice. Next to them was a squat bottle with a picture of a pirate on the label. No, not *that* pirate. It had already been unsealed, so Cray popped off the top and poured us each a couple of fingers of the dark gold liquid. We stood and took our glasses off the tray.

Cray held up his. "To pirates and rogues." He winked at me, and I barely suppressed a smirk. Most of the time, I didn't mind indulging flirting from crusty old collectors, especially when they were handing out rum that smelled this good. I swirled it around the glass, noting its heavy legs as it dripped down the sides, and took a sip. I held it on my tongue for a moment—vanilla. Banana? It burned gently on the way down.

Neil looked up with a sigh. "That'll do."

Cray chuckled. "Yes, it's quite *nice,* isn't it?" He threw my word back at me.

"Very nice, though maybe not the best rum I've ever had," I said.

"Oh-ho! Peppery response from Pepper. And she's right, of course," Cray said. "But it's been twenty years in the making on a lovely little island in Spain, and I'd say they were well spent. Someday I'll show you the vault, and we'll pick out something more to your liking. But for now, I believe you wanted to ask me something?"

Neil knocked back his rum, lifted the glass in salute and set it back on the tray. "Thank you. And yes, we had an incident yesterday with some bad whiskey, and we'd like you to test it."

"You intrigue me!" Cray set down his half-full glass. I drank down the rest of mine as Neil had and returned the glass to the tray. Maybe I'd been a little snooty about the rum, but it was still pretty damn good, and I didn't want to waste it.

"Can I be assured of your confidence?" Neil asked Cray.

"I'm like a priest. A priest of rum." He made the sign of the cross in the air. "Come with me, darlings."

We followed him on a journey up the sweeping staircase and then up another to a third-floor landing with a lone door. Cray withdrew a key from his pocket, unlocked it with a click and pushed it open.

We followed him into a marvelous chamber of light and modernity. It was a clean, roomy lab, with glass beakers and test tubes and flasks and microscopes arrayed on stainless-steel tabletops. There were bright lights overhead, enhanced by small dormer windows set into the slanted ceilings.

"Invented anything lately?" Neil asked.

"No, just playing around a bit with paper cocktails." He bent down and pulled out a small tray from a short refrigerator. "Try one?"

Neil picked up a translucent piece of orange paper embedded with darker fragments of color, about the size of a stick of gum. He broke it in half, put half in his mouth, and handed the other half to me.

Pleased and surprised, I took it and laid it on my tongue just as Neil said, "Scotch?"

"Very good!" Cray exclaimed. "And?"

"Orange," I said, chewing. It had the consistency of dried seaweed and a citrusy bitterness that teased my tongue. "And an amaro of some kind."

"Aperol, and a few other things. She's good," Cray said to Neil.

"I know." Neil nodded at my bag. Enough fun. Time to find out what was really in the Bohemia whiskeys. I extracted the bottles.

"Oh, my!" Cray said when he saw my elaborate wrapping and skull and crossbones. "That doesn't look good."

Neil looked like he was swallowing a laugh. "It isn't good." He explained about Barnie and the suspected methanol poisoning. "We just want to confirm that's what it is before we go further."

"Then let's not waste any time." Cray grabbed a bottle and began unwrapping it. I did the same with the other. Soon, the attractively rotund Bohemia Beachside Bourbon and taller Bohemia Rye bottles were staring at us from the counter. "You haven't opened these, I see."

"One empty bourbon bottle was on the floor next to Barnie," Neil said. "I pulled another bourbon randomly from a case and opened it. We tasted it and confirmed it was off. Pepper grabbed these from other cases. Right?"

"Right. I raided four cases in all, two bourbon, two rye. So I guess it's possible these aren't contaminated. I would've brought the one we opened, but they'd already dumped it."

Neil pulled his wine key from his pocket, but Cray held up a hand. "Allow me," he said. From a drawer, he extracted a razor knife and began cutting delicately through the wax on the bourbon, peeling pieces away with his fingers. Then he eased the stopper out slowly. He brought the whiskey to his nose and sniffed. His eyebrows lifted. He grabbed a beaker and poured an ounce, then lifted it to his lips.

"But shouldn't you—" I said, alarmed.

Cray raised a hand to stop my protest and took a sip. Then he spit it back into the beaker, much as Dash had done. "I'll be more scientific about it, I promise, but that there is alcohol abuse. I expect it would be quite tasty without that nasty additive."

A corner of Neil's mouth lifted. "Additive?"

"Oh, well, it might have happened in the distillation, but then it might not be so obvious. The poor man who fell ill must not have much of a palate."

"He works for Dash Reynolds," Neil said, "but he doesn't have anything to do with distilling. He drank a whole bottle of the stuff, so he must not have much restraint, either, regardless of whether he has taste."

The edge of judgment in Neil's voice surprised me. "Or he was bored to death," I replied, then bit my lip. "Hopefully not literally."

"Indeed." Cray donned goggles and gloves and waved us back. I followed Neil's lead and went to the far side of the next table to watch the mad scientist work.

First he went to the wall and flipped a switch. I heard a hum and looked up. A powerful vent was at work.

Cray poured a dollop of the bourbon into a clean beaker, dipped in an eyedropper, and measured out ten drops of the whiskey into a test tube. He went to shelves along the wall and pushed bottles around until he found a small one containing a bright orange liquid.

"Tang?" I asked as he brought it back to his table.

Cray chuckled. "Let's just say I wouldn't feed this to astronauts. Sodium dichromate solution. Nasty stuff. But we don't need much."

In another test tube, he measured a tiny amount of the orange liquid, then went to the shelves again and brought back a small brown bottle. He measured an even smaller amount into another test tube, then poured it into the tube with the not-Tang.

"Sulfuric acid," he explained. He took the tube with the mixture and swirled it around. "Not nearly as fun as an Old-Fashioned. But here's where it gets interesting." He took another dropper and filled it from the mixture. Then he leaned over the test tube with the bourbon and began adding drops, counting aloud to ten. He put the additive aside and picked up the toxic cocktail, swirling this one, too.

Then he held it about a foot from his face and fanned the top.

His nose scrunched up immediately. "Ugh. No doubt. Methanol. Only a reaction with acidified sodium dichromate would stink this badly."

It took me a minute, and then it hit me. "Whew!"

"You can smell it over there? Well, that's not good at all," Cray said. "Neil?"

"Not really."

I held my nose and sounded kind of funny when I replied. "I should mention that I have a doglike sense of smell."

Cray was busy capping the tubes. "I didn't need any special powers, unfortunately. The only thing I can't tell is if this occurred through the process of making the whiskey or whether it was added later. But I believe the concentration is high, suggesting an additive."

Neil frowned. "I'm having my doubts about this having

occurred by accident. I've gotten to know Dash pretty well, and he has a top-notch operation. Plus the whiskey we've bought outside of their event stash has been fine."

"Different batch, different results," Cray said, beginning work on the rye.

A few minutes later, after the same process, he held out the final concoction and waved his hand over the top. A vaguely fruity odor wafted my way.

Cray grinned when he saw my reaction. "Ethanal. From ethanol and my witch's brew. This one isn't tainted."

"Huh," Neil said. "Maybe it *was* a product of distilling. A disturbing result."

His reasoning clicked in my brain. "Because only the bourbon is affected. At least if these bottles are representative of the whole stash."

"It happens all the time in places where regulations aren't so good," Cray said as he cleaned up and stoppered everything. "A traveler picks up a bottle from a street vendor and doesn't even know he's poisoning himself. A moonshiner who doesn't know what he's doing or wants to up the alcohol content can end up killing his customers. Something could have gone wrong in Bohemia. Or perhaps," he said with a raised eyebrow, "someone just wanted you to think it was an accident."

Neil narrowed his gray eyes at the older man, who'd pushed the goggles up onto his head and was pouring himself a generous dollop of the Bohemia Rye in a clean beaker.

Cray took a sip and sighed. "It's really very good. Why are you looking at me like that, my friend?"

"What do you know?"

Cray tittered. "Come here. Look at the mouth of the bourbon bottle."

We both walked over to Cray's table, and Neil picked up the bottle, held it at a slant and rolled it slowly under the lights.

"Holy shit. It's scratched, isn't it?" I asked.

"It's very subtle," Cray said, "but I believe so. I was very careful in removing the wax to be sure I didn't scratch it. Of course, a bottle can be damaged any old time, but someone in a hurry to take off the wax and the stopper might not be so careful, especially if they were doctoring several bottles."

Neil ran his finger along the neck of the bottle. "And then they could add their poison and stopper it and wax it again."

"But who? Why? And how?" I asked. "We need to figure out where this bourbon has been or who might have had access to it."

"We can trace its history," Neil said, pouring a little rye into two small glasses Cray produced and handing me one, "but it comes down to the hotel problem. Anyone can get into a hotel room if they really want to."

"But Barnie was guarding the stuff."

"Was he? The whole time? We're going to have to ask him."

I sipped the rye, savoring its peppery sweetness, but in the back of my mind, I couldn't get over the nagging worry that it might be tainted, in spite of overwhelming proof this bottle was fine. It was a creepy feeling. I shook my head. "I don't like this. We have almost four more days of events, and we're going to have to guard any whiskey we've got 24/7."

"The smart thing might be to go ahead and store our stuff with everyone else's," Neil said. "Cocktailia's security isn't screwing around. They've got at least two beefy guys watching that room at all times. Forget the private suite."

"Good plan," I said. "Though I'm not sure how Dash is going to take all of this."

"If I were him," Cray said, "I'd be pissing in my pantaloons."

"Exactly. He has a problem." Neil sipped his rye and shot me a look. "We all do."

Chapter Seven

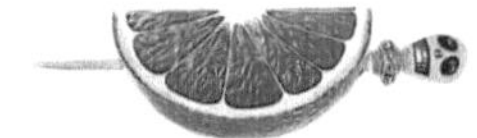

Neil was right. Bohemia Bartenders' reputation was on the line as much as Dash's was. And I wanted this event to be great for the Bohemia Bartenders. For Neil. For me. I liked these guys. And I needed this, a way to stretch my wings, get out of Bohemia once in a while, prove myself.

Of course, this wasn't just about being great. We had to make sure we weren't the bartenders who poisoned the entire convention. That could've been us last night, if Neil hadn't taken a moment to test the bourbon. Everyone was in such a hurry to get to the tasting, it all might have ended very differently. Suppose it had been just me getting the bottles to the floor? Would it have occurred to me that Barnie might be more than just dangerously drunk? Methanol would've been a lot harder to detect once the whiskey was mixed up in our cocktails.

"You OK?" Neil asked. "You look pale."

"Sure," I said, but I set what was left of the rye down on the metal tabletop. "I'm just thinking about tonight. I'd like to see the restaurant and maybe taste the whiskey."

"If you have any more to test, let me know," Cray said. "Or if you come across any interesting rums I simply must have."

He showed us downstairs and had us wait a moment under

the monster chandelier while he vanished into the parlor. He came out with the bottle from Spain and handed it to me with a wink. "Take this and think of me when you drink it."

"Oh, I can't—"

"Thanks so much," Neil said, shaking Cray's hand. "Will we see you at Hookahakaha?"

"Can an old rum man resist?" He waved us out the door and shut it.

I shot Neil a look as we headed down the sidewalk toward the gate. "I didn't appreciate your speaking for me back there."

"I'm sorry, but if I hadn't just thanked him, we would have been there all day arguing with him. This is what he does. He's generous. I never leave his presence without some kind of rum."

"Yeah, but he doesn't flirt with you."

"He might've if you weren't there hogging all his attention."

My mouth dropped open, and then I saw the twinkle in his eye. "Oh, I get it. You're messing with me, right?"

Neil grinned. "Maybe. He knows not to flirt with me, but I think he'd have trouble resisting Barclay."

"Oh, is Barclay—"

"Barclay likes girls," Neil said. "But that doesn't stop guys from drooling all over him, too."

"Well, he is rather picturesque," I said as we went through the gate and Neil started tapping on his phone to summon an Uber.

"You think so?" Neil's face was impassive as he tapped, but there was an edge to his voice.

Suddenly I discovered that I wanted nothing more than to get under his skin. To break that eternal composure. "Yeah, Barclay's pretty." I sighed dramatically. "Those green eyes?

That bone structure? Then again, Luke is nothing short of gorgeous."

Neil huffed, put his phone away and stared down the street as if willing our ride to materialize. "All the girls think so," he said resignedly.

I burst out laughing, and Neil looked over at me. He quirked his mouth. "You're messing with me?"

"Maybe. But they *are* pretty."

"Oh, shut up. So is Melody."

"If you like Barbie, sure." Don't get me wrong, Melody was a friend, but Neil needed a kick in the ass.

"Ha!" was all Neil said as a purple SUV rounded the corner and pulled up next to us. We got in, and the driver said hello and confirmed the address of the restaurant. Jazz was playing on the radio: "Do You Know What It Means To Miss New Orleans?"

"Louis Armstrong!" I said with a happy sigh.

"Yeah, my mama says he's my very distant cousin, about ten times removed, but talent runs in the family," the driver said as he rolled away from Cray's house.

Something was bugging me. The driver looked familiar. And I felt a presence behind me. I turned around and looked in the far back of the car, where a big, black shape crouched.

"Is that an instrument case?" I asked.

"Tuba," the driver said. "I make a few bucks down on Royal Street at night with it. People love the tuba."

BACK IN THE busy French Quarter, we walked to a café near our destination to grab lunch before thinking about the real work of the day. It had a checkerboard tile floor and scary machines swirling with neon-colored frozen drinks. Neil got a shrimp po'boy, and I ordered a muffuletta. We both got Cokes. Neil made a brief phone call to Dash to update him on what we'd learned and to tell him that we should have fresh whiskey straight from the distillery no later than tomorrow.

Neil nodded at my lunch. "That thing's bigger than your head," he said as he added some Crystal hot sauce to his sandwich.

"Ginormosity is a requirement for a muffuletta. I'll find someone to give the other half to. I have to have one every time I come to town. With a handful of Tums, usually. For heartburn," I said to his curious expression.

"Stress?"

"Sometimes." I shrugged.

"I hear you. It's hard running a business. And then I decided to run two, for some reason. Millie's been a godsend, though."

"Oh, yeah. She arranged today's shipment. She seemed really efficient. Half the work I was supposed to do for you here was already done. She'd placed a lot of the orders for yesterday's garnishes and stuff in advance."

"She's great. And I appreciate you, too. That you could help us out this week."

Uh-oh. We were back to just "this week." And I wanted to go to that next event in Fort Lauderdale. "What was that Hooka-whata-whata you mentioned to Cray?"

"The tiki convention in Fort Lauderdale in June. Hooka-hakaha. I think you'll love it." Neil moved on to the second half of his sandwich.

Pshew. I was still in. "Sounds great. Emphasis on tiki drinks, right?"

"I can't wait. But tonight, it's whiskey." He went on to

describe the four cocktails we'd be making to go with each course of the dinner, plus a welcome drink.

"By the way," I said after I'd finished the first and only half of my sandwich that I was capable of eating. "Will we be doing the welcome drink before or after the press conference?"

Neil stopped chewing and stared at me. He finished chewing and swallowed. "What?"

"The press conference. Actually, I think it's a just a few of the bloggers who've signed up for this particular Distiller Dinner."

Neil put down his sandwich and chased it with a big gulp of soda and a frown. "I didn't know there was a press conference."

"I helped set it up at Dash's request earlier this week. But I think I know what you're thinking."

"That this is a really terrible idea?" Neil said.

"I know. If someone heard something and gets the wrong idea about the bad bottles—"

"Or the right idea."

"I know. It's a risk. But Dash is here to promote his brand. And if any kind of rumor comes up, he has a chance to defuse it."

Neil nodded slowly. "Maybe. I want you to brief him. Help him find the right words to say, just in case."

"What? Why me?"

"Because you have an idea of how to do it. Right?"

I took my own sip of cola and tried to look intelligent. The eyeglasses helped, I think.

"Sure," I said. "I'll do it."

Chapter Eight

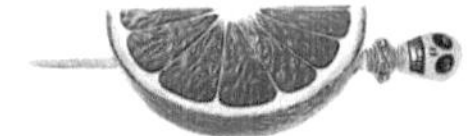

We found our team had already delivered the fruit, garnish fodder and liquor-store whiskey to La Bonne Vie, along with a hefty canvas bar tool bag. They'd left again, probably to get dressed for tonight. I didn't have to change, but I wrapped myself in a big apron I found hanging in the kitchen before I went to work.

The restaurant was an old-school New Orleans kind of place, with lots of red drapery and gold trim and white marble. The main dining area was downstairs, with an adjoining bar. The restaurant would be closed tonight because of the special event, though the bar was open already. Closing the bar would be akin to sacrilege in the Quarter.

The Distiller Dinner was slated for the upstairs dining room, which sat about sixty. We set up in the small upstairs kitchen while the staff cooked downstairs in the big kitchen for the four-course meal.

Neil began by opening the upstairs freezer and removing a large block of ice. After he let it sit for a few minutes so it would be more friendly to his tools, it was beautiful and clear. I was distracted from all of my juice-squeezing and peeling as he scored the big block with his hand saw, then used a mallet and chisel to break away a chunk. He repeated the process with smaller chunks and still smaller ones until he had lovely fat cubes, and then he chipped the corners off those. All of them went back in the freezer for use in the bourbon cocktail we were serving with the steak course. Which meant we had a bunch of lemon twists to do.

By the time he was done with a second block of ice, I'd squeezed a ton of grapefruits thanks to a thundering industrial-size squeezer, and my glasses were spattered with droplets of juice. I stacked up lots of grapefruit twists on layers of wax paper—curly strips of peel for garnish in the Blinker we were making as the welcome drink. We'd shake the juice up with raspberry syrup and rye whiskey later.

We were taking a quick water break when we heard a commotion downstairs.

"Guess who's here!" Luke said as he entered the kitchen, hauling two cases of bourbon.

"Besides you?" I asked. Then behind him came Barclay and Melody, each hauling whiskey. "But we already have whiskey."

A woman with round cheeks and dark hair, cropped Betty Boop style, was right behind them struggling with another box.

"Millie!" Neil exclaimed, rushing over to take it from her. He set it down and gave her a hug. "What on earth are you doing here?"

"It was proving difficult to get the courier you wanted on such short notice, and I figured it might be fun to do a weekend in New Orleans with Bennett. So I got started early."

"This is above and beyond," Neil said, shaking his head and smiling.

"We were glad to do it," came another voice. A guy with unruly brownish hair and a scruffy beard entered into the room, hauling a couple more boxes. "I'm Bennett."

Ah. The boyfriend. I'd heard of him. He was usually traveling the world doing sand sculptures at festivals. Quick introductions were made all around.

"There's a lot more in the car," Millie said.

"We'll take care of that," Barclay said.

Neil held up a hand. "I think we have plenty here for now. Millie, can you and Bennett take the rest to the hotel and talk to the Cocktailia staff about stowing them in the guarded storage room that everyone else is using? But first, take one bottle of the bourbon and one of the rye to this address. It's in the Garden District." He texted the information to Millie. "I'll let him know it's coming. Wait for an answer, then text me the result."

Millie looked puzzled, but she didn't hesitate. "We're on it. Let's go, Bennett!"

"Anything, my love," her boyfriend said with a twinkle, and they were off.

Neil gestured to the newly arrived boxes. "Put them in the corner, separate from the stuff you bought earlier today. I don't want to use them until we hear back from Cray. We're going to have Dash sample the stuff you got at the liquor stores just to be sure. He knows his whiskey better than anyone, and I'm confident they're OK anyway or we would've heard of other people getting sick."

With that, Neil made a quick call to Cray to give him a heads-up, and everyone pitched in to squeeze juices and make garnishes for the other four drinks. We batched what we could, but some stuff would be shaken or stirred as we mixed and poured on the fly.

Dash and Travis strolled in at five, both looking dapper. Dash sported a light-blue suit and a white hat with a blue band, while Travis wore a black vest over a dark blue button-up shirt, black pants and fun sky-blue high-top sneakers.

"Your sponsors have arrived," Travis declared with a grin and a bow.

"I hope that smile means Barnie is doing better," I said.

Dash's smile faltered a bit, but he still looked a lot better than he had the previous night. "The doctors say there's slight improvement. He was briefly awake while we were there but didn't make much sense, and then he was out again."

"We have a few more cases for you to test," Neil said, pointing to the two stacks of boxes.

Dash blanched.

"Don't worry," Neil said. "I think just a sip per case will be plenty."

"Thank God," Dash said, settling on a stool next to an out-of-the-way sink.

Neil nodded at me. Funny. He hadn't mentioned that some of the boxes had just arrived from Bohemia.

As the others worked and Travis went downstairs to check on the dinner prep, I methodically pulled and opened bottles from the cases. I poured Dash his first taste in a glass I found in one of the cabinets. He spit it out almost immediately.

"Whoa no!" I said, and everyone in the room stopped what they were doing and looked up in horror.

Dash glanced at me and then at everyone else.

He laughed. "You all look like goldfish at feeding time. It's fine. It's great! I just don't want to be smashed before the dinner."

"Oh!" My face heated. "Well, there's nothing like a quick heart attack to get the evening rolling."

Though Dash spit out most of the samples and rinsed the glass each time, he still managed to imbibe a bit. Gradually the whiskey took the edge off his stress, and he tilted toward relaxed.

When he was tasting the last of it—the last of the batch that had come straight from Bohemia—he pushed his hat back and sighed. "I feel better. This is really good stuff. I'm proud of my whiskey, no matter what."

Neil's phone buzzed. He glanced at the screen and came over to Dash and me. "We're good," he said quietly. "Cray says the new bottles are clean. Those last several cases came today from the distillery."

Dash's eyes widened. "Then the problem wasn't at home. The stuff we had at the hotel is from the same batches in the warehouse at home. That's great news!"

"Yes and no," Neil said. "The logical conclusion is that there was deliberate tampering of the stuff at the hotel. We're taking extra precautions."

I liked how Neil took the responsibility, sliding it away from Dash as naturally as a cat tricks a dog.

Still, Dash's face fell when he processed the fact that there was someone out there with evil intentions.

"There's good news," I said to Dash. "If anything happens to come up in your Q and A with the bloggers, you can dismiss the idea that anything's wrong with your whiskey."

"Do you think they'll ask?" exclaimed Dash, aghast.

"Oh, no. Absolutely no chance." And then I chickened out of further coaching because I didn't want him to freak out. Neil raised his eyebrows at me, and I offered him a weak smile.

It turned out that Travis had arranged for the press to arrive twenty minutes before the doors opened, so we didn't have to worry about serving the crowd during their chat. The journalists consisted of three bloggers and a reporter from one of the foodie mags that did a lot of articles about cocktails, and Dash and Travis sat with them around a big table in the unoccupied restaurant downstairs while Neil and I loitered in the background.

The first question for Dash was, "I heard that you might have a problem with your whiskey. Can you tell us about that?"

To his credit, he smiled and answered in a partial truth. "One of our employees had a little too much to drink and we had to get him medical attention," Dash said. "It happens. It's Cocktailia."

That got a laugh out of them, and they didn't push for more. Travis looked like he was biting his tongue, but he kept mostly quiet except when one of the women—all but one were women—asked about whether being at the beach influenced their distillery's identity, and then he launched into some nonsense about the sun and the attitude and how the best things happen where the land meets the sea and she really ought to come to Bohemia to take a tour sometime.

Neil declared the interview over at five minutes to show-time and invited the journalists to go upstairs and claim their seats and welcome cocktail. A couple of restaurant staffers stood at the front door to check tickets and usher the guests directly up the stairs, and Neil and I practically flew up there ahead of Dash and Travis to help the others get the Blinkers poured and garnished to welcome the horde.

I paused for a minute at the top of the stairs, watching the crowd come in, a foolish hope in my heart. I'd sent a note to my parents telling them about the dinner, offering to buy them admission. They hadn't responded, but I thought maybe they'd get tickets anyway.

When it was clear they hadn't, I headed back to the kitchen and the bartenders.

"Hey, who's that?" Luke asked as we worked, looking

through the window of the kitchen into the dining room, where the window was disguised as an antique mirror.

We all looked up to see a highly polished blonde in a little black dress enter the room with an entourage of two guys in dark suits.

"I can't decide if those are goons or lawyers with her," I said, "but they look protective, don't they?" The suits hovered while she shook hands with Dash, who looked uncomfortable, and she allowed Travis to kiss her cheek after he and she exchanged a warm smile. The Travis charm at work.

"That's Raquel Tocks, one of the prime sponsors of Cocktailia," Neil said. "Big developer throughout the South. So let's make her really good drinks, OK?"

We took the hint to get back to work and redoubled our efforts at mixing and garnishing. We lined up the welcome cocktail on trays for the servers to take out as I snuck glances at Ms. Tocks, who'd seated herself next to Travis. Maybe if I looked like *that,* was a bigwig in some company, my parents would've come to dinner.

Then again, I was used to disappointment when it came to my parents. Running a bar and going on adventures with the Bohemia Bartenders was enough for me. I was pretty sure I knew what made me happy.

My eyes drifted to Neil. He perched the grapefruit-peel spirals on the bowl of each coupe, those classic champagne-style glasses that mixologists loved. They gleamed with the reddish-brown Blinker cocktails. As if he felt my gaze, he glanced up at me and smiled before diving back into his task.

Whew. That'll make a girl tipsy.

The dinner went surprisingly well. It was what came later that had me shaken, not stirred.

Chapter Nine

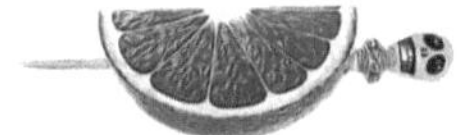

Dash and Travis welcomed the crowd with their origin story and introduced Neil and the Bohemia Bartenders, and then the real fun began—mix, pour, stir, pour, shake, pour, garnish *everything*—in a different type of glass for each drink—so three hundred glasses passed through our hands. The meal was over by eleven, and the room was happy, so we were, too. Truth was, even if our last couple of drinks had sucked, which of course they didn't, half the crowd wouldn't have known it because they were as obliviated as a muggle by the dessert course. This wasn't like a wine dinner. Those were for amateurs. Distiller Dinners were not for the faint of liver.

A string of cabs lined up outside La Bonne Vie afterward to haul off the hammered. Some of the tipsy guests chose to ensconce themselves in the restaurant's adjacent bar and pile on, but the mostly sober Bohemia Bartenders were ready to rock. We cleaned up what we had to, leaving some of it to Cocktailia volunteers, and Millie and Bennett reappeared to escort the leftover whiskey back to the secure room at the hotel.

"We're going out, and I'm buying!" Travis announced to us as we gathered outside the restaurant. His cheeks were a bit flushed, as he and Dash, unlike us, *had* partaken of the dinner. We bartenders had only engaged in strategic taste tests.

"Hell, no, cuz. I'm going to crash," Dash said.

"Nonsense. You are coming out. We're celebrating. And we're treating these fabulous bartenders for making us look even better! You don't want to seem ungrateful, do you?"

Travis's remark seemed a little manipulative, but I was like everyone else, in a party mood. "You should come," I said to Dash.

"What about tomorrow's workshop?" Melody asked, shooting a sidelong glance at Neil.

He quirked his mouth. "It's not until two. Surely you can recover by noon."

"Yes!" Luke and Barclay shouted simultaneously.

"I heard there's a great bar nearby," Travis said. "Can't quite remember the name. They serve little drinks or something. Do you know the one I mean, Pepper?"

"Snaiquiri! That's a great place," I said. "We can walk there."

"Ooo, I've heard of it," Melody said as we started walking. "Do you know how exciting it is to be in a place where I don't have to make pink frozen drinks all day?"

"You can always get a job on Bourbon Street if you miss the sugar bombs of Bohemia Beach," Barclay said.

"Shut up," Melody told him. "I won't be working in that hotel bar forever. Right, Neil?"

"You know your way around a cocktail. That's why I asked you to join us," Neil replied. "Have you talked to the managers there about starting a real bar program?"

"They're letting me do one special cocktail a night. It's driving me crazy. But when the tourists order a daiquiri, I always ask if they want a real daiquiri or the stuff in the machine. Maybe one in ten asks for the real thing, and then at least I get to make a Hemingway daiquiri."

"Now you're talking," Barclay said.

"Rum," Luke pointed out.

"Well, you're going to get a mini daiquiri with the first drink you order in here," I said as we reached the bar.

In other words, a snaiquiri. The seven of us settled around the elbow at the end of the bar so we could all sort of see one another, with the help of the mirrors tilted above and behind the rows of bottles in the back. I ended up near the end, with Dash on one side of me and Neil on the other. Travis and the others were seated on the straightaway, ordering from another bartender.

It was hard to hear much of the extended conversation because of the noise: lounge music with a slinky beat and tipsy chatter from the fair-size crowd, many of whom sat at tables or in comfy clusters of chairs and couches. The décor was a funky mix of old and new—brick walls and LED lighting, wood-beam ceilings and bright orange folding screens.

The most important element, of course, was the cocktails. Infusions with fruit and spices were steeping in elaborate jars against the back wall, promising great craft flavors. And everything was super-fresh.

I ordered a Last Word. It seemed like chartreuse was showing up in everything these days, but this was a classic that also had gin, maraschino liqueur and lime juice that the bartender squeezed right in front of me. He had a devilish charm, with rumpled black hair and dark eyes, a hint of scruff and intricate tattoos wrapping around his arms and up the sleeves of his black shirt. He smiled at my rapt attention as he worked on three drinks at once, all different, then shook and strained my pale yellow-green elixir into a pretty little coupe glass and pushed it toward me. I sighed as he set a shorter classic rum daiquiri next to it.

"Happy?" Neil asked, taking hold of his Ramos Gin Fizz in a tall Collins glass.

"There's nothing better than having a handsome man serve you a handsome cocktail," I said dreamily, kind of wrapped up in the moment, and then I lifted my eyes to see both Neil and the bartender looking at me with huge grins on their faces. "Oh, crap. Did I say that out loud?"

"Works for me, pretty lady," the bartender said with a wink. "Let me know how you like it. There's more where that came from." And then he went back to work on his next round.

"Was that a come-on?" I whispered to Neil when the bartender was out of earshot.

"Definitely," said Dash, happily sipping his Sazerac.

"Don't think too much about it," Neil said. "Drink up. You know what they say. Drink it quickly, while it's still laughing at you."

I held up my snaiquiri first. "To Bohemia Whiskey and Bohemia Bartenders."

Dash and Neil clinked their short glasses against mine. It took me two delicious sips and them just one to make the tiny daiquiris disappear. Then I tasted my heavenly gin cocktail and basked in the beauty of it all.

Twenty minutes later, Travis checked his phone and exclaimed over the time. "I know you were the tired one," he called to his cousin, "but I'm beat, and I have to make some phone calls home tomorrow."

"Always working," said Dash, who'd now relaxed into his Sazerac and had asked the bartender for a Vieux Carré. He was definitely into his whiskeys. "Stay for another. Plus, you're buying."

"Can you get it, Dash? I'm good for it. And I may or may not have promised to meet a girl at the French 75."

"Ah, I love that place," Neil said.

"We'll get there," I answered. "It's OK, Travis. Have fun, and we'll see you tomorrow at the awards ceremony."

"Best craft distillery!" Dash said.

"Don't count your bourbons before they're batched," Travis said. "It's bad luck."

"And *someone* is up for a Best New Cocktail Book award." I elbowed Neil.

He looked a little embarrassed, but he elbowed me back, leaning into me for an extra second of electric warmth that shot to all my extremities. Or maybe it was the cocktail.

"We'll catch up," Travis said, waving.

We had another round, then two, and everyone was feeling pretty happy by the time Neil's frenemy Alastair waltzed in. He carried the kind of cardboard tray that normally held four coffees. Only this one had four rocks glasses in it, each covered in plastic wrap.

He was dressed in a gray tweed pants-and-vest combination with a burgundy collared shirt, and his blond hair was curling out from under his hat like a fountain of silk. He looked like the frontman for a Brit-pop boy band who'd forgotten he was ten years too old for the part. He scanned our crowd.

"Where's your other merry man?" Alastair asked in his crisp accent as he approached the bar. "Too bad. One of these was for him."

"One of what?" Neil sounded more curious than annoyed.

"Sent from La Bonne Vie as kudos for your dinner tonight.

Which I'm sure wasn't as good as Frilly Fairy's, but I had to take their word for it."

He handed a glass to Dash, Neil and our devilish mixologist behind the bar. "And since the other ingrate isn't here, I'll have to drink his myself." Alastair pulled off the plastic wrap, which had "Congrats Travis!" written on it in black marker.

The Snaiquiri bartender's wrapper said "Boomerang me" on top, confirming this was what I thought it was. Boomerangs had only recently crept into NOLA from New York, so they were probably still a long way from Bohemia.

The writing on Neil's wrapper said, "Well done. You belong in NOLA!" And Dash was holding his so closely, I couldn't see it. But he had a ghastly, ghostly look.

"Dash?" I touched his arm. "You OK?"

"What?" His voice shook, and he set the glass on the bar. Neil was up in an instant and coming to stand between us. We leaned over to read the tiny hand lettering:

KATRINA MEMORIAL
AT MIDNIGHT IF YOU
WANT TO KNOW
THE TRUTH

We turned to look at Alastair, who was halfway through his drink. "A reasonably competent Old-Fashioned. What? Did I belch?"

"Did you write this?" Neil asked.

"Write what? I got these straight from Nicki at La Bonne Vie. Mark and I were grabbing a drink, and she asked me to bring them over. I think she wanted Mark to herself, if you know what I mean. He was all over her. Randy bastard."

"And you didn't write on them?" Neil pressed. "Didn't read them?"

"Oh, you know I can't read after attending *Oxford*." He laughed in a giddy, high-pitched giggle that had me shaking my head to dislodge the sound from my ears. "Look, she handed them to me with specific instructions on who was to get what. That's it."

"I'll call over there," I said quietly to Neil. I slipped off the barstool and stepped out into the street, where small groups of partiers were moving up and down the sidewalk under the streetlights, floating from bar to bar. I called La Bonne Vie, asked for Nicki and was told she'd left for the night.

When I got back inside, Neil was trying to convince Dash not to drink the cocktail.

"Nonsense," Alastair said. "It's perfectly fine."

"I concur," said our devilish mixologist, who took the last sip of his and licked his lips. "Nicki sends these all the time. I'll be sending one back."

"I don't think you need to bother," I said. "She's not there."

"I'll catch her tomorrow, then," he said with a smile and moved down the bar to fill another order.

Neil frowned, uncovered his cocktail and took a sip. "It tastes fine, but I don't want to drink anything else if I'm going with you to the memorial."

"What memorial?" Alastair asked.

"You really didn't read these?" Neil asked.

"I told you, *no*, except to identify who got what. That one was a dreadful scribble anyway. And it was dark. Besides, I don't care what it says. You lot are no fun at all." And he huffed and moved down the bar, waving down our mixologist as he went.

Luke, Melody and Barclay were now on their feet and moved closer. "What's going on?" Melody asked.

"There's a message on the boomerang," I explained, and they read it, too.

Dash was still and pale, but he finally spoke up. "I have to go. And I'm going alone."

Neil shook his head. "I'm going."

"I'm going, too." It probably wasn't the smartest thing I'd ever said, but there was no way I was going to miss this.

"We can all go," Luke said.

Neil shook his head. "The whole troupe might scare off this person. If they have information, we need to talk to them."

"But you might need muscle," Luke said, and Melody and Barclay burst out laughing at their slender friend.

"Actually, if I remember right," I said, "the memorial is in a cemetery. I need to look up which one."

"Don't go," Barclay said, frowning at me in particular, as if I was the troublemaker. "No one in their right mind goes into a New Orleans cemetery at night."

"Ghosts?" Melody asked.

"People," he said. "Much scarier than ghosts. But probably ghosts, too."

Barclay was right about the people. I didn't believe in ghosts, except for maybe a few spots here in my hometown. If any city had them, it was New Orleans. I also hadn't ruled out resident vampires.

I found the memorial on my phone. "Charity Hospital Cemetery. I don't remember anything about that one."

"Dash and Pepper and I will go," Neil said. "I'll text you when we arrive, Luke, and I'll text you when we're done." The implication being, if they didn't hear from us, call in the cavalry.

"All right," Luke said. "Keep us in the loop."

"Here." I took the bottle Cray had given us out of my bag and handed it to Barclay. "Take this. It would be a shame if something happened to it."

It was as if I'd sprinkled fairy dust on him. He took in the label, and his scowl transformed into a smile of wonder. "Dude. Really?"

"Cray gave it to us. Glad to share. Dash, are you up for this?" I asked. "Would you prefer to just call the cops?"

"And tell them everything? Besides, they'll laugh at this ridiculous situation. Let's go check it out." Dash tightened his hat on his head, a new determination on his face. "I need to know who's out to get us."

Chapter Ten

We flagged down a cab to take Neil, Dash and me to the intersection nearest Charity Cemetery. Dash and I sat in the back, Neil up front, and I read up on the memorial as we motored to Canal Street.

"Have you received any other notes?" Neil asked Dash.

"No! Honestly, I was hoping this was over."

"Maybe it will be after tonight," I said, expressing optimism I didn't really feel.

We didn't say much else for the rest of the ride, but my tummy was not entirely happy, and I was wishing I'd had some snackery with my snaiquiri so I wouldn't feel quite so tipsy. Dash seemed a little fuzzy, mostly anxious, and Neil was a rock. Heck, when wasn't he a rock?

"Um, is it just me, or are there a lot of dead people around here?" Dash whispered after the cab dropped us in front of a dilapidated white structure with a gate at Canal Street and City Park Avenue. The car peeled rubber getting out of there. This was a weird, not-quite-square three-way intersection, and the traffic lights and occasional headlights weren't bright enough for me.

"This is kind of the nexus of dead people here," I said. "This is the gate for Odd Fellows Rest, an old secret society cemetery. Lots of tombs. And there are people buried in the walls."

"Atmospheric," Neil said with grim humor.

I pointed out Cypress Grove across Canal Street and Greenwood in the opposite direction.

"What the hell is that?" Dash asked in alarm as a car's headlights caught a bizarre shape atop a small hill in Greenwood.

I suppressed a semi-hysterical giggle that was half fear. "I think that's the Elks mausoleum. That's an elk. I saw it on a field trip when I was a kid."

"Well eff me and eff their elk," Dash said, and I laughed for real this time at the unexpected vitriol.

"We might want to take it down a notch," Neil said quietly, tapping his phone, probably sending his text to Luke. "How far away is this place?"

I whispered this time. "Just up Canal." We walked in the direction I indicated, side by side like Dorothy, the Tin Man and the Scarecrow. Only we weren't worried about lions, tigers and bears. It was more like muggers, ghosts and killers. I clutched my messenger bag tightly and tried to look fierce.

"But everything's closed," Dash said.

"So maybe we meet at the gate," I said.

Dash sounded hoarse. "I hear voices."

"Is that a—bus?" Neil asked.

A short, white bus was parked just up and across the street. We crept across the streetcar tracks and behind it, then peered around its bumper.

About ten people were passing through a black iron gate topped by the words "Charity Hospital Cemetery."

"It's open!" I said.

"For a tour," Neil said. "Let's follow them in."

"Maybe our source is one of the tourists," Dash murmured as we strolled in behind them like we owned the place.

Neil didn't say anything, just led us up the path and then off to the side and behind a chunky white structure faced in shiny black panels. The voice of the tour guide drifted back to us from where the group had stopped in the center—the eye of the hurricane, according to what I'd read online. I only heard a few words, but I knew the story all too well.

"Are you sure this is the right place?" Dash asked as he clung to the wall, out of sight, looking around at more blocky structures set in a rough circle and an expanse of grass that rolled away into the darkness. "This doesn't look like a cemetery. I don't see any graves."

"It was basically a potter's field," I said. "Poor people were buried here. Victims of yellow fever and flu epidemics. And then they built this memorial. You're leaning on a grave."

Dash jumped back, and Neil's mouth twitched.

"There are dozens of victims of Hurricane Katrina buried in here, including some who were never identified." I'd known only a few of the fourteen-hundred people killed in the storm, but I never got to mourn them. Once my parents sent me to Aunt Celestine, I came back only for short visits, much later. My aunt and I stayed in a hotel every time, and my parents were too busy talking about all the good work they were doing with their church and hurricane victims and their missions to Central America to discuss all that we'd really lost. For them, the hurricane was like crack. It gave their needy souls a focus they'd been unable to find in me.

"OK, now I'm creeped out," Dash said.

"You should be," I agreed.

"Maybe hiding isn't the right thing to do." Neil glanced at his phone and pocketed it again. "It's midnight. Let's give them a chance to contact us." The tour guide's spiel had ended, and now the tourists were wandering through the memorial. Following Neil's lead, we also wandered for several minutes, but we stuck together.

No one came up to us. Couldn't our informant see us? The dead seemed like they were crowding in. And now the tourists were gathering back at the gate, getting on the bus. If we didn't get out of here soon, we might be locked in, and the last thing I wanted was to spend the night with Katrina's glorious dead.

We got to the large black plaque in the middle and pretended to read it, but all of us were looking around, knowing our time had run out.

And then I heard a *whoosh* and a clatter.

I jumped back instinctively and looked up at Dash. He held a hand to his forehead. Crimson rivulets of blood trickled through his fingers.

"What the—?" I sputtered.

"We're leaving *now*." Neil yanked on the stunned Dash's arm and pulled him toward the entrance. I walked quickly behind them, then heard another *whoosh* past my ear.

"What the hell is it?" I asked, finishing my sentence this time as we broke into a run. I spied Dash's hat caught in a bush in a strip of vegetation. I grabbed it and kept going, then saw another hat lying on the grass. Maybe *that* was his? Without thinking, I grasped the brim and had to give it an extra yank to free it—from the arrow that had pinned it to the ground. Another *whoosh* by my head as I bent to grab the arrow told me I didn't have time to extract the shaft from the ground, so I leapt up and stumbled after the others as we made a run for the front gate. We got a funny look from the rosy-cheeked tour leader, who was hovering there looking for the rest of his tourists.

"Do you have room on that bus?" Neil asked him.

I shot Neil an *Are you crazy?* look. "I don't care if there's room. We're getting on it!"

Neil shrugged his assent, caving to my panic, and we both pushed Dash forward and onto the bus. The tour leader apparently grokked our urgency, because he boarded right behind us and plopped into the driver's seat. He cranked up the motor as the three of us stood in the middle of the packed bus, Neil and I steadying Dash between us.

There was a loud crack as something hit one of the side windows, greeted by screams from the tourists. The glass cracked but didn't break.

Neil didn't look especially concerned. "Oblique hit, maybe?"

"Your play-by-play for tonight's *Hunger Games* provided by Neil Rockaway," I quipped, and Neil quirked his mouth at me. OK, so stress made me sarcastic.

"Hang on, everyone!" the leader-driver said. The bus jumped away from the curb and hurtled down the street. "Everyone OK? As you can see, we go all out on our ghost tours, and so do the ghosts!"

There was nervous laughter. A few people stared at us, since it was kind of obvious we weren't part of the tour. Others pulled out the cocktails and flasks they'd stowed on the bus and took generous swigs.

"We're taking a slight detour, but we'll return to our BYOB Midnight Ghost Tour in just a few minutes," the driver said. I caught his eye in the rearview mirror. He didn't look happy.

Hey, it wasn't our fault some maniac with a bow and arrow shot up his bus. Probably.

I plucked the handkerchief poking up from Dash's jacket pocket, pushed his hand away from his forehead and pressed the cloth against his skin. The white fabric blossomed scarlet, but even minor head wounds were big bleeders. At least that's what I told myself.

"I can hold it," Dash said softly, taking over and putting pressure on his wound. "I should've thought of the hand-kerchief."

"You had other things on your mind. How do you feel?" I asked.

"Stupid," Dash said, and a rush of empathy warmed my heart. "You got my hat?"

"Um, yeah. I think." I held up both of the hats and picked the most familiar one. "This is yours?"

"Yes," he said, his eyes widening.

There were two holes in the fine straw mesh, one in the front, one in the back.

"That ventilation should come in handy back in Bohemia," Neil said.

I raised an eyebrow at him and couldn't suppress a smile. "I'll tell you more when we stop," I murmured. There were too many interested parties on board. For a second, I wondered if maybe one of them was the archer—but then, that last arrow had struck the bus as we were leaving, so that didn't make sense.

"Anybody missing a hat?" I called out, waving the one that wasn't Dash's, a natural straw fedora-style hat with a band in an alternating gray and white triangle pattern. No one bit.

The driver ended up dropping us off at the same hospital where Barnie was staying. The guys got off first, and I leaned over to the driver and whispered, "You didn't leave anybody behind back there, did you?"

The driver turned as pale as one of his ghosts and snapped his gaze up to his mirror. He mouthed numbers as he counted, and then his face relaxed. "All here. I hope your friend's going to be OK. I'm going to report this to the cops when the tour's over. You should call in your report, too."

"Great idea. Thanks a lot." I grabbed one of his tour brochures from a holder on the dash and stepped down to the street. At least if the driver reported what happened, we had the option of not being involved at all. I wasn't sure what the right thing to do was anymore. There was more at stake than some bad whiskey now.

Neil had already taken Dash through the doors of the hospital, and I followed, wondering if someone had really been trying to kill Dash. Or maybe all of us.

Chapter Eleven

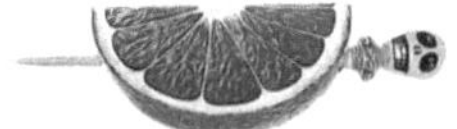

When Dash was finally taken back for examination amid the busy flow of incapacitated drunks and mysterious injuries, Neil and I sat on the uncomfortable emergency room chairs to wait. His arm rested lightly against mine. The contact was comforting after the scare we'd just had.

I held the two hats out, one in each hand. "I got Dash's hat and this other hat. What I wasn't able to pick up was the arrow that carried Dash's hat off his head."

"You actually *saw* an arrow? I wasn't sure. I don't know much about guns, but I wondered if a gun with a silencer might have been used."

"That's a grim thought. But the arrow had poked right through the hat. I think there's no doubt that's what injured Dash."

"And no one on the bus claimed this other hat," he said thoughtfully. "Oh, damn, I need to text Luke." He pulled out his phone, and I couldn't resist looking over his shoulder as he tapped out, "We're OK. Complications. More later."

"Complications. Ha." I looked up at him.

Neil's eyes arrested mine. Normally so hard to read, those blue-rimmed grays seemed to say a lot tonight. They held concern. The camaraderie of shared danger. A spark.

I swallowed and looked away, then placed Dash's hat on an empty chair and turned over the other one in my hands until I thought it was safe to look back. "What if this belonged to the shooter?"

Neil ran a hand over his trim beard and took a moment to answer. "Maybe, since it didn't belong to anyone on the bus. Not that any of them admitted, anyway."

"So maybe we need to find out who it belongs to."

"Tall order. Everybody wears a hat like this."

I lifted a shoulder. "At least at Cocktailia."

"True," he said. "Plus it might've been in the cemetery before we ever arrived. Before the shooter ever arrived."

I shook my head. "It wasn't far off the path. I think we would have noticed it when we came in."

"So we need to find someone who's lost their fedora and is good with some kind of bow and arrow."

"Sure. Easy." I returned Neil's wry smile and continued. "The style is somewhat distinct. The rim is short and rolled a little." I turned it over to look inside. "And it has a pretty lining."

"Gray silk. Nice. Is that a label?"

I looked more closely at the small, dark gray square sewn into the lining. "Chapeau Brothers. There's another tag." I fingered the tab that had been tucked under the sweatband inside. "Size large."

"So our shooter has a big head. Not surprising."

I grinned. "Now judging his brains by the size of his head?"

"His ego." Neil leaned back and crossed his legs and sighed. He looked tired.

"What is it?"

"I have a big workshop to give tomorrow. I'm worried for me and for you, since you guys have to make the drinks. I'm tired. And more relevant right at this moment, someone is trying to kill us. Why?"

I shook my head. "I don't see why anyone would want to whack us. Or Dash. But if I had to guess, I'd say he was the target. As for the bad whiskey—that could have been so much worse."

"Again, why? We need to ask him some questions."

"Cripes!" I pulled out my phone. "I should text Travis."

"I texted him when you were helping Dash check in. He was worried and asked if he should leave his date and come here. I told him Dash had a minor accident and would be OK."

"I think that's accurate. Hey, should we go see Barnie?"

"Not now. I hope he's asleep. We'll try to see him tomorrow."

"OK." I was too tired to argue, now that he mentioned it. The alcohol had worn off, and it had been a hell of a long day. I slouched in my seat, too, adding the mystery hat to Dash's on the other chair, and dug around in my messenger bag until I found my little tin of jelly beans. I sort of wished I was still carrying around a bottle of rum.

"Want one?" I held the box out to Neil.

"Oooo, licorice." He took one and popped it in his mouth.

"Good. You're a freak like me. Black jelly beans are my favorite."

He chuckled. "I'm into green, too, but licorice makes me think of absinthe."

"And absinthe makes me think of New Orleans." The good parts, anyway. I closed my eyes against the waiting room's fluorescent lights and tried to picture myself in the Carousel Bar, slowly spinning, high on Sazeracs.

I was awakened from a doze by Neil's elbow. "Dash is out."

"He is?" I sat up, groaning from stiffness. I straightened my glasses, which had gone cockeyed on my face. The clock on the wall said it was one forty-five. Great.

Dash came over to us, patting a small bandage on his head, and we stood to greet him. "Six stitches," he said, "and a lot of questions."

"What did you tell them?" I asked.

"That I bumped into a grave. What could I tell them? I have no idea what's going on."

Neil gestured toward the door. "I just summoned a ride. Let's get you back to the hotel, and we can all get some sleep."

"OK." Dash noticed me picking up the hats. "My hat."

"You want it?" I held it out.

"No—no, you keep it for now. I think I need a new one."

"New hat. New memories." I knew what that was like. New town. New memories. Which I found in Bohemia Beach, with its easygoing pace and blue ocean. It had hurricanes, yes, but none yet like the one I'd left behind. More to the point, it had my aunt and my dog, who were all the family I had left.

The cab ride went quickly. Neil didn't ask Dash any questions, and neither did I. We were all exhausted, and there wasn't much we could do tonight. We'd start fresh in the morning.

"Do you want us to go with you to your room?" Neil asked Dash once we were back in the lobby of the Hotel Lebeau, which still had a few revelers walking around.

"I'll be fine. Travis is next door if I need anything. That is, if he's not out with his new amour."

"Or in with her." The guys looked at me, and Neil was suppressing a laugh again. "Ew. I mean, that didn't sound right. Sorry."

Dash gave us a small smile. "Probably an accurate assessment. We'll touch base tomorrow to make sure everything's ready for Saturday, but I know you have your workshop. We'll get through this."

"If you see anything that doesn't seem right, call us. Call security. Call 9-1-1 if you have to," Neil said. "All right?"

"I will," Dash said. "For now, all I can think about is sleep. I'll be OK in my room."

Neil looked at him intently. "Text me once you're locked in there, OK?"

"You make me miss my dad," Dash said.

"Great," Neil answered, and I laughed as Dash headed for the elevator.

"OK if I walk you to your room?" Neil asked me.

"Me? Um, yes, sure." Why was I so flustered? He was just making sure I was OK. "I'm on four."

"We all are, I think. Our team, I mean." Oh. Well, then, that's why he was walking me to my room. We were on the same floor.

We headed toward the back stairs, which had the easiest access to our section of our floor. This was a big hotel, fifteen stories tall, with a pool on the roof and a maze of rooms and ballrooms. And so many stairs.

"Damn Dionysus," I said, pausing halfway through the ascent.

"What?"

I caught my breath for a moment. "Do you hear that?"

"What?"

"It's Tuba Guy."

He grinned as we started climbing again. "I'm surprised you haven't tuned him out yet."

"Impossible! He plays right across the street from my room."

The carpeted hallway was deserted as we turned a corner and found the alcove that held the doors to two rooms, including mine. Neil's phone pinged, and he glanced at it and stowed it again. "Dash is back in his room."

"Good."

Neil looked around. "How nice. Your room is next to mine."

"I—" I got caught up in those piercing gray eyes again. "I hadn't realized that. I just asked them to put us as close together as possible."

He smiled. "Convenient if you need me."

I gulped.

"Hey, look, you got a note." He reached over to my door, popped off the folded piece of paper that had been taped there and handed it to me.

I flipped it open, read it and clutched my stomach.

"What is it?" Neil took it from my hands, which shook as he read it aloud. "'Stay out of it or the next mark will be you.'" Neil's eyes were almost wild when he looked at me this time. "Pepper! We have to call the police."

"No. No! If we do, then everything comes out. The whiskey. How will it look for you if that happens?"

"I have no worries about that. We found the bad batch, and professionally, everything is fine."

"That's not how the gossips will see it. Your reputation, your business is on the line too. People are just getting to know how awesome you are." I was babbling, I knew it, but personally, I didn't like the idea of being under the microscope, either.

He slipped his arms around me and pulled me close. "Pepper, it's OK. It's OK. We'll sleep on it, all right? And we'll talk about it in the morning." His arms were warm and strong and comforting, and I returned the embrace, needing the hug, surprised by the muscular feel of him. He caressed my hair with one hand, as if I were a cat, and in spite of everything, my body slowly relaxed into him. I tilted up my head to ask him something and got distracted by his faraway look. He threaded his fingers into my hair, behind my neck. My breaths came short as his gaze locked with mine.

I must've imagined him leaning in to kiss me, because his lips weren't connecting with mine. So I grabbed his collar and did it for him.

His apparent reluctance shattered when my mouth touched his. Hesitance became hunger as he pulled me closer. Coming on top of the drinks and the adrenaline and the new rush of fear, his mouth coaxed a wave of euphoric dizziness from me as my lips opened to his. I tossed my glasses to the floor so nothing could get between us. A flare of heat shot through my body as he caressed my back and sipped at my mouth, tasting me the way I liked to savor a Sazerac. And then, all too soon, he pulled away and let me go.

I took a deep breath, not sure what to make of that—the kiss. Him stopping the kiss. I wanted a lot more of that kiss.

"Open your door, and we'll make sure everything's OK," he murmured.

He could come in and make everything *really* OK.

I picked up my glasses, pulled my badge out of my bag and held it up to the lock. It clicked, and I pushed open the door, Neil right behind me.

I set down my bag and the eyeglasses. He looked around, opened the closet, checked out the bathroom, met me back in the middle of the room. "Looks OK."

We just stood there for a minute staring at each other. My

lips were hot and needy and telling me to do something about it.

And then Tuba Guy, whose mournful bellows had been relatively quiet when we entered the room, burst into a lively rendition of "I Ain't Got Nobody."

A corner of Neil's mouth lifted. Good old steady Neil was back, wry and cool, though I caught a hint of turmoil behind the mask as he spoke. "I'll see you in the morning. Breakfast at nine if you feel like it."

"If you make it nine thirty, I'll be there."

He nodded. "And call me right away if you need anything. *Anything.* I'm right here."

"OK," I whispered, afraid to say what I needed just then.

He touched my cheek. "I'm right here."

And then he wasn't. He left, and I heard his door open and close.

There I was, alone, geek girl gone wrong. Again. I'd misread his invitation or acted too late to do something about it.

It was going to be a long night with Tuba Guy.

Chapter Twelve

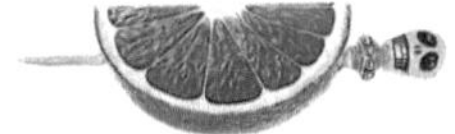

I didn't sleep well, and it wasn't just because of the tuba, which ceased its elephant mating cries around 4 a.m. I dreamed about someone trying to kill me with a gigantic whiskey drink that had an arrow for a swizzle stick. First they were forcing me to drink it, and then I was drowning in it. For a mixologist, getting killed by a cocktail is a particularly unpleasant way to go. I mean, you can always choke on a cherry or an olive, but poisoned? Ick. It was almost enough to turn me off alcohol.

Almost.

The truth was, like Neil, I'd never been into *alcohol* per se. I was into the glamour that surrounded it, the classic cocktails and the lush life that was especially thriving in New Orleans. Sure, the underbelly could be sordid and even sad, and NOLA had quite the muffin top when it came to booze. But I saw the gorgeous old bars, heard the great stories, soaked up the traditions. I watched the best bartenders in the world come to the French Quarter and make everything from delicate champagne cocktails to kick-ass tiki drinks, each creating a safe and pleasurable world of flavors for their drinkers. Not the neon nightmares on Bourbon Street, but sophisticated, balanced potions whose quality was almost magical. I was into the craft. Art, really. For every trendy vodka filtered over diamonds extracted from the belly buttons of Scandinavian virgins, there was a naturally fruity liqueur that had been made in some Italian valley for three hundred years or a boutique rum crafted by an ancient genius on a paradisiacal Caribbean island the size of a postage stamp. The newly minted foodies who watched chefs on TV all day long were only just waking up to how wonderful cocktails could be with their cuisine, and I wanted to show them the way.

Small steps.

I let the shower finish the wake-up process and donned black pants; a white button-up shirt that I didn't button up all that high; a subtly striped vest with a deep, rounded V-neck and four buttons in a diagonal, off-center line; black leather boots with a short heel, and Snow White-caliber red lips. And the glasses, of course. This hot geek was going to kick some cocktail butt today.

That said, I peeked out of the door before undoing the chain, and not seeing anyone, I sighed in relief, exited and closed the door behind me.

When I looked up, Neil was standing there, and I almost rocketed out of my skin.

"What the hell!" I clutched my bag as if it were some sort of anchor and tried not to feel stupid.

"Sorry. Timing. You're meeting me for breakfast anyway, right? I can walk you downstairs."

"Yeah. OK." As my heart settled, I stole a second glance at him as we walked toward the stairs. His beard looked freshly trimmed, crisply defining those sculpted cheekbones. He wore matching gray pants and vest, a crisp white shirt and a black skinny tie. In other words, he was completely edible.

Stop it, Pepper. First of all, he hasn't even touched you this morning.

No hello kiss or anything. Though now that I thought about it, that would've been kind of awkward. *OK, we're pretending last night didn't happen, I guess. The kissing part, anyway.*

"Any developments?" I asked as we trotted down the stairs.

"I pinged Dash, and he said he had a headache and was going to sleep in this morning but would try to catch my seminar this afternoon. Travis called to ask me details of what happened. Other than that, no news."

We got the same table at the restaurant in case any of the others showed up. This morning was a French toast morning for me. That and lots of coffee. Neil went with protein—an omelet and bacon, plus more coffee. The bartender's friend.

"I feel like I have to clear the air," Neil said.

Uh-oh. "Yeah?"

"I shouldn't have let what happened happen last night. You were shaken up, and besides that, I've hired you to do a job. I don't want to be that kind of guy."

I let the spoon clink into the cup where I'd been stirring in my sugar. "Look, I'm not your employee." He raised his eyebrows. "Not really. You hired me, yes, but the way I look at it is, I'm your partner. We all are. Most of us work at different bars. I own half of mine, for God's sake. And we're grownups. And if anyone's to blame, it's me." Crap. That wasn't exactly how I wanted to say it.

"I don't know," Neil said.

"That didn't come out right. There's nothing to blame anybody for. I mean, what happened wasn't bad. I mean, it was good. Oh, hell, somebody please shut me up." I took a big gulp of my coffee and spit half of it back out, it was so hot.

Neil looked like he was trying not to laugh. "I just want to make sure we're OK."

"We're OK. I hope you don't act like this every time a girl wants to kiss you."

This time he laughed out loud. "It doesn't happen all that often."

"Then maybe you should enjoy it when it does." *Christ, he's going to think I'm a total man-eater.* "Before I say anything else that makes me want to move to a desert island, I have some ideas on how to track down Robin Hood."

"Mm-hmm," Neil said over his own sip of coffee, his eyes twinkling.

"I'm thinking I'll go to the hat shop after breakfast and see what I can find out. Maybe they'll know who bought that hat, even have a record of it."

He quirked his mouth. "It could be anyone's."

"True. But we don't have a lot to go on. I also want to talk to Nicki, the bartender at La Bonne Vie, and see if she knows anything about the boomerangs."

"Good thinking. I wish I could go with you, but I have some last-minute prep to do for this afternoon. You can be back by noon?"

"As close as I can. We're all meeting in the kitchen that's linked to the ballrooms on the second floor, right?"

"That's right. The workshop starts at two." He did that looking-out-the-window thing again. Unspoken words hovered between us like an unwanted drone at a nudist camp. Fortunately, our food arrived, giving us an excuse not to talk.

"So," I said after a few minutes of delicious French toast inhalation, "why do you think I got a threatening note last night and you didn't? You were there, too. You've been there all along."

Neil stopped eating for a minute and looked me in the eye. "Maybe because this psycho knew that threatening you would have the same or worse effect on me. He didn't need to threaten me directly."

I stared at him. What was he saying? Was he worried about me?

"I feel responsible for my people," he continued, bursting my bubble. *It's not all about you, Pepper.* "This whole thing makes me really angry. There are a lot of people that could have been hurt last night. Even more with the whiskey stunt. And I still can't figure out why anyone would target Dash and Travis or us, for that matter."

"What about your frenemy? He threatened you at the tasting. He had possession of the boomerangs. And he seems pretty nuts."

Neil snickered. "Alastair talks a good game, but it seems unlikely. He was at the bar when we left. Wait a minute." He pulled out his phone and tapped it, took a sip of coffee, and glanced at it again when it chimed. "Luke says Alastair left just after we did, complaining he couldn't get his drinks fast enough."

"So he had opportunity." Boy, those *Law & Order* marathons were paying off. "I guess the next question is, does he hate you that much?"

"I don't know. I don't think so. But he did hate that I was better than him in school and behind the bar. So he endlessly delights in giving me shit about dropping out."

"You left. That's different."

He smiled. "I appreciate that. He makes me question whether I would've been better off as an astronomer. But I had this insane affinity for cocktails, for making great ones, and once I got a part-time job doing it, I knew I didn't want to do anything else."

"When did you start making drinks?"

"Officially, college. But I was making whiskey sours and gin martinis for my grandfather when I was ten years old."

I almost choked on my coffee. "He sounds like fun."

"I would say I'd like you to meet him someday, but I'm not sure you'd ever forgive me."

I laughed. "Then I definitely have to meet him."

"He has this bad habit of showing women his ancient dildo collection."

"His *what?*"

"He's a treasure hunter. Shipwrecks. His house is full of all kinds of interesting artifacts, including the dildos, though he keeps those in his private office. Most of the family is still trying to figure out if he's got a stash of gold somewhere."

"Do you think he does?"

Neil shrugged. "He helped me buy The Junction Box. I think he knows more than he's telling."

"Intriguing." We'd finished our food. I pulled my phone from my bag and checked the time, then fished around for my wallet. "I should probably get going."

He waved me off as I extricated the wallet. "I've got this. I'll write all this off, anyway."

"Oh. Thanks! That's awfully nice of you."

"I'm definitely not being nice." He raised one eyebrow, staring at me as he sipped his coffee. *Oh, my. Maybe ...*

I couldn't help a small smile, remembering last night's kiss. And then I popped a pin in that thought when I remembered all the crazy stuff that was going on, the problem we had to solve before I could think of anything as frivolous as Neil's mouth on mine.

I tried to assume a serious expression. "I wish I had time to see Barnie this morning, but I don't think I do."

"We'll try to go after my seminar. I'll have my head in the

game then. We should have enough time before the awards tonight." The waiter dropped off a bill, Neil signed it, and we got up and headed toward the lobby.

"Are you nervous about your seminar?" I couldn't quite believe it. Neil wasn't nervous about anything.

"Let's just say a shot might be required."

I grinned. "Nerves are good for you."

The faintest of smiles touched his lips. "Then you're good for me. Listen, Pepper—" What? *I* made him nervous? "Be careful out there. I mean it. Don't go into any dark alleys."

"Or cemeteries."

"It's not funny." His voice had an edge now. We paused at the fringe of the busy lobby, and he moved closer, lowering his voice. "Take cabs if you have to. I'll pay for it. Just be careful."

"Now you're making *me* nervous. It's not a far walk to either place. There are tons of tourists around. It's broad daylight." I was trying to convince myself more than anything. "I'll be OK."

"You'd better be." He zapped me with what could only be called a smoldering glance, then turned on his heel and walked away. Nothing more to say. Or he'd gone verklempt. Actually, I kind of had, too. Maybe Neil did care about me, a little.

I headed through the throng toward the main doors and almost ran into Dash.

"Pepper!" A new straw hat with a broad white band covered most of his bandage.

"How are you feeling?"

He smiled. "A lot better. Sleep helped, and I took some ibuprofen and a shot of bourbon."

Distiller medical insurance must be as bad as bartender medical insurance. "What are you up to?"

He shrugged. "I thought I'd ask the same of you."

"Heading out to learn more about the mystery hat and the boomerangs."

"Mind if I join you?" His enthusiasm charmed me and impressed me, too, given all the stress he was under.

What the hell. Two targets were better than one, right?

Chapter Thirteen

The streets were already bustling with tourists, and there was a commotion at the end of the block with parasols and musicians. "What's that?" I asked.

Dash smiled. "They're having a jazz funeral for the Long Island Iced Tea."

"Of course they are." We headed off in the other direction. I kept an eye on the map app on my phone to make sure we didn't miss a turn. "Is this your first Cocktailia?"

"I went once as a bartender."

"You're a bartender?" I exclaimed.

"Briefly. It was part of the journey, you know? That and a Kentucky bourbon tour I did when I turned twenty-one. I worked at one of those distilleries for a couple of years. When my dad made it clear I would inherit the building in Bohemia's industrial district, the first thing I thought of was a distillery. He loved the idea. He's the one who got me loving whiskey in the first place."

"I've only seen it from the outside, but it's got a cool vibe. Lots of brick."

"Yeah, it's an unusual building for Bohemia in that regard," he said. "I'm the fourth generation in our family to run a business there. Unfortunately, we're not the only ones who think it's cool. I've had a developer on my ass since I started renovating, wanting to turn it into condos. We've been in business for nine years, and I'm still getting letters asking if I'll sell."

"Who's bugging you?"

"Oh, a big corporation," he said. "Tocks Development Group."

"Tocks ... why is that name familiar?"

"Because Raquel Tocks was at our dinner last night?"

"Oh, yeah! She's a sponsor. And I've seen that name around Bohemia, too. They've built some new apartments out on the north end of town. I guess they're trying to get into the old industrial district, since it's not really industrial anymore. A couple of my friends live in another building kind of like yours that another developer remodeled, the old ice plant."

Dash nodded. "That's a gorgeous building. It would have been fantastic for us. We could have even made our own ice, like that distillery up in St. Augustine. But the factory building was what we had to work with. My dad closed the paint business a few years after his brother died, but he wanted the building to stay in the family, since their grandfather started the paint factory there. My mom had passed by then—"

"Oh, I'm sorry."

"Thanks. It's OK. Basically, the only family my dad had left was me and my cousin, so he set up a family trust to help me start the distillery."

"You and Travis?"

"Travis didn't come on board until about a year into it, around the time my dad passed. The story we tell everyone is that we started it together, but the truth is, Travis just wasn't interested at first. He's moved around a lot. Always had something more glamorous cooking, though he never seemed to settle anywhere. I made him some promises to get him on board."

"That's interesting." With Travis's charm, I figured he could walk into any business and be owner of it before long. "So he's your partner?"

"He will be soon," Dash said. "My lawyer is drawing up the papers. I think he really likes the job now, even if he wants to turn it into a vodka factory." Dash rolled his eyes.

"Nooo!" I said, and we both laughed.

"I could have started with vodka, but I started with gin while we got the whiskey going. He thinks we can make big money if we make vodka, and he's probably right. He was always the practical one."

"Why is that?"

"He's a survivor. Travis had a tough time as a kid. His dad—my uncle—was an ass, frankly. Always cutting Travis down. And his mom kind of withdrew into herself, didn't intervene, and she and Travis were estranged until she died last year. He was strong, though. He protected me from bullies, and I did everything I could to get him away from a bad crowd. Both of our families lived up the road in Cocoa Beach, even though our dads' paint business was in Bohemia."

"Turn left here," I said, and we shifted direction. "I wondered why I hadn't seen you in school."

"I'm also a few years older than you, I think, but that's why." He smiled. "I would've remembered you."

Now Dash was being dashing. "So you and Travis were friends as well as cousins."

Dash looked thoughtful. "Almost like brothers. When we were kids, we did everything together. We loved adventure stories, not just *Star Wars*, but the classics from my dad's library—C.S. Forester, *Lord of the Rings,* Howard Pyle, that sort of thing. Especially that medieval stuff by Pyle. Great illustrations. And any old movie with swashbuckling, swordplay, you know, and we were always acting them out. My dad even paid for us to take fencing lessons together. For me, it was plain old fun. For Travis, those stories were an escape."

"I loved those kinds of stories, too. Lots of fantasy. I still wish I had a dragon of my own."

Dash chuckled. "We kind of grew out of them. We didn't hang out as much when we got older, especially because he was a few years older than me. He was a junior in high school when his dad died. It was hard on him, even if the old bastard wasn't much of a loss."

"I get it, believe me." My remark sounded more bitter than I'd intended.

Dash looked at me with sympathy. "When I started the distillery, I wanted to get Travis involved. He's not only the brother I never had; he's a charming guy and perfect for marketing, a total extrovert, the yin to my yang. Everybody loves him. We wouldn't have come this far without him."

We approached a doorway where a guy played a melancholy jazz tune on tenor sax. We listened for a couple of minutes, then Dash produced five bucks and tossed the bill into the instrument case before we moved on.

"It's so nice to hear jazz on every street corner," he said. "Music seems like the perfect life to me."

I chuckled. "Sure, playing for a few bucks at a time, playing at all hours ..."

Dash's smile was fleeting. "It just seems like an easygoing kind of existence. The distillery—it's a lot of pressure. There were days when I thought I didn't want to go on."

His comment surprised me. "And now?"

"It's been kind of a struggle to get going, but we're just hitting what I think of as the second level. Our gin held us over while we developed the whiskey, but it's all taken a ton of time and effort and investment. Now we're getting good press and better distribution. I even got an offer from a British distiller who's looking to partner with an American firm, but after all of our hard work, I'd like to keep the business in the family and reap the success we've earned. I figured it was time to make a splash here, which is why I talked to Neil about you guys helping us. I was pretty excited about it until we almost poisoned the convention. Do you know how hard it was to dump out all that whiskey we brought? It was like watching my dreams go down the drain. I know that was only one batch, but—I don't know if I can take another setback like that."

My blood still ran cold thinking about it. "That was scary."

"It still is. And now I'm worried about you, too."

Damn. "Neil told you about the note, didn't he?"

Dash nodded. "He's concerned. Someone is messing with us. I can't imagine what's going to happen next, but I don't think it's going to be good." He turned to me and offered a strained smile. "But I know we can figure it out. We'll look out for each other, OK?"

"OK. Honestly, Dash, I'm more worried about you than me. I think someone is harassing me because they don't want me helping you. Here, give me that hat." I paused on the sidewalk, and he handed me his hat. I examined the inside, then stuck it on my head for a moment as I rummaged in my bag. I extracted a slim object sheathed in leather and a mini roll of pink duct tape and secured the sheath into the sweatband inside the hat.

"What's that?" he asked.

"Cocktail knife."

"In case I have a lime emergency?" Dash grinned.

"No, silly. In case you need a weapon. It's sharp as hell."

He put the hat back on his head, wiggling it into place.

"Seems like overkill. You have a whole cocktail kit in that bag? And duct tape? Rope, too? Should I be worried?"

I laughed, a little embarrassed. "I like to carry a few things, just in case. A small shaker. Et cetera. But no rope. Usually. Does it feel OK?"

"Just fine," he said, patting his head as we continued walking. "You sure you don't want to hang on to it?"

"The knife? Are you kidding? If I did need it, it would take me ten minutes to find it and dig it out. You can give it back to me later." I glanced at my phone. "We're here. Maybe we'll find out what we want to know from the Chapeau Brothers."

Chapter Fourteen

The "brothers" might have been a fanciful branding invention, but there was no doubt this store had an impressive assortment of hats: luxurious felt, smoothly woven straw and saucy cloth, mostly for men but a few for women that ranged from broad-brimmed sun blockers to elaborate going-to-church-on-Sunday confections. They were displayed on tall, dark wooden shelves and central tables, beautifully arrayed, hinting of luxury, their invisible tentacles reaching out to nearby pockets for a wallet they could pluck.

"That's a nice sipping-mint-julep-on-the-porch kind of hat," an elegant young man said to Dash in a studied Southern accent. Or maybe he wasn't so young, but he had a youthful appearance that I suspected was enhanced by makeup. The accent might not have been all that authentic, either, but the slim-fitting pants, crisp shirt and suspenders made his attire perfect for the shop. "Have you tried something in blue? It would match those pretty eyes."

I sighed. It figured that of the two of us, Dash was the prettier one.

"I had a nicer hat, but it suffered an accident," Dash replied. "I could probably use another one."

"What are you looking for? Another straw hat? This one

has a robin's-egg-blue band and sharper lines. I think it would set off your eyes *and* your nice square jaw."

I struggled not to roll my eyes and tapped my phone to pull up a photo of the hat we'd found in the Charity Hospital Cemetery. I showed it to the salesman. "What about something like this?"

He glanced at the phone and turned his attention back to Dash. "Oh, we do carry that one, but we only have a couple left. I sold one just a few days ago, in fact."

"Really?" *Tamp it down, Pepper.* "I mean, do you remember what the person looked like who bought it?"

"Well, *that's* an unusual question." Our salesman finally tore his gaze away from Dash and raised an eyebrow at me.

"I wouldn't want to commit a fashion *faux pas* by having the exact same hat as someone else at Cocktailia," Dash said, drawing the guy's eyes again. "He might've been from the convention. Do you remember what he looked like?"

"Oh, I see. As a matter of fact, I believe this young man was wearing several buttons from Cocktailia on his jacket. Paid cash. Told me he'd been saving his tips for this hat. He looked like a bartender. Big beard. Might've been squirrels nesting in it. You definitely don't want to dress like him. I can help you find another style you'll *love.*"

"That is disappointing," Dash said, getting into his role, "but nothing else here is getting me excited."

"Well," our salesman said, *sotto voce,* "*excitement* isn't really our job here. We're more into *elegance.* But if you want some real excitement and entertainment, you should come see me in my other job." He slipped us a card.

Dash glanced at the card, swallowed and handed it to me. It advertised a drag show on Bourbon Street.

"I bet you're fantastic," I said to our sales guy and meant it.

"You've *got* to see my new gown for this show, which we're calling 'Wham Bam Thank You Glam.' I've got big sequins. *Big* sequins. Silver, silver, silver. It practically blinds people when I come on stage."

"My brother here is a huge fan of female impersonators!" I squeezed Dash's arm and tried not to grin at his glazed expression. "When do you perform?"

"Friday and Saturday night. The midnight show is the best. I hope I see you, sugar," he said to Dash. "Let me know if you need a new hat for a night out you won't forget." He winked and walked away, and Dash grabbed my elbow and practically pushed me out of the store.

"What was that about? I've never seen a drag show in my life," he said as I shook him off and took the lead, steering us toward La Bonne Vie.

"You should. They're fantastic here. Anyway, I just wanted to make his day. He was flirting with you so hard I thought his mascara would flake off."

"Mascara?" Dash said with a squeak.

I laughed. "Does your masculinity feel threatened?"

"Absolutely not." He straightened his hat and slipped his arm in mine. "I have a beautiful woman with me, after all."

It took me a moment to de-fluster. Dash's flirting was way more obvious than Neil's, which was kind of a relief. At least I didn't need psychoanalysis to figure out what it was. I let myself enjoy the feeling of his warm body brushing against mine as we walked briskly toward our destination.

"So someone actually bought a hat there that looks like the one we found," I said. "Sound like anybody you know? Buttons? Beard?"

"Half of Cocktailia? But no, no one I know personally."

"Fake beard, perhaps?" I asked.

"That seems far-fetched. It's not like the guy anticipated losing his hat in the cemetery, if it was even the same hat or the same guy."

I frowned. "I don't know what I expected from the shop. We could've asked for a name, maybe."

"He paid cash. Tips, the guy said."

"But they have a mailing list. I saw the register on one of the tables, like a guest book. Very old-school."

"I saw that, too," Dash said, "but there's no way to match the hat with a name. I didn't see dates in it."

I frowned. "Damn it. OK, we're here. Let's hope Nicki is working today."

La Bonne Vie had light traffic mid-morning on a Friday. A few people sipped eye-openers at the bar. I went up to the seasoned barman and asked for Nicki.

"She should be here in a couple of minutes. Y'all want anything?"

I looked at Dash, and we each took a stool. It was early for me, especially since I had to work, but hey, it was New Orleans.

"Bourbon milk punch," I ordered.

"Bourbon. A girl after my own heart," Dash said. "I'll have the same, with Bohemia Beachside Bourbon, if you have it."

"We do," the barman said. "Had a great event with those folks just last night, one of those Distiller Dinners. Super bartender team. They sent a couple of each drink around to us here at the bar, so I had a taste. Good choice. I'll have these right up for you."

"There you go. Right from the expert's mouth," I said after he'd walked away.

"I didn't know Neil did that," Dash said.

"Honestly, I didn't either. But it was a brilliant marketing move. Now these bartenders know your whiskey, know the kinds of drinks they can make with it, and are talking about it to their customers."

"And that may explain why Nicki sent the boomerangs."

"Good point. Oh, look, here comes a woman who might just be who we're looking for."

A female bartender had entered from the restaurant side of the house and slid behind the bar. She was pretty, with pinned-up reddish-blond hair and freckles, and she wore a tight, short black skirt and a silky green blouse.

"Y'all being taken care of?" she asked us.

"He's got it." I nodded to our guy down the bar. "Hey, are you Nicki?"

"Yeah." There was hesitance in her voice.

Dash rushed to reassure her. "We just wanted to thank you for the boomerangs. I'm Dash Reynolds from Bohemia Distillery."

Her face lit up. "Oh, you're Dash? Nice stuff. I was only too glad to send over those drinks for you. Only I wish I'd thought of it."

"You—you didn't?" I asked.

"Another guy asked me to send them. He said he enjoyed the dinner so much, he wanted to say 'thank you.' He said he heard you were headed to Snaiquiri and marked them so they'd go to the right people."

"That's really nice," I said, though that's not what I was thinking. Who the hell sent the drinks? "Did you read the notes after he marked them?"

"No need. Alastair Markham was in the bar, so I asked him to take them over."

"So Alastair didn't send them?" I asked.

She laughed. "Uh, no. Not his style to compliment another

bartender." She looked down, picked up a bar spoon and began rearranging the garnishes. Almost like she didn't want to say anything else.

"What did the man look like?" Dash said. "I'd like to thank him."

"Oh, not remarkable," she said. "I don't even really remember. We'd had a few ourselves that night. Excuse me." She moved down the bar as our bartender brought over our lovely white cocktails and set them down. He produced a UFO-shaped gadget and turned its crank over each drink, generating a sprinkling of aromatic nutmeg that fell prettily on each foamy white surface.

"Enjoy," he said before going to check on another customer.

"Do you think Nicki is hiding something?" I whispered to Dash after a moment.

"Maybe she just didn't want us to know how drunk she was, especially since I have a professional relationship with her place of employment." Dash took a sip. "Wow, my whiskey is delicious."

I couldn't help but smile as I tasted mine. "I detest false humility. It's true. It is delicious." I took a deeper sip, savoring the cold, smooth texture of the cocktail. It was like a boozy vanilla shake, only not as thick. "Maybe you're right. But it's frustrating she couldn't tell us anything else about the guy who wrote the message."

"A random diner from the dinner? I mean, that could've been any one of sixty or so soused people, talking to a tipsy bartender. Somebody who overheard us saying we were going to Snaiquiri. I don't think we're any closer to finding out who he is."

"Say he's the one who bought the hat, and he's from Cocktailia. And maybe he's the same guy who did the dinner. We can look at the guest list and try to narrow it down."

"I have a thought. Nicki?" Dash called out. She came over to us, but this time, her face was more guarded. "Did the man who asked you to send the boomerangs have a beard?"

Her eyes widened and shifted to the door as someone came into the bar, and then she looked back at us. "You know, I think he might've had a beard. But it was dark. I really don't remember. I'm sorry."

"What about a hat?" I asked.

"Oh, yes, he had a hat."

"What did it look like?" I pressed.

"Kind of like yours," she said to Dash. "I don't really notice things like that. Excuse me." And then she was off to attend to the new customer.

"Well, that narrows it down," I joked.

"Look at it this way," Dash said. "At least we got a killer drink out of it."

I shot him a look.

"Maybe not the best choice of words," he said, downing the rest of his. He plunked down the glass and felt around in his jacket pockets, pulling out his buzzing phone. "Give me a minute. I'll be right back. Hello?"

He went out the door, and I waved at our original bartender, miming the writing of a check. I was only halfway through my drink, but that was plenty. I had way too much to do today, and it was already warm and humid outside. "Could I have a glass of water, too?" I asked when he dropped off the bill. I left cash inside the billfold, drank down half the glass of water he brought, and headed out to see if Dash had abandoned me.

He was standing outside the restaurant like one of those

performance artists who pretends to be a marble statue, and was almost as pale.

"Dash?"

"It's all gone."

"What?"

"Our checking. The Bohemia Distillery account. It's been cleared out. All the money is gone."

Chapter Fifteen

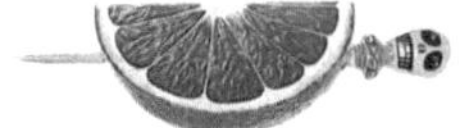

I flagged down a cab to carry Dash and me back to the hotel. He was about as responsive as a marble column and in no condition for another stroll through the Quarter, though he did tap on his phone as we rolled through the sunny streets. I wanted to get him somewhere relatively safe. And find out what the hell happened.

I texted Millie on the short ride back. "Still in town?"

"We just had brunch. About to see if Neil needs anything. What's up?"

"Meet me in the lobby in 5."

She and Bennett met us just inside the doors, and I asked Bennett if he would show Dash to his room and stay with him for a minute while I talked things over with Millie.

Dash looked at me. "I need to talk to Travis." It was the first thing he'd said since he'd lapsed into shock outside La Bonne Vie.

"Good idea," I said. "Did you text him?"

"He's not answering."

I touched Dash's shoulder lightly. "Why don't I find him and send him to your room?"

"OK." Sounding defeated, he let Bennett lead him off through the busy lobby.

"What happened?" asked Millie, looking cute in a short

dress. Her bobbed hair, a few shades darker than mine, was as smooth and efficient as she was.

"Dash got a phone call and said that someone cleaned out the Bohemia Distillery checking account."

Millie's eyebrows rose, and she blinked a couple of times. "Forgive me if my first reaction is to say, thank goodness they paid us for most of the work already. And my second reaction is, this sounds bad."

"Really bad."

"Like 'someone is out to get them' bad. After the toxic batch of whiskey—Neil told me about that—"

"And the cemetery," I said.

"What cemetery?"

Crap. I lowered my voice and filled Millie in on the attack, leaving out the note I found on my door.

"Damn. OK. What can I do?"

"Get as many details as you can from Dash about what happened and his theories on what might have happened. I have to help Neil and the others with the workshop cocktails, and I don't want to get Neil upset before his presentation."

"Does anything get Neil upset?" Millie asked wryly.

I snickered. "You have a point. But I don't want to test his limits right now. Talk to Dash, and I'll find Travis and send him up. See if he has anything interesting to say."

"You got it. Let me know when you're out of the seminar."

"Cool." I gave her a quick hug, watched her go and thought about where I might find Travis. If he was schmoozing with press or distributors, the bar seemed like a good choice. I headed that way.

The Hotel Lebeau's bar was less traditional than its restaurant and more twenty-first century bordello. Mirrors alternated with tall windows in the lounge area, where overstuffed couches and chairs in black and taupe and stripes fought for space with low tables. The bar itself was curvy and luscious in dark wood and onyx, the stone's creamy veins lit from beneath. Generous shelves of liquor lined the wall behind it, and velvety taupe barstools with high backs invited customers to linger. Clusters of different-size Edison bulbs, the filamented things that everyone seemed to have now, hung overhead like hipster chandeliers.

Travis was ensconced in a corner with a couple of guys who seemed a lot like him, all of them relaxing on the plush furniture and sipping whiskey. Bohemia whiskey, I figured.

"Pepper!" Travis called out as soon as he saw me. Lightly soused, I was pretty sure. "Come on over and meet my friends."

"Hey, Travis." I shook hands with the men as he introduced them, but I was too distracted to process their names. Distributor types. "Have you seen Dash this morning?"

"I was letting him sleep in. I should get him down here, though."

"Actually, he asked if you wouldn't mind stopping by his room." I didn't want to say more in front of these guys.

"OK, sure. I'll check in with him later. We're getting along too well to stop now!" He wiggled his eyebrows, clinked glasses with the other guys and waved at the bartender to bring more.

"He's a little under the weather this morning," I said, trying to insert some emphasis so Travis would get my hint. "He really needs to talk to you."

"No problem," he said blithely. "Why don't you sit down and have a drink with us? Tell us about your favorite whiskey cocktails."

Any other time his merry drunkenness would've been kind of cute, but Dash was hurting, his company was in trouble,

Travis was oblivious, and I was annoyed. "I have a workshop I have to get to. Please check on Dash, OK?"

"He'll be fine. But sure, I'll go. One more drink, OK?" Travis's gaze focused on mine, he gave me a small nod, and I finally got a sense that he saw more than he was saying. Like he'd finally picked up on my urgency and didn't want to clue in the dudes.

"Thanks." I waved awkwardly and beat it out of there.

Several minutes later, after a leery visit to my room (where there were no more nasty notes, to my relief) to dump my bag and pick up the hat we'd found, I made a stop by the front desk to leave it at the Lost and Found and have a word with the clerk.

Finally, I got to the massive kitchens that adjoined the second-floor ballrooms. It took me a minute to find the remote corner where Melody, Luke, Barclay and Neil were huddled. Neil was reminding everyone how to make one of the cocktails he was featuring in his seminar, and he nodded at me when I came in. Luke and Barclay both shot me quizzical looks, and Melody elbowed me in greeting. Nearby, convention interns were setting out hundreds of small cups on trays and prepping blood-orange slices to garnish the first drink.

"This is going to be great, but I can't wait until this is over," Neil finally said to our surprised laughter. I was relieved to see he'd left printouts of the recipes, since my brain had apparently stepped out for a smoke. "Pepper, have a minute?"

"Oooo, you're in trouble," Luke said, and Barclay smacked him upside the head. Melody just grinned.

Neil led me out of earshot, not far from where another team was prepping a variety of tiny, fancy gin and tonics for another seminar. Not just any team. Alastair was directing them with curt, loud commands.

Neil shot a disapproving side-eye in their direction, then turned to me. "What did you learn?"

"Not much from the hat store, except that someone from Cocktailia bought a hat like the one we found. I dropped it at Lost and Found and tipped the desk to let me know if someone picks it up."

"Good idea. And the boomerangs?"

"Someone asked Nicki to send the boomerangs and wrote on the plastic. She was low on detail, maybe deliberately so. But I didn't get a sense there was malice in her. More like she was worried about her job or something. And she said the guy who suggested it wore a hat and maybe had a beard, though she wasn't sure."

Neil searched my eyes. "There's something else."

"I don't want to distract you. Let's talk after the seminar."

"Well, now you have to tell me. I won't be able to do a damn thing if I don't know what you're hiding."

I allowed him a brief smile. "Dash said someone drained the distillery's checking account. He just found out. I asked Millie to talk to him and Travis and see what she can find out, and we'll catch up with them afterward. I hope that's OK."

"Damn it." He shut his eyes and rubbed his temples before looking at me again. "Having Millie talk to them is brilliant. She's methodical and smart. But that's not the best news, is it?"

"And it raises a lot more questions. Who did it? Was it just a theft? Coincidence?"

Neil let out an exasperated sigh. "Coincidence? It's hard to believe, given everything that's happened. They'll have to get the police involved now, at least with the money missing."

He checked his watch. Yes, an old-fashioned watch with moving hands and everything, drawing my eyes to his forearms, dusted with rusty hair and wiry with muscle visible where his shirtsleeves were rolled up. My attention wandered to the rest of him, still sharp in the vest and tie, the trim beard, the thick hair.

I stopped at his gray eyes. He was looking at me funny. I cleared my throat and tried to appear focused and efficient and not curious and horny.

"I've got to get in there and make sure the multimedia is ready," Neil said. "You OK?"

"OK and ready to work," I said with authority.

"See you after?"

"Smelling of whiskey and citrus, no doubt."

He grinned. "My favorite perfume."

NEIL'S SEMINAR WAS PACKED, and it was all we could do to keep up with the cocktails. Trays of petite drinks were brought out for each talking point as he shared the history of classic cocktails and ways to give them modern twists, along with tips on how to experiment and create them from scratch. We only got to watch the last ten minutes or so, after the last trays of cocktails were delivered, but he didn't seem nervous at all. It was love I saw up there on the dais as he went through the slides of his presentation—love of the craft, the history, the flavors.

The convention interns cleaned up while a dozen guests lingered to chat with Neil and get him to sign books.

"We're going to a new bar down the street," Melody said to me. "Want to join us?"

Barclay and Luke watched me expectantly. This was a chance to get to know them better, and I really wanted to go.

But I shook my head. "I think I have to see what's going on with Dash and Travis."

"Oh, no. What now?" Luke asked.

I gave them the highlights version of the morning's events and the bank account. "I feel like I'm in the middle of this, and I know Neil will want to find out what's going on."

Melody elbowed me. *Ooops.* I'd been staring at Neil. "Groupie," she said. The guys laughed, and my face heated.

"Am not! *That's* a groupie." I nodded toward the svelte blonde in the tiny dress gushing over Neil as he signed her book.

OK, maybe I was a groupie, too. But they didn't need to know that. "How about I text you and catch up with you when we're done? I think I'm going to need a drink after this afternoon."

"We're all going to need a drink, and I'm buying," came a voice at my elbow. Neil. He'd finally shed his last fan and looked happy with himself. "But not until after the awards. They go from seven to nine, which means we can actually go out and have fun. It's about time we had a night off."

"Now you're talking," Barclay said. "I want to go to Latitude 29 tonight."

"Done." Neil nodded. "You know I dig tiki."

"Well, we're going to get a head start. We'll see you at the ceremony," Luke said to Neil.

"I need a quick break, too," Neil said as the others scattered. We picked up his bag of bar tools and his laptop, and we headed through the busy corridor toward the stairs. My tummy fluttered. Maybe I *was* too clingy. A groupie?

I looked up at Neil. "Would you rather go see Dash and Millie alone?"

His eyebrows rose, and a hint of a frown played around his lips. "Why? If you'd like to go out with the others, that's fine."

"Oh, no, that's not it. I mean, that would be fun. But I don't want you to feel like I'm—I mean, I'm new to the Bartenders, and I—"

"No, no. I absolutely need you to be there. You were there when Dash got the news this morning. You've been there all along during this mess. But I don't want you to feel like you're in danger. If you're worried, I'll be happy to do it myself. Well, not happy. But I feel like our fate is entwined with Dash's, not to be melodramatic or anything—"

"So do I! I want to be there. I want to help sort this out."

"And I want to make sure you're safe." He laid a hand on my arm, lightly, but I warmed through at his touch. What was it about this guy? "Speaking of which, no more threats?"

We'd reached our rooms, and I glanced at my door. "Not yet."

"Good. Five minutes, OK?"

I nodded. "OK."

In the calm of my room—and yeah, I checked all the corners to be sure no arrow-wielding poisoners were lurking—the bellowing tones of Tuba Guy and the racket of traffic reassured me that mercurial New Orleans had my back.

I met Neil in the hallway, and we headed toward Dash's room.

Chapter Sixteen

As it happened, Neil and I ran into Millie, Bennett and Travis in the hall outside Dash's room.

Travis looked grim. "I gave him one of my sleeping pills. He'll be out for a while. He's shaken up."

"I can see why," Neil said. "Have you found out any more about what happened?"

"The bank says it's some kind of check scam. I talked to our accountant. One of our vendors didn't get paid. Probably someone stole a check we'd written to them, forged a new one with a new payee and a much bigger amount, then deposited it into their own account."

"Then you can find out who has that account, right?" I asked.

"It was a fake account," Millie said, "and they emptied it right away. This probably happened two or three days ago."

"While we were here," Travis added. "No one had really been looking at the account until this morning, when the automatic payment for the power bill didn't go through."

"Do you have any idea who could be doing this?" I asked Travis.

He ran a hand through his unruly hair and stared at the crazy corridor carpet as he replied, his voice edgy. "No idea. Listen, I've got to think. I've been on the phone for the past two hours. I'm going to take a walk." He looked up at me. His normally mischievous eyes were dark. "I'll check on Dash when I get back and make sure he's OK for the awards tonight. He's been so stressed about the business, maybe this is a sign he needs to get out. But I can't be the one to tell him to forget his dream."

He walked away toward the elevator. None of us said anything until after it dinged and we heard the doors close, and then we all looked at each other, questions hanging in the air.

"I think this calls for a meeting over booze," Bennett said.

"I have no idea where you'd get booze around here," I replied.

The others laughed. I knew just the right spot to get a drink and a snack, too.

Ten minutes later, the four of us were seated at a table in a dark oyster bar that smelled faintly of dank whiskey barrels and crustaceans. This wasn't the kind of place where Cocktailia folks would hang out, and that's why it was perfect. The tables were topped with chipped, dark green laminate, the floors were scuffed black-and-white checkerboard, the ceiling fans bore dust chunks that clung to the twirling blades like cliffhanging mice, and the walls were crowded with photos and memorabilia with about as much aesthetic sense as a hoarder house.

Millie eyed the decor dubiously as she ordered a club soda from our tired-looking waitress.

"Aw, come on," said Bennett, who ordered a beer.

"Not until later," she said, winking at him.

"Should I get a cocktail?" Neil asked me. I knew what he meant—not whether he should drink but if it was likely he would drink well.

"They're good here if you stick to the classics," I said, then told the server, "Pimm's Cup, please."

"I'll have the same," Neil said. "And an oysters Rockefeller for the table."

"Not the raw stuff?" Bennett asked.

"It's not a month that ends in 'R,' " Neil pointed out.

"Too snotty for me no matter what month it is," I said to Millie's "Eww."

"I like all the snot. All that delicious, tasty oyster snot," Bennett said.

Neil snorted. We perused the menu and ordered more snacks when the server returned with our drinks and the oysters Rockefeller.

I sipped my Pimm's Cup. "Ahh." Gently tart lemon and herbal gin flavors embraced my taste buds.

"Good choice," Neil agreed after a long sip of his. "Now that we have alcohol, I have to ask: What do you think is happening here? Someone's out to get Dash, it looks like, but was the theft the same person?"

"We had the police on speaker phone while we were in the room," Millie said. "The chances of them figuring out who had the account, the one where they deposited the check, aren't great. It was established almost a year ago, and the security footage doesn't go back that far. And the money was transferred out electronically."

"So someone was planning this for a year? That doesn't seem random," I said.

"The victim could've been random," Millie said. "The cops said this is standard practice—set up the account, find a victim or victims, close the account once the bank gets wise. Though a year is a long game."

"How'd they get the Bohemia Distillery check?" I asked.

Bennett swallowed a bite of cooked oyster while he waited for his raw ones. "They're looking into it, but it was probably forged, like Travis said. You can go into an office supply store and buy supplies to make checks. All you need is the account number, which you can get from a stolen check or a little social engineering."

"Well," Neil said, "it just seems peculiar that this is all happening at the same time. It's like someone wants Dash to fail."

"Big-time," I said. "And I forgot to mention, Dash said there's someone at home bugging him to turn his building into condos. A developer in Bohemia. They want him to move out, if not fail altogether. And Dash said another distiller was interested in buying into the company."

"Interesting." Neil stared into his drink as we all watched him.

"What is it?" I asked.

"Something Travis said about how stressed Dash has been. You don't think it's possible that he—?"

"Is sabotaging himself?" Millie asked. "Good lord."

"I'm sorry, but that makes zero sense," I said. "I mean, he did mention feeling overwhelmed this morning, but I think he loves what he does. Plus he could just walk away, sell out. He also doesn't seem like the kind of guy who would poison a whole convention."

"He could've stopped us at any time that night if we didn't do it for him," Neil said. "Maybe he doesn't want to admit to failure. Would rather blame it on external forces."

I shook my head. "No way. I've got to go with my gut here. Plus he'd have to hire someone to shoot an arrow at us. And send the boomerangs."

"He could've arranged that before he left La Bonne Vie.

Him arranging the arrows, well …" Neil smiled, and I saw a hint of mischief there. "It's absurd. But then again, so are the arrows. Just playing devil's advocate. I wanted to see what you thought, since you've spent more time with him."

"What about Travis?" Bennett asked as our dishes arrived. "He could have done any of those things, too."

We pondered that thought for a moment as we enjoyed the array of appetizers, which, like the drinks, were definitely several notches above the decor.

"What I got from Dash is that Travis might be hard up without the job at the distillery," I said.

"Doesn't he own part of it?" Neil asked.

"Apparently not. Travis's father and Dash's father owned the building when it was a paint company. Dash's father inherited it and passed it down to Dash, though Dash mentioned that family was really important to his dad. I think Dash wanted to help out his cousin, who didn't have much of a career going. But Dash is making him a full partner, so that should make Travis happy."

"Maybe we need to talk to the woman he was going to meet up with the night of the cemetery attack," Neil said, "just to be sure."

I laughed. "Good luck getting that information."

Bennett grinned. "Let me try guy talk. See if I can find out who it is."

"So are there any rivals that might be out to get Dash or Travis?" Millie asked.

"There are so many new distilleries," Neil said. "It's not like anyone's out to get anyone else. It's friendly rivalries, or behind-the-scenes bitchiness, but nothing that warrants attempted murder."

"Poor Barnie," I said.

"Yeah," Neil said. "Want to check on him after this? Maybe he can tell us who was in the suite with him and all of that bad whiskey."

WHILE MILLIE and Bennett went off to conspire, Neil and I headed back to the hospital to see Barnie. He was curled up on his side, asleep, when we entered the half-lit room. Machines beeped, and bags delivered fluids into his body. This time, there were no other visitors.

"Kind of a crappy way to end your big trip to Cocktailia, alone in a hospital," I whispered to Neil.

"It could be—well, I'm just glad he looks better." *It could be worse* was what he was going to say.

"Should we stay for a minute?"

Neil nodded. I sat in the chair next to Barnie, between the bed and the window, where the afternoon light was turning gold. Neil hovered beside me, and we waited.

"And how are we this afternoon?" came a voice from the corridor, preceding the appearance of an attendant with a tray. The young woman, wearing scrubs with little cats all over them, did a double-take when she saw us. "Oh, he's sleeping again?" she asked in a lower voice.

"Not now I'm not," came a croak from the bed.

I turned back to Barnie, who'd rolled onto his back and was looking up at the ceiling.

"Then let's get you sitting up. You need to eat something," the attendant said, pressing a button that pushed Barnie up to a sitting position. She adjusted his pillows and rolled the tray closer. "Maybe your visitors can help you? I'll be back in a few minutes after I deliver the other dinners."

"What is it?" Barnie asked.

"Hmm?" I replied, not knowing what he meant. He hadn't even looked at the tray.

Neil moved around the bed and lifted the cover off the plate. "Hot turkey sandwich. Open-faced with lots of gravy. Mashed potatoes. Jell-O."

"At least there's gravy," Barnie said. "Is there a roll?"

"Yes. Want it?"

"With butter."

Neil looked amused but patiently buttered the roll and held it out to Barnie. Barnie turned his head slightly and reached out his hand but didn't connect.

Neil's eyebrows lowered, and I sucked in a breath.

"Here." Neil placed the roll in Barnie's hand and watched as the patient took a big bite, chewed and swallowed. Then Neil asked softly: "How bad is it?"

Barnie looked toward Neil's voice. "Severe ocular damage is what they told me," he rasped. "Mostly blurry. I can see movement. Every once in a while, there's this little patch of clarity, like at the center of a tunnel."

"Oh no. Barnie, I'm so sorry," I said.

"Pepper?" Barnie turned his head toward me. "I really wanted to go to the showcase, you know? It was so boring in the suite. I didn't think a little drink or two would hurt." He took another bite of roll. "Is there ginger ale? I asked them for ginger ale."

Neil handed the cup to Barnie and resumed his position next to me as the patient slurped his straw.

Neil's expression was dark and inscrutable. "Was anybody drinking with you?"

"Naw, no. It was my job to get the stock and get it ready to go for the event. And there wasn't much to do, so I just hung out and watched TV in the suite. Travis and Dash checked on me once, late morning."

"Was anybody in there after we moved in the liquor the night before?" I asked.

"I don't think so. I don't see why anybody would've been." Barnie still didn't get it. Still didn't understand he'd drunk tainted whiskey. "I mean, that Brit fop was hanging out around the suite when I showed up in the morning, but—"

"Who?" Neil asked sharply.

"What's his name ... Markham. Alastair Markham. Said he was curious about the Bohemia whiskey and wanted to try it."

"And did he?" Neil asked.

"Am I in trouble?" Barnie asked. "I mean besides the fact that I'm fecking blind."

"No, Barnie," I said, resting my hand on his arm. A small smile crossed his lips. "We're just trying to figure out what happened that day before we found you."

Barnie slurped to the dregs of his cup, and I took it from him. "He brought a bottle of the Frilly Fairy. I like gin. I wanted to try it. He said he'd give it to me if he could have a taste of the bourbon. It didn't seem like it would do any harm. We'd brought a lot of extra so Dash and Travis could give it away or whatever, so we wouldn't run out. So I invited him in and opened a bottle."

"Alastair drank the bourbon?" Neil asked, surprise in his tone.

"Hardly," Barnie said. "Kind of a snob, that one. Took a sip and said, 'Well, that's nothing to worry about,' and then he left."

"Scouting out the competition?" I asked Neil.

"Maybe." It was what he wasn't saying that had me curious.

"I didn't even get to try the gin," Barnie said. "I'll probably drink gin from here on out. Not sure I'll touch bourbon again. Uh, you don't, you know, have anything with you, do you?"

I stared at him in shock while Neil uttered a firm, "No."

"I thought you might," Barnie said sadly. "You know, since you're a bartender. That's OK. Shit. Talk about a fecking hangover."

Neil shook his head. Barnie really didn't get it. He'd almost died, and he still wanted a drink?

"Did you leave the suite at all after we loaded in the whiskey?" I asked.

"No, not at all," Barnie said, perhaps too emphatically. "I love room service, you know? And they have HBO at the hotel."

I got up and brushed past Neil so I could return Barnie's cup to the tray. At that moment, the attendant came back in, precluding further questions.

"You've got to have some of this gravy!" she said gaily. She either deserved an Oscar or a humanitarian award for one-tenth of the cheer she was showing. "Better let him eat," she said to us, and we nodded, said our goodbyes and left the room.

My guess is we were both thinking the same thing: Alastair Markham had just stepped to the front of the list of suspects.

Chapter Seventeen

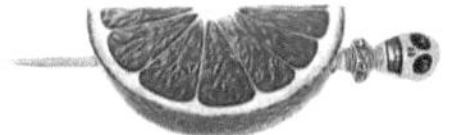

"**P**oor bastard," I said once we escaped the hushed misery of the hospital, reached the street and started walking. "Blind. Actually drank himself blind."

"With methanol, yeah," Neil said.

"What the hell was Alastair doing in the suite?"

"Maybe he was just checking us out. The tasting was that night, plus the cocktail competition is coming up."

"You don't think—"

"That he was checking to see if the batch was tainted? That maybe he'd engineered the tainted batch and was just making sure?" Neil shook his head. "Why? It's all so far-fetched."

"This whole thing is far-fetched," I said as we turned toward Canal Street. There weren't many tourists around, just a few businesspeople wrapping up their work week. "Say Alastair, maybe with help, replaced the good whiskey with the bad stuff. When?"

"It would've had to be overnight, right?"

"But Barnie slept there and never left the suite."

"That's what he says. But could a serious drinker like him really resist sampling one of the greatest drinking cities in the world?" Neil's cynicism had a ring of truth to it.

"You have a point."

"You said you helped them move everything into the suite the night before the event—that would be Tuesday," he continued. "How was it shipped from Bohemia?"

"Dash paid a transportation company to take a van-load of the stuff from home to here. Dash actually complained because it arrived late afternoon the day before the event, several hours after their plane landed in the morning. It was supposed to be there the night before, or at least in town, so it was ready for them when they arrived. He was tired and wanted to get it loaded into the suite so they could relax."

"So he was stressed even then."

"Yeah, I guess he was," I said.

"Why was it late?"

"Travis called the company, and they told him they'd had car trouble. He tried to cheer Dash up, talked about how this was the event they'd waited for. That seemed to help. When we met downstairs again at six, the bellboy said a bunch of cases had arrived and were waiting for us in a storage room."

"Holy hell," Neil said. "So the stuff was just unguarded there in the storage room?"

"Not for long. They said it had arrived within the hour. There's no way somebody could have gone in there, uncrated the bourbon, opened the bottles, put in the bad stuff, and closed and resealed everything."

"And the cork stoppers have plastic tops under the wax," Neil mused, "so no one could have easily injected the methanol. Plus there was enough poison in the bad bottles that I'm guessing whoever did it had to take some whiskey out of the bottle to get the methanol in."

"Yeah," I said. "And if you think about it, we still don't know if every bottle was tainted or not."

"If they weren't, then Barnie was especially unlucky. The

irony is, if he hadn't been a drunk, we might not have found out."

A drunk. It wasn't the first time Neil had said something like that. It made me wonder where that fleeting bitterness came from.

"Maybe we need to find out more about the delivery company." He took out his phone and started tapping. "I'll ask Millie to look into it."

We turned up wide, busy Canal Street. Here the huge stores, restaurants and streetcars competed for eyeballs and tourist dollars, reminding us that a big city surrounded the quaintness of the Quarter. We walked for a few minutes in silence, taking in the rainbow of tourists in their crazy clothes, the business types, the cabs, the buskers. One human statue—his suit and his face tinted in shades of shiny bronze—attracted a lot of attention as he stood on a box holding out a crystal ball. Every sixty seconds he performed improbable maneuvers with it and shifted position, then stood eerily still. I swear his dark eyes followed me as people moved around him, posing and chattering. Creepy. At least he didn't have a bow and arrow.

"Watch your wallet," I said under my breath.

Phone already stowed, Neil laughed as we turned again toward the heart of the Quarter and the hotel. "Front pocket, close to the family jewels."

I guffawed. "Not a phrase I expected from you."

Neil grinned. "We really do have family jewels, or at least I think we do, thanks to my treasure-hunting grandpa. Not that anyone knows where they are."

"Ha! One assumes you know where *yours* are."

"I'm all too aware of mine at the moment," he joked, but the joke had an edge, and it was all I could do not to glance at his treasure chest. "So do you think they've dumped the rest of the bad booze?" he asked.

Oh, good. Change of subject. "Dash mentioned that this morning. It's gone. The good with the bad," I said, remembering that the rye was untainted, at least the rye that Cray tested.

"I hope Dash has recovered enough to attend the awards ceremony. He might get some good news there, and he needs some good news."

"And Alastair will be there too, right? His bar in London is up for an award."

"Probably. Let's keep an eye on him. As long as you're careful."

I glanced over to see Neil eyeing me with concern, and I got a little chill. Attraction? Fear? Maybe both.

PEOPLE DRESSED up for the Cocktailia Awards, but it wasn't like the Oscars. The looks tended to be vintage. Women who showed skin also showed a lot of tattoos. Men were split between bow ties and skinny ties, and at least half wore hats, but few wore jackets. A few bar teams who were up for awards dressed alike. We weren't up for an award, except for Neil and his book, but the Bohemia Bartenders had agreed to acknowledge our Florida roots. Hence the guys sported tasteful aloha shirts, with only Barclay in a straw hat, and Melody and I wore tropical dresses. Printed with deep red hibiscus and green leaves, hers was two pieces and showed a few inches of annoyingly flat belly; a slit in the long skirt went high enough to reveal most of one thigh.

Mine was more suited to my shorter stature, sleeveless

with a knee-length skirt that I puffed out with a pink crino-line. It was printed with palm fronds that matched my eyes, and its low-cut front was drawing a lot more looks than my eyes were. I hadn't remembered it being that revealing in the thrift store, but then again, I might've tried it on over a T-shirt. I forwent my big bag in favor of an adorable, sparkly bowling-bag purse.

We four were chatting amid an ebullient crowd, waiting for Neil. A film crew, interviewing people for a documentary about the cocktail world, or so they told us, asked if they could chat with us on camera. I motioned for the others to grab their moment in the spotlight. I was too new to the group to speak for the Bohemia Bartenders. Besides, I was still looking for Neil.

Finally, I spotted him across the second-floor lobby. I wandered in his direction and became even more convinced of the power of my dress when his eyes widened and he glided toward me as if pulled by a magnet, his mouth open. He held out a hand, palm forward, but didn't touch me, as if an electric field was keeping him back. He pulled it away as if realizing he was about to commit a faux pas.

I frowned. "You're horrified." Meanwhile, I couldn't help but admire his lush hair, bow tie and natty, nerdy plaid vest and pants. Especially the pants.

He shook his head. "Not horrified. Just stunned."

"Gee, thanks."

"In a good way. My God, Pepper." He scanned me one more time. "Do you want me to be able to breathe tonight or what? I'd rather not pass out before they announce the awards."

I laughed, more secure in my boobaliciousness. "I'll hold you up. You ready?"

He nodded. "Have you seen Dash and Travis?"

"Here we are," came Dash's voice, and I turned to take them in. Dash was in a creamy white suit; Travis wore a sleek black one.

"How are you feeling?" I asked Dash.

"Embarrassed."

"Embarrassed?" I asked.

"Because I've let a few stupid things happen," he said. "I'm not sure I even deserve to be running this distillery."

"Well, you're wrong," I said, and Dash looked just a bit stunned. "What I mean is, you absolutely deserve your business, and you deserve the best. You've built a wonderful distillery, and you're making delicious whiskeys. You're having problems because of something that's really outside your control. Are you going to let the bastards get you down?"

A flurry of emotions crossed Dash's face, and then his jaw set.

"No," he said. "No, I'm not going to let them get me down. My whole life is wrapped up in Bohemia Distillery. We're going to solve our problems and make it even better."

"The unsinkable Mr. Reynolds," Travis said. "He always was the one with the heart of a lion, even when the kids picked on him in school."

"Because you helped me."

"And you couldn't help helping me," Travis said with a wry smile.

"I'm glad to hear it, Dash," Neil said.

"And we're going to help you figure this out," I pledged as we strolled toward the rest of our group and headed inside.

The hotel provided a portable bar to supply the audience with drinks, but unlike so many generic hotel bars back home —akin to the one poor Melody worked for—this one knew what it was doing. By the time the ceremony had progressed to the award for best craft distillery, we were all relaxed and enjoying our drinks and hors d'oeuvres.

Still, we were disappointed when Dash didn't win best craft distillery. He smiled graciously when his company's name was mentioned among the finalists, especially when it was greeted with hearty applause by those who'd no doubt tried our cocktails during the showcase the first night. But his irrepressible spirit was visibly dampened when Fairyland, the distillery that made Frilly Fairy Gin and Vexatious Vodka, took the medal.

His loss curtailed our expectations, so when Neil was announced as the winner of best new cocktail book, the surprise was exhilarating. We all leapt to our feet and shouted and cheered, and he went up to the stage and took the award with just a few words about what an honor it was to be among the legends of the craft. That didn't hurt his audience appeal, either, and there was a lot of clapping as he returned to his seat.

Notably, Alastair's bar, a finalist for best international cocktail bar, didn't win, and the cold, sharp look he shot Neil had all the charm of an ice pick. Neil and I exchanged glances. Alastair wasn't winning any points for warm-fuzziness.

His sponsor, however, was more generous. A handsome guy with a quirky smile, dark red hair, appealing chin scruff, golden-brown eyes and a rugby player's body approached our table as the awards ended. He introduced himself to Dash in a delectable British accent, not so posh as Alastair's, with just a touch of gruffness to it.

"Mark Fairman. Pleased to finally meet you in person. I'm a fan of your whiskey, mate. You should have been up there with us."

Dash mustered a smile for him. "That's kind of you. Congratulations on your win. The gin is fantastic."

"Your gin is *almost* as good as ours." Mark chuckled at his own joke. He turned to Neil. "Well done, my friend. Is this your crew?"

Neil introduced the bartenders, ending with me.

"*Hot* Pepper?" Mark asked as if he hadn't heard correctly. His grin said otherwise.

"Just Pepper." My goodness, his handshake was firm. As firm as the rest of him appeared to be.

Still clasping my hand, he leaned in to speak low in my ear. "Hot Pepper it is," he murmured, then released my hand, winked at me and headed out with his friends while I resisted the urge to fan myself. There was something dangerous about Mark Fairman. Dangerously sexy.

Neil—was he *scowling?* I couldn't help but giggle.

As the crowd surged around us on the way out and we prepared to leave, a familiar figure, sharp in a plum suit with a creamy-white silk ascot, approached our table.

"Mr. Cray!" I said, and the old man winked at me.

"Oh my God." Barclay's eyes were as big as lime slices. "I'm such a fan. And that rum you sent along with Pepper—how can we thank you?"

Cray subtly looked him over. "I'll think about it," he said with a twinkle. "I just wanted to meet the fellows behind Bohemia Distillery."

"Then you want to meet Dash," Travis said, his brisk tone belying his sullen expression. Still stinging from the loss, no doubt. But he put a hand on his cousin's shoulder, and Cray reached out his hand to shake Dash's.

Dash took it. "I understand we owe you a debt. Thank you."

"Not at all. It was a pleasure drinking your rye, especially." The untainted whiskey. No one was mentioning the tainted one. "I wanted to have a word with you," Cray said, lowering his voice. Neil leaned in at the same time I did. "The judges were planning to give you the award, but they were unsettled by the rumors they'd heard at the start of the convention."

Dash went pale. "But that's terrible. Will we ever get out from under this cloud?"

"I tell you this not to distress you," Cray said. "There was a lot of argument about it. I wanted you to know that you do have fans and supporters, and they—and I—wish you well."

Dash nodded and shook Cray's hand again. "Thank you for those words and for telling me what happened. We have a couple more opportunities to shine while we're here, and we'll take advantage of them."

"That's a good fellow," Cray said warmly. He turned toward Neil and nodded at the medal now around the bartender's neck. "Nicely done, my friend." And then he was off into the flow of happy people streaming out of the ballroom.

Luke, unaware of the whispered conversation with Cray because he'd just returned from the restroom, was practically bouncing on his feet. "We need to celebrate! Want to come to the tiki bar with us?"

"I'm done for the night." Dash turned to Neil. "But I want us to outshine everyone at the big party tomorrow night. You'll be ready?"

"Absolutely," Neil said, and the rest of our crew murmured agreement. "We have fabulous cocktails in the works. Bohemia's whiskeys are going to be very popular tomorrow."

"Unforgettable, I'm sure." Travis patted Dash on the back. "Come on, cuz. Let me buy you one in the bar."

"Just one, and then I'm going to bed. My head still kind of hurts."

Travis chuckled. "I'll be going to bed later, too, if she shows up, that is."

Barclay and Luke laughed, but somehow I couldn't bring myself to join them. Playboys annoyed me. And I wondered if Bennett managed to figure out who Travis went out with the other night so we could talk to her. If we followed him now and happened to track her ...

"I know what you're thinking, and the answer is no," Neil whispered in my ear. His heat and nearness gave me a nice little buzz, at least until his words penetrated my brain.

"What?"

"Not now." Then louder, "Goodnight. Don't worry, Dash, Travis. We'll touch base in the morning."

The cousins walked away. "Why can't we follow them?" I whispered furiously to Neil.

"Because we have no reason to," he murmured back, "and Bennett is on it. I'll make sure he knows what's happening even if he hasn't found out who she is."

We looked up from our secretive conversation. Barclay, Luke and Melody were staring curiously at us.

"Sorry," Neil said to them as he pulled out his phone and tapped out a message.

"What Neil is trying to say is that I want to kick his ass," I said, and they all burst out laughing. "Don't ask why."

Neil looked at me as if he didn't know what to think. I'd provoked him, but I'd also defused their questions.

"What I want to do is buy all of you a drink," he finally said to their hoots of approval. "It's time we took a night off. A real night off. And I could use one or two myself."

Chapter Eighteen

I t was not long after nine, but that left plenty of drinking time. We waved at Tuba Guy on our way out the door of the hotel, and he tipped his instrument toward us as he played "When the Saints Go Marching In," because by law, you cannot spend a day in New Orleans without hearing that song at least once. Its relentless ubiquity prompted the Preservation Hall Jazz Band to charge tourists extra to hear it.

Half a block away from the tuba player was that same bronze statue guy we'd seen earlier on Canal Street. Several people were gathered around him, watching him perform. No rest for the buskers, I guessed.

I was glad my low heels were chunky and comfy given we had to walk several blocks. The streets were crowded now, and bars and restaurants along the way were hopping.

"Do you have room for this in that little bag?" Neil asked me, pulling the heavy medal off his neck and handing it to me.

"You don't want to wear it?"

"I'm not a 'Look at me' kind of guy," he said. "Do you mind?"

"Not at all. I can build up my arm muscles carrying this thing." I squeezed it into my bowling-bag-style purse next to my phone and wallet.

He grinned. "Want me to carry it for you?"

"No way. It totally would not match your plaid."

He laughed, and the sound made me buoyant. The pleasantly cool evening helped restore our sobriety to a degree so we could lose it again at Latitude 29, the tiki bar no mixologist could resist. Neil's eyes widened as he took in the Polynesian Pop decor, and they filled with pleasure when we all grabbed a table and he got ahold of a menu.

Bohemia Bartenders' first order was an elaborately built communal drink punctuated by several straws, the Snake vs. Mongoose. A taller cocktail sat in the center of a triangular bowl that held its own drink, each point of the vessel supported by a stylized moai.

Neil could barely tear himself away from the menu to try the bowl drink. A smile had attached itself to his lips and wouldn't go away, at least not until he pursed his mouth around a straw and took a sip. Then the smile got even bigger.

"Ahhh. I've been wanting to come here ever since it opened," he said.

"Are you glad you did?" I asked.

"Do Canadians like maple syrup?" We laughed. "This one and the next round are on me, guys."

Over exotic snacks and another round of rummy drinks—I soaked up a Nui Nui, a rum punch invented in 1937 by Don the Beachcomber and resurrected by Latitude 29's Beachbum Berry—I could almost forget Dash's bank account and Barnie lying in the hospital seeing nothing but blurry colors. So after that was done, I ordered a Mai Tai, which helped me focus (well, maybe focus was the wrong word) instead on my new friends, who were flush and chatty and enjoying the best of the craft.

Neil was entranced, insisting on a sip of everything we

ordered. For himself, he got the new-fashioned drinks but exclaimed just as much over the classics.

As the other three argued about how much mint a Mai Tai should have and just how hard it should be spanked before it was plopped into the glass—mine had a sprig but was enhanced by an orchid—I turned to Neil. "Having a good time?"

He rolled his eyes around in an expression of ecstasy that I'd never seen him wear. "This is what cocktails are meant to be. This is what I'm trying to bring to Bohemia, and so are you. Balance. Creativity. A symphony of flavors."

"Yeah. They're *good*." I sucked on my straw, and I swore Neil seemed distracted for a moment, his gaze drawn to my mouth.

"Good?" He refocused. "So much more than good. Great. What this place does is take the classic formula and then it elevates it to delight and surprise your mouth, your nose, your eyes." He caught my eyes then, and even though I was a bit giddy myself, I got a little lost in his blue-edged crystal-gray pools. I was pretty sure Neil wasn't a hundred percent sober either.

"One of sour, two of sweet, three of strong, four of weak," I recited. "And by 'good' I meant 'delicious.'"

"YES!" Neil bellowed, and Barclay, Luke and Melody all stopped chattering and turned to gape at him. I could've sworn Neil colored slightly. "She gets it!" he said by way of explanation, and they laughed and went back to arguing about garnishes.

"It's fun seeing you tipsy," I said in a low voice.

"You won't see it very often," he said, "but it's hard to enjoy all this place has to offer without a little buzz."

"Just a *little* buzz." I giggled. Oh, yeah. I was buzzed.

He grinned, catching my eyes again, but only after what he probably thought was a surreptitious glance at my bosom.

"Look," Luke said, "if we don't get Barclay out of here, he's going to move in."

Barclay shook his head. "Because they know how to do rum. Please, just one more round."

"And I want to hear Melody sing," Luke added.

"Melody sings?" I asked. "How did I not know this?"

"Terrible confirmation that naming is destiny." Melody drained the last of her Mai Tai. "I told you I lived in New York before I came to Bohemia, right? I was working in one of those restaurants where the wait staff is expected to sing."

I crinkled my brow at her. "And this was by choice?"

She laughed. "I was trying to become a Broadway star. It didn't work out."

"But she's awesome," Luke said. "It's time to move on!"

Neil seemed as reluctant as Barclay, but everyone was still in a good mood and ready to roll with the evening, so we settled our bill and headed out into the night.

We wandered over to the relatively quiet riverfront and took a look. The water glimmered in the clear night.

"The mighty Mississippi," Neil said as we resumed our stroll. He was walking next to me again—I thought, hoped, not by accident.

"Mighty and mercurial," I said. "We keep trying to contain it, and it keeps showing us who's boss."

"Katrina," Neil said.

"I guess I shouldn't blame the river. It was a levee breach on the 17th Street Canal that got my neighborhood."

"Are you going to see your parents while you're in town?"

"Maybe. Not sure if there will be time." The truth was,

between my dinner invitation and a couple of phone messages, they hadn't called me back.

"I'll go with you if you want," Neil said. "We might have time tomorrow before the party."

I looked up at him, startled. "Um, thanks. I guess we could do a drive-by if we're out picking up supplies."

A weird little chill crept up my spine, and I turned around, looking behind us. We were just getting back into the crowds, but the street behind us was dark and empty.

"What is it?" Neil asked.

"Heeeere we go!" Luke called out, interrupting the moment. He was surveying the dark and weathered front of a bar with an open door, the sounds of saxophone, horns and piano leaking out. "This place has music."

Melody looked dubious. "They have a jazz band. It's not karaoke."

"It's an open mike jam!" Luke pointed to a sign in the window. "Aw, come on. One drink and a song."

"Nobody's singing," Barclay said, peering in the door. "They need you."

"OK, one song, but only if it's something I know *really* well," she said.

"That won't be hard," Luke said. "I don't think there's a song you don't know."

Melody grinned at the compliment, and we all piled in. There were only a couple of tall, skinny tables in the back, the kind designed to hold a few drinks and that's about it, so we worked our way through the crowd, closer to the low stage.

The bar was dark and loud, but in a good way. The band was jamming—trombone, trumpet, tenor sax, guitar, standup bass, drums. I didn't recognize the song, but it had some tempo, and a few people were dancing in the tiny bit of space left near the front of the room.

"Whaddaya want?" Luke asked, then went to the bar and came back with beers for him and Barclay, Cokes for Neil and I, and a water for Melody. We needed a breather between serious cocktails.

"Well, hello, trombone," Melody said, sipping her water and glancing at me with a gleam in her eye.

I spoke in her ear so she could hear me. "You have a thing for trombonists?"

"I have a thing for *this* trombonist." She caught the eye of the sandy-haired, clean-shaven guy wailing on the horn and gave him a little wave. His eyebrows rose as his cheeks puffed out. "I know just what I want to sing, if they'll let me."

The band wrapped up its tune, and Melody darted to the stage and said a few words in the ear of the sax player, who appeared to be leading the group. He took in her tropical attire, nodded and leaned close to the other players to impart instructions. Melody, looking every bit the diva in her midriff-revealing dress, parked herself in front of the retro microphone and winked at the trombone player, who smiled. And then they launched into a bluesy song, the trombone player getting the raunchiest sounds out of his horn, Melody's voice a powerful instrument as she caressed each word and flirted with him as she did it.

Luke appeared fascinated. Neil wore an appreciative smile. I was agog at the sexual tension on stage, and Barclay was chuckling, probably because he recognized the tune. I didn't figure out until the chorus that it was "Big Long Sliding Thing," aka "The Trombone Song." No wonder the trombonist loved it, and the crowd was getting into it, too, whooping and clapping.

A strange vibration at my hip made me jump. I realized it was my purse or, more specifically, my phone. I took it out but didn't recognize the number.

"I'm going to take this outside," I said in Neil's ear. "It might be the hotel lost and found." Or some other crisis, though I didn't want to entertain that idea.

I stepped out onto the empty sidewalk, walked toward the corner and swiped to answer the call. There was nothing. No sound. No voice. I stared again at the phone, puzzled. The call ended as I watched the screen, and I caught a movement out of the corner of my eye.

It was the bronze statue guy, several feet away, standing absolutely still, his face paint gleaming under the streetlights. He wasn't standing on a box this time, and he wasn't carrying a crystal ball, either.

But he was holding a phone.

My still modestly drunk brain took a second to put it all together. By then the statue had sprung into motion and was running toward me faster than my mascara during Snape's big scene in the last Harry Potter movie.

I turned and ran.

Chapter Nineteen

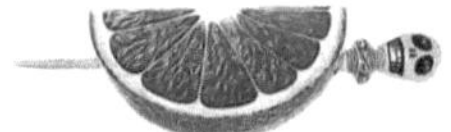

The statue was already between me and the door of the bar, so the only way to go was in the opposite direction. I tore down the narrow street and into the next block, which was slightly busier with pedestrians who seemed oblivious to the fact that I was running away from a statue. I ricocheted through a party of drunk bridesmaids wearing tiaras, bumped into a couple of frat boys and rocketed around a corner. I had no idea where I was. The street was lined with houses with balconies and the occasional bar, where I didn't want to be trapped. But there was noise in the distance, and a couple of blocks down, I saw barricades. *Bourbon Street.* There were always cops on Bourbon Street.

And then a pedicab popped out in front of me at the next corner and I almost got a face full of bicycle chain as I stumbled to avoid it.

It was already gone when a strong arm grabbed me around the waist. "That's the most runnin' I had to do in a year, bitch," said the deep voice in a strong Nawlins accent. Meaning his voice sounded almost New Yorkish—but we natives would call him a Yat, as in, "Where yat?"

I elbowed him and started to scream, but he clasped a hand over my mouth. I could smell the paint, the makeup.

"You're done interfering," the statue said in his gruff voice, dragging me toward a dark doorway. "And you're a pretty little doodle bug, too, aren't ya? Ah, I might get me an extra bonus tonight before I drop you in the watah."

No. *No!* I was not going out this way. And I had to do something before he got me somewhere even darker and scarier. I tried to stomp his foot with my clunky heel, but since my feet were barely touching the ground, I wasn't doing much damage. This guy was big. Brawny.

I'd dropped my phone in the street, but I still had my purse in a death grip. It wasn't much of a weapon. Then again, it had Neil's medal in it.

We were almost to the doorway. Mustering the strength I had left, I tried to calculate my swing and whipped the purse up and over my shoulder.

"Unh!" he grunted, dropping me immediately. He clutched his bronze forehead, but he was still on his feet. So I swung again, hard, catching him solidly on the back of the head. He dropped to his knees, looking only moderately dizzy, and then I ran like hell.

I got past the barricades of Bourbon Street and found myself drowning in drunks. It didn't have to be Mardi Gras to be a wild and wacky party here every single night. I didn't like it. Didn't like the volatile nature of the crowd, the terrible drinks, the seedy carnival atmosphere. But I knew there were cops here, and I looked around wildly, trying to find one.

There. I ignored the police on horses and ran toward two officers who were standing in the street, hands on their belts, surveying the crowd as if they'd rather be battling alien invaders instead of monitoring this smelly bacchanal. I ran up to them, a man and a woman, and tried to keep it simple. "I was attacked. He tried to pull me into an alley. Up there. Up there!"

"Show me," the woman said, running in the direction I'd pointed. I tried to keep up, pointing again so they'd know where to turn. "Was he armed?"

"Not sure. I don't think so," I puffed. "Maybe." Yikes. What if he had been armed? One gunshot, and I'd—I didn't want to think about that.

The two cops went ahead of me. "Here!" I said. "It was here." They had guns drawn, and they moved up and down the street, around the intersection, while I hid behind a column that hid approximately one-third of my cheese-diet-enhanced hips.

Finally, they stopped, and I started to breathe properly again. The male cop was talking on the radio. I spotted my phone in the street and grabbed it. The screen was marred by a crack but still working. It was covered in texts, but I didn't have time to read them before I was interrupted.

"Can you describe him, ma'am?" It was the female cop again. More cops showed up on foot and in a squad car, and the scene got kind of crazy.

"He was bronze."

"Bronze? Black, you mean?"

"No. I mean, he might've been, but I don't think so. He was bronze. Painted bronze all over."

This information didn't seem to faze her in the least. "Like this?" She pointed at my dress. Damn it, the bastard had ruined my dress, too. There were smudges of bronze makeup all over it.

"Yes! He was one of those statue guys. This was the third time I'd seen him today."

"Statue guys?"

"A street performer. You know what I mean?"

She sighed. "I know what you mean. Have you been drinking tonight?"

Duh. It's New Orleans. "I was drinking earlier," I admitted.

"Are you sure about what you saw?"

"You see the paint on me, right? Yes, I'm sure."

"Are you hurt?"

I took a moment to take inventory, starting to feel pretty stupid about the whole thing. "I'm OK, I think. I mean, I'm fine. A little bruised but OK."

I shivered when I thought about what might have happened. And then she asked me a lot of questions. I didn't give her the whole backstory of our struggles this week, just stuck to the statue sightings and the attack. Finally, she asked if I needed help getting where I was going.

"I think I'm good, if you'll just walk me back to Bourbon Street." I didn't want to be in the crowd again, but I really didn't want to be alone on a dark street again this evening.

"No problem. I'd suggest you get back to your hotel and get some rest, and take it easy on the booze."

I bit my tongue. Yes, inebriation was the cause of most of the problems these cops encountered, but it's not like it was my fault a statue attacked me.

I thanked her when we parted ways at the barricade, and then I looked at my phone. Crap. A bunch of texts from Neil asking where I'd gone and one from Melody saying she and the trombone player were going to make a night of it, and she'd chat with me in the morning. And there was a voice mail.

"Pepper," Neil said. "I'm really worried about you. Are you OK? Call me as soon as you get this."

For the first time tonight, tears pricked my eyes as his

concern broke down the walls I'd thrown up around myself after the attack. I stumbled into a long, narrow, neon-lit bar, sat on a stool and called him back.

He answered on the first ring. "Are you OK?"

"I am now." I sniffled and tried unsuccessfully not to sound like I was crying.

"Are you sure? Where are you? What happened?"

"I was attacked. I'm OK. The police talked to me. I'm in a bar on Bourbon Street. I don't want to walk home alone."

"Tell me which one. I'll be right there."

ONCE I GOT off the phone with Neil, I really started crying.

"What's up, sugar?" asked a skinny young man behind the bar with glowing umber skin and a friendly smile. "Looks to me like you need a drink."

I looked up and around, noting with horror the colorful frozen drinks swirling in round windows, lined up behind the bar like miniature washing machines from hell.

"Give me a shot. Tequila. Good stuff," I added. Tequila was the drink of choice for memory erasure, but it was better to go for premium to soften the hangover the next day.

Neil found me perched on a stool, two shots in. He came over to me and cupped my chin and looked me in the eyes. "Are you OK?" He was so quiet I almost didn't hear him. Or maybe it was just that everything else was so loud.

My tears had dried up by then, and the tequila had taken the edge off. "It was the bronze statue guy."

"The busker?" he asked in surprise.

"Yeah. He attacked me outside the bar. I think it was him

who called me to get me to go outside. He had a phone in his hand."

"How'd he get your number?"

"I don't know. It's one of the numbers on my bar's website. It's listed on various records online. Easy enough."

"Why didn't you come back inside?"

"I was too far from the door. I tried to run away, but he caught me a few streets over."

"Oh, Pepper. What did he do?" Neil took one of my hands in his.

"He grabbed me and tried to drag me off the street." I shuddered. "I don't know what he was *going* to do, but I stopped him with this." I pointed at the bag still looped over my forearm.

"Your purse?"

"Your medal in my purse. Just stunned him enough so I could run away."

A corner of Neil's mouth quirked up. And then he wrapped his arms around me and pulled me close. He was warm and comforting and something more, projecting an intensity that made me dizzy. Or maybe that was the tequila. Heat suffused me, along with the strangest feeling of well-being, especially given the night I'd had.

"Be careful," I muffled into his vest.

"What?" He pulled back.

"Be careful. You'll get the paint on you, too."

He held my hands and looked me over. "Your poor, beautiful dress. I want to kill him just for ruining it. I want to kill him, period." His gaze darkened. "Tell me what he said."

I told him, and fury lit in his eyes. "Interfering? How are you interfering?"

"It all has to go back to Bohemia Distillery. I'm interfering because I'm helping Dash, encouraging him."

"We all are. But I think whoever is doing this knows that targeting you will have an effect on all of us. Attacking you affects *me*," Neil said. The connection between us crackled. He *did* care about me, and he was pissed.

"You don't think the statue guy is out to get us?"

"I think he's a tool. I don't think he's the guy who drained Dash's bank account or is trying to ruin his reputation. Why would a thug want to—to attack you?" *Or kill you* was unspoken. "Unless someone has connected you with Dash and thinks they can get to him through you. *You* don't have any enemies, do you?"

"Not that I know of, though Marian the librarian has threatened to pull my library card if I return another book late."

That earned a small smile from Neil.

"So what's the end game?" I asked. "They're trying to break Dash, ruin him?"

Neil nodded. "It's the only thing that makes sense, given what's happened. The 'why' eludes me. We need to look into that developer more, the one you said he talked about back in Bohemia."

"And see if Fairyland Distillery has anything to gain by hurting Dash, given that Alastair is doing work for them and hates you."

"Well, I don't know if he *hates* me," Neil said puckishly.

I laughed. It felt good to laugh.

"We're not going to worry about any of it tonight. I'm taking you home." He turned to the bartender and took care of the bill, and I didn't voice one iota of protest. "Not your usual kind of place, is it?" he asked me, looking around at the daiquiri machines, a hilariously distasteful expression on his face.

"I went for the straight liquor. I can't handle those froufrou frosties in colors not found in nature."

"Thank God," he said, putting an arm around me and escorting me back into the river of insanity that was Bourbon Street. "I thought I was going to have to fire you."

Chapter Twenty

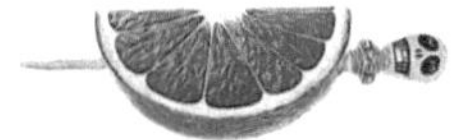

As we exited the bar, we passed a hawker for a drag show. "Opening tonight! *Wham Bam Thank You Glam!* See our gorgeous ladies sparkle!" A poster looked out at me from the window of the club featuring a glamorous creature in a dazzling all-silver gown. The hat store clerk. Too bad I wasn't in the mood for theater.

Within a block of elbowing our way through the loud, unruly crowd and spotting no less than five bridesmaid and bachelor parties, one arrest, and three instances of tit-flashing, Neil pulled me off the main drag and onto a quieter street. I looked around nervously at every face, every car. It didn't help that the tequila had made me just a little bit fuzzy. It had caught the last bubbles of my drunkenness from the tiki bar and whipped them up into a froth, a weirdly giddy mood enhanced by exhaustion and spent fear. A mood lightened by having Neil next to me.

Neil's arm was still wrapped around my shoulders, protective if not possessive. "Are you OK?" he asked again.

"Yes. I'm OK. Now I'm just kinda drunk."

He laughed. "I shouldn't be laughing."

"Please laugh. If we don't laugh, then we have to cry, and I've had enough of that for the night."

"I'm sorry," he whispered, pulling me more tightly against

his body. His noticeably firm body. He'd been hiding a hunk of sexiness under that nerd wardrobe, I was sure of it.

"Don't be sorry. I'm having a great time."

He laughed again. "We're almost to the hotel. Then you can get some rest."

"I don't particularly want the evening to end on a note of dread," I said. "Maybe one more drink?"

He looked at me askance. "You sure that's a good idea?"

"You!" came a deep, island-accented voice from behind us, and I jumped halfway out of my skin as Neil whirled, pushing me behind him.

I peeked around him to see a group of eight or ten bewildered tourists led by a colorfully dressed woman wearing a head scarf. "You!" she said again, pointing to Neil, then waving at him to move aside. Yeah, she meant me.

"I don't think so," Neil declared.

"Oh, stop it now, my boy, and let her come forward. This is what I was telling you about, my friends!" she called to her little tour. The men and women seemed pale and dull under the street light as they crowded up behind the dark and beautiful woman in her flowing gown, dozens of necklaces and jangling bracelets. "Sometimes you can see in the aura a person in need. My child, come here."

"I think it's OK," I whispered to Neil. Besides, I didn't think this voodoo priestess or whatever she was would woo-woo me with all these people watching. I stepped gingerly out from behind Neil.

"You are in danger!" she said.

My mouth dropped open. "How did you know?"

The tourists gasped at this validation of her talents. She stepped closer. "Take this, my dear." She lifted a black leather cord from around her neck strung with a pointy tooth wrapped in silver wire, flanked by colorful beads. "From the ancient creature of the swamp. It will give you protection."

"Creature of the swamp? Do you mean an alligator?" I barely managed to avoid blurting out that I could get gator-tooth gear at every beach-towel emporium in Bohemia Beach.

"You are skeptical. You must believe!" she bellowed as I tried to hold my ground, flashing back to my father's preaching in his storefront church. "This is special. Blessed by me. Wear it." She looped it over my neck. Then she looked at Neil. "Protection is very valuable."

What a scam! Neil shrugged, a smile playing about his lips, and dug out his wallet. He handed the woman a ten. She gave him a hard look, and he handed her another ten.

"Go in peace and love," she shouted, looking from him to me, and in spite of myself, a shiver ran down my spine. She leaned in close to me and whispered in my ear. "You cannot get back what the wind has taken away."

Then she was herding the tourists down the street. "To my shop, where we will ask for blessings!"

We waited until they'd turned a corner and then looked at each other.

"What the *hell* was that?" Neil asked.

I was still mulling the priestess's remark about the wind. "I don't know, but I'm wearing this thing every day until I get home. Thank you."

"You're welcome, though I didn't really feel like I had a choice," Neil said with good humor. He took my hand this time and led me toward the turn that would take us to the hotel. His grip was strong and dry and warm, and it sent a slow-burning thrill through my entire besotted body.

I was nervous. On one level I was scared after tonight's attack. On another I was gently blitzed. On a third I was freaked out by the voodoo tour guide. And lastly, I was wondering where things were going with Neil. Were they going somewhere? It felt like it. I was up for the ride.

I knew we were close to the hotel when I heard the tuba chugging bass notes on a tune I didn't recognize. We were back among the ceaseless activity outside the Hotel Lebeau.

"Where'd everybody go?" I asked, suddenly remembering our fellow bartenders.

"Oh, crap, I was supposed to message them. They were worried about you, too." To my regret, he dropped my hand, pulled out his phone and tapped. My phone pinged in my purse as well.

"Was that you?" I asked, pulling it out to read it: "Pepper's OK, but she was threatened. Be careful, everyone. Don't go out alone."

"I added you to the Bohemia Bartenders message group," Neil explained.

"Thanks." Warmth above and beyond the alcohol suffused me, and then I thought of my friends and whether they were in danger. "Are they going to be OK?"

"I think the trombonist will look out for Melody," he said wryly, stowing his phone again. "He couldn't keep his eyes off her. The guys were talking about hitting a couple of the high-end craft cocktail bars."

"Damn it, I'm sorry."

"What? Why?"

"I'm sure you would've wanted to go with them."

He paused outside the lobby doors and put his hands on my shoulders. "All I wanted to do was make sure you were all right."

His hands on me, the laughter nearby, the gleaming facade of the old hotel, the cabs coming and going—every sensation coalesced into a whirlwind around us, and we stood in its calm center, looking at each other. He was going to kiss me. Again. I closed my eyes.

"We'd better get you inside." His hands had left me, and my eyes flew open to see him holding the door for me as people shifted around us.

Damn it. I swallowed and followed. I was off-kilter. I didn't want to go to bed feeling like this, even if I was going to bed alone.

"One more drink?" I suggested again.

"All right." Neil had a helpless look on his face. "People have been giving me samples left and right. I have some interesting stuff in my room. Would that be OK? Or would you prefer the bar?"

Huh. So what did that make me if I chose his room? I didn't care. "I'd love to try some new stuff."

"Cool. It's hard to find time to sample everything." He led the way to the elevator.

"What, no stairs? And how is it that you are not drunk?"

"It's been a while since the tiki bar," he said. "Nothing sobers me up like worry. And I have a feeling my tolerance is better than yours."

"Bigger isn't necessarily better," I scoffed.

"That's not what I hear."

I looked at him in shock, then nearly collapsed in a gust of laughter. He laughed, too, helping me into the elevator when it opened. We joined eight other revelers in the tiny space. I swear, at this point, everyone and everything in the Hotel Lebeau smelled of alcohol, but we survived the packed bodies and popped out at the fourth floor.

"I need to stop in my room," I said when we reached our little corridor.

"Sure. I mean, if you want to go to sleep ... "

"Two minutes."

"Do you want me to check it first?"

I shook my head. "If you hear a scream, come running." But he did have a point. I opened the door cautiously, turned on the light and checked the closet before using the bathroom. I caught a glimpse of myself in the mirror, and the horrors of the night came back to me. Among them, my hair. And the ruined dress, tainted with paint, a reminder of how close I'd been to—to something *very* bad. I yanked it off, kicked off my shoes, removed my glasses, washed off my face, combed out my hair and slipped a soft, casual, sleeveless tropical dress over the crinoline. It paid to have emergency outfits.

Feeling better, I took Neil's medal out of my purse and opened my door.

"Sorry I took so long," I said when I realized Neil was still standing in the hall.

He smiled. "I wanted to be sure I could hear you scream."

"At least the tuba player isn't as loud tonight."

"I think he's around the corner." He held his key card up to his lock, then opened the door for me to enter. As he ducked into his bathroom, I looked around. The room was a mirror of mine, small but elegantly old-fashioned. The bed was perfectly made. That's the beauty of hotels and also the trickery. I wondered if Neil made his bed at home. Was he a neatnik? A horrible slob? Hell, I didn't even know where he lived.

Personally, I didn't make my bed at home, but I pulled the duvet up so it was more or less neat, and I tried to keep the main rooms of my duplex clean. As for the closets—it wasn't a bad idea to wear a helmet when opening them.

Neil emerged and gestured to the desk, which was almost covered in little bottles. "So what do you want to drink?"

"Holy shit," I said.

"Yeah. They used to have a lot more of this kind of stuff at the seminars and tastings, but now most of it exchanges hands behind the scenes. Bar owners like me get a lot of it. Everybody wants us to carry their liquor."

"But I'm a bar owner. Half of one, anyway."

"But you didn't register till the last minute, right? I've been registered for months, plenty of time for people to add me to their lists, plus I was a presenter, which means I got a nice swag bag."

"And this." I handed him the medal.

"You sure you don't want to keep that in your purse?"

"Ha ha," I said without humor. "You have the Frilly Fairy? We've been talking so much about it, I want to try it."

"Yes. It's really nice. Even their Vexatious Vodka isn't bad, but don't tell anyone I said that." I giggled as he produced a couple of rocks glasses with logos on them—more swag—and poured us each a finger of the gin.

I took the glass and sat on the end of the bed. Neil sat in the desk chair at an annoyingly courteous distance, eyeing me as I sniffed the gin. The botanicals tickled my nose, floral and spicy. I inhaled deeply, then took a sip.

"Oh, yeah," I said. "I guess their award wasn't undeserved."

"They're good," he said. "They have a Navy strength gin, too, and they're experimenting with rum, but that has a little ways to go."

I knocked back the gin. "What else you got?"

"Well ..." He had this look like he wanted to caution me. Whereas I shot him a look that said, *If you lecture me about drinking right now, I will stab you with a pair of ice tongs.* And yes, I knew ice tongs weren't particularly sharp. Which would make them all the more painful as stabbing instruments.

He drank down his gin, too, and set down his glass. He loosened his tie and slipped it off, dropping it over the back of his chair. I held my breath. Then he unbuttoned a button. Then another one. Then he popped open the buttons of his vest. Then he stopped loosening things and picked out a flask-size bottle. *Damn it.*

"This is a wicked good bourbon out of Kentucky. Twelve-year-old. Want to try it?"

I swallowed, maintaining my buzz, trying to maintain my composure. "Got ice?"

"In the mini fridge."

I was closer, so I set my glass on the desk, opened the fridge and pulled an ice tray from the tiny freezer. It was a red square silicone tray divided into fourths, so it made four big cubes, the kind that were perfect in a glass of whiskey. "I can't believe you have this."

He grinned. "I'd like to say I remembered to bring it from home, but it was in the swag bag, too."

I rolled my eyes and plopped a cube in each of our glasses, then put the tray back in the fridge. "Hit me."

He chuckled and poured enough whiskey into our glasses to almost cover each fat cube.

I sat on the end of the bed again, a little closer to him this time, and held up mine. "To new friends." Only the way I said *friends,* it implied a lot more. Hey, I was almost drunk.

Neil looked me in the eye. "Here's champagne to our real friends and real pain to our sham friends."

I guffawed. "Did you just make that up?"

"Francis Bacon," he said, taking a deep sip of the whiskey.

I followed suit. "How do you have all this stuff in your head?"

"Slow nights behind the bar. Gotta read something."

"Cocktail books," I said. "I need to do more of that. I mean, I read yours, of course."

"You did?" He visibly brightened.

"Well, duh. Of course I did. You're freaking brilliant." Only I didn't say "freaking." I drank some more to cover up my embarrassment. Now I *was* drunk, for real and sure and true. And when I was drunk, my halfhearted campaign to clean up my language really went out the window.

"That means a lot, coming from you," he said, his voice low and warm.

"Aw, stop it."

"I mean it. What are you doing?"

I was wrestling the crinoline out from under my dress. I pulled it off my legs and dropped the puffy, frilly pink thing next to the bed. "Sorry. It itches."

He looked like he was torn between laughing and—*oh, my.* That spark of heat was back in his eye. He took another sip of bourbon.

"Are you drunk again?" I asked.

"Not nearly enough," he said.

"Enough for what?"

"For this." He put the glass down and sat next to me on the bed. He took my glass and set it on the desk as well, then cupped my chin, searched my eyes, leaned in ...

The kiss was even better this time, because he initiated it. Because I knew he wanted me. Because he chose this moment, and I dove into it, opening to him, to the delicious bourbon and Neil cocktail that made me higher than a parasailing parrot over Bohemia Beach.

I wasn't making much sense.

I pushed his vest off his shoulders, and he let it drop. He

moved his mouth to my neck, the sensitive spot behind my ear, and I moaned.

And he jumped back as if he'd been stung. "What the hell am I doing?"

"I don't know, but I liked it," I said, breathless, reaching out for him.

He dropped back into the desk chair. "Whoa, now."

"You started it! Are you going to lecture me about human resources again?"

He laughed, and then I laughed.

"Come here," I said.

He shook his head. "We can't do this now."

"We damn well can."

"Pepper." He moved slowly and sat next to me on the bed. "You're drunk. I don't want to do this—I mean, I do want to do this, OK?"

"So what's the problem?"

"I don't want to do it when you're drunk. I want you to know what you're doing."

"Baby, I know what I'm doing," I said in my best Mae West accent.

He exhaled. "Oh, boy. No. No, you can't do this." Talking to himself. I could relate.

"Neil, honey?" I ran a hand over his trim beard, leaned in and nuzzled his neck, wrapping my arms around him.

"Not tonight, Pepper," he said, but his tone said he was struggling. And a glance down confirmed my conclusion.

Good, damn it. I wanted him to struggle if he was rejecting me again.

He gently disentangled my arms from his person and stood. "You'd better go. We'll have breakfast in the morning, OK?"

"Oh my *God*. I cannot believe you are throwing me out."

"It's not like that—"

"Yes, it is. Yes, it is!"

"Pepper, please. It's because I respect you."

"I don't want you to freaking respect me! I want you to—" When I realized what I was about to say, I put my hand over my mouth to keep it in. He had a pained look on his face, and I felt dizzy. The liquor hit me hard, all of a sudden, and all the stress and terror of the evening came rushing back to me. I looked up at him and spoke in a small voice. "Listen. Just listen for a second. If you don't want to ravish me, fine. But don't let me sleep alone tonight, OK?"

He let out a long breath, his face softening. He sat next to me again and gathered me in his arms. "OK, Pepper. Stay with me. I'll keep you safe." He kissed my neck again, but this time, it wasn't as hot. Not *quite* as hot.

"Undress me."

He pulled back a little, his face still reflecting his inner struggle, and looked me over. I leaned forward and cocked my head, expectant. After a moment, he ran his hands over my bare shoulders, checked out my packaging, then reached down and grabbed my hem. Awkwardly, as I shifted my body, he peeled the dress over my head and handed it to me. I tossed it to the side.

"Jesus," he said, his eyes wide as he scanned me in my matching green bra and panties.

I was just drunk enough to pop off my bra as he stared, drop it to the floor and slip under the covers. Half asleep, I watched him as he tried to put his eyeballs back into his head. He slowly took off his formal shirt, shoes, socks and pants, leaving on his black boxer briefs *(oh, my!)*, which were noticeably strained, *thank you very much,* and a clingy, plain white T-shirt that suggested a lean, muscled torso. But I didn't get to savor the sight. He turned off the light and slid into bed next to me.

If I'd been a little braver, I would've tried to make something happen then, but things had shifted again between us. I didn't know where they were going, and I was too tired to worry about it. But in a moment, he pulled me close to him, wrapping an arm around me, warm and strong.

I relaxed into him, liking the feel of my breasts rubbing up against his shirt, his hard chest.

He probably liked it, too.

"Goodnight, Pepper," he whispered.

Chapter Twenty-One

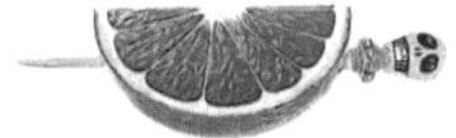

The morning after a night of drinking can go a number of different ways. I was pretty good about not getting hangovers, because I usually drank a lot of water along with my alcohol. Except for last night.

And usually, on the rare occasions when I succumbed to the charms of a guy, I had zero expectations about what would come next, other than a quick trip home to shower and nap. Or, if I really liked him, brunch.

Except this morning, I woke up alone *and* hung over, and it took me several seconds to realize why my room looked backward. It was because I was in Neil's room, and there was no Neil in it. I'd not only failed at seduction; my behavior had been so excruciatingly embarrassing that he'd fled the room before I even woke up.

I glanced at the digital clock. Just after eleven. *Crap.* Brunch wasn't even an option. Now I was going to need lunch, if the snakes in my tummy ever stopped doing the samba.

At least the walk of shame was relatively quick. Right across the hallway. And what did I have to be ashamed about, anyway? I worked hard on rationalizing last night as I took a nice, hot shower. I'd been attacked. I'd been drinking, which one absolutely must do at Cocktailia anyway. And Neil had kissed me. I mean, he'd started it. Sort of.

By the time I'd donned stretchy gray jeans, a low-cut white T-shirt, a tight black vest and my gator-tooth necklace, along with shockingly red lipstick, I'd come to terms with my failure as a floozy. The priority at this point was finding and stopping whoever was targeting Dash and me. Us. All of us. Or else I wouldn't be able to sleep at all without the aid of a whole lot of whiskey.

That said, I didn't much want to be alone. I thought about texting Melody, but I figured she might still be sliding the old trombone, if you know what I mean. As for Neil—OK, I was a big chicken and wasn't ready to face Neil. So I texted Millie instead.

Fifteen minutes later, I met her and Bennett in the hotel restaurant, and we ordered lunch. None of our crew was in evidence, which was just as well.

"I didn't see you guys at the awards ceremony," I noted as I stirred sugar into my coffee.

They exchanged a disgustingly sweet smile. "We wanted to spend some time alone, and we didn't have tickets anyway," Millie said.

"Millie likes hotel rooms." Mischief gleamed in Bennett's eyes, and Millie elbowed him hard, prompting an *"Ooof!"* He recovered enough to add, "Though our *evening* was interrupted when Neil sent me to track after Travis."

I smiled at his teasing. "What did you learn?"

"Millie and I saw him go to the hotel bar, where he had a drink with Dash. We hung back. Then Dash left, and we followed Travis to Napoleon House. A woman met him there, and they had a drink, and then they went back to our hotel."

"That was fast," I said.

"I got the feeling they'd met before," Bennett said, making me wonder about the friend Travis had enlisted to go with Barnie to the hospital. "I'd had no chance to quiz him about his love life earlier, before we started playing Sherlock Holmes. I assume they went right to his room, or at least I think that's where they went. They got in the elevator, and so he wouldn't catch on, we went up the stairs to the floor where the elevator stopped. We didn't see anyone in the halls, so we went to our room. And then we were—kind of busy."

Millie's smile got even wider, and I sort of wanted to scream. Well, I'd been chased and mugged and touched by a voodoo priestess and also flashed my boobs at Neil to pretty much zero effect, so yeah, I was sure our evenings were comparable.

"Would you recognize the woman if you saw her again?" I asked.

"I think so," Millie said. "Pretty. Light hair caught up under a hat. Hard to be sure of the color."

That narrowed it down. *Not.* I looked around. Light-haired women everywhere. Blondes. Redheads. A few in between like me. And every other person wore a hat. It was a target-rich environment.

"I got a picture," Bennett said, and I almost tore the phone out of his hand. It was shot on the dark street outside Napoleon House, and it was blurry and grainy. Travis had his arm around the woman, and her face was obscured. So much for instant identification. "I know it's not that great," he said, echoing my thoughts. "What did you hope to get from her anyway?"

I sighed. "We were just curious about where Travis went after we got the boomerangs the other night. Whether he hooked up with this woman in particular. Just to rule him out."

Our server arrived with our food. I was going with a burger

and fries that cost almost as much as my car payment, but this was a hangover emergency.

Millie lowered her voice after the waitress left. "Here's the thing. If Travis had wanted to do anything to his cousin, wouldn't he have had a thousand opportunities even before he got to Cocktailia? And why would he do it anyway? They seemed chummy last night."

"All good questions," I admitted, rummaging in my brain for other ideas as I devoured my burger. "Did you find out anything about the delivery company, the ones who were late with the whiskey?"

Millie nodded. "The office manager at Bohemia Distillery gave me their number, and I called and asked them what happened with the delivery. They said what you already know —the driver had mechanical trouble. They were very apologetic. They wouldn't let me talk with the driver. I think they were afraid I'd chew him out." She laughed.

"Hey, Dash mentioned a developer had been bugging him about selling his building for condos in Bohemia. Tocks Development Group, owned by Raquel Tocks, a sponsor of Cocktailia. Ever heard of it?"

"I guess I've seen her mentioned in the news," Millie said. "Want me to see what I can find out?"

"That's exactly what I was going to ask." Relief filled me. It was good to have friends like these who could back me up, back us all up, and get things done.

It was also good to have french fries.

My phone buzzed in my bag—I was back to the bigger bag, sans medal—and I checked the screen. The number looked familiar. "Hello?"

"Ms. Revelle?" came the soft female voice, so soft she was whispering.

"Yes?"

"This is Sherry at the lost and found. You asked if I could give you a call if someone picked up that hat you left. A gentleman just picked it up."

"Sh—I mean, sorry. Which way did he go?"

"Toward the stairs. I'm not sure where he was going, but a few seminars are ending and starting. Maybe— "

"Thank you!" I cut her off and ended the call. "I've got to catch the guy with the hat. He might be headed for the ballrooms. Oh, crap, the bill—"

"I've got it," Millie said. "I'll charge it to Neil. And he'll charge it to Dash."

"If he has any money left," I muttered under my breath, leaping out of my seat.

"I'll go too!" Bennett said, glee in his voice, following me as I ran out of the restaurant and across the lobby, bumping into people as I headed for the stairs. "What are we looking for?"

"A guy with a hat. I mean, hang on—" My phone was still in my hand, so I zoomed through galleries, retrieving the photos as I ran. And tripped on the stairs.

Bennett caught my elbow before I face-planted. "Easy there."

I found the photo of the hat and showed it to him. "Stop anybody who's wearing this hat. Probably a guy with a beard, but it might be someone else. A guy picked it up. That's all I know."

"And this guy is?"

"There's a small chance he tried to kill Dash and me and Neil the other night."

"Good to know," Bennett said, deadpan, as we got to the second-floor lobby with its handful of ballrooms and a huge crowd of people waiting to get into them.

"Yeah. Be careful. I hate being short. I can't see a damn thing." I jumped up, scanning the crowd with each hop.

"Is that it?" Bennett asked, pointing to a far corner.

I jumped once, twice, and got a good look. "Looks like it. Let's get him!"

We started pushing our way through the noisy crowd, to grumblings and occasional elbows in our bellies. And then the double doors of the biggest ballroom opened, and the crowd starting pouring out.

All wearing hats. Straw hats with patterned gray and white bands.

"What the—?" I choked out as I tried to get through the crowd to the guy we'd targeted. But it was hopeless. We were adrift in a sea of hats, people trying to get to their next seminar or lunch. The hats might not have been the fancy product of Chapeau Brothers, but they were awfully similar.

"Is this a joke?" Bennett asked with a breath of laughter. At least he appreciated the absurdity of the situation.

"Look closely. See? The band has a logo on it. They're vodka swag."

"I'd rather have vodka," he said.

"I'd rather have whiskey, but we can talk about that later. Maybe we can still get our guy if we can tell them apart."

"Let's split up," Bennett said. "I'll move toward the elevators, see if I can intercept him. You keep headed in the direction we first saw him."

"OK. Text me or shout if you get him."

"Ditto," he said, and we split up.

Now I was barely moving through the crush as the seminars switched out. Every once in a while I hopped up to get a better view, but I still couldn't see the bearded guy with the original hat. At least I didn't know if I was seeing him or not.

Another ballroom began disgorging its guests as some of the folks who'd been hanging out in the lobby moved into the room. And everywhere were the damn gray-and-white-banded straw hats. Actually, faux straw, I was pretty sure. But it's not like I had the time to check the weave and the stitching. I glanced at each hatted head. Beard? No. Logo? Yes. Move on. Move on. Move on.

As I was looking in one direction, I ran into yet another cursed mixologist. "Sorry," I said, looking up to find myself face-to-face with Neil. "Oh."

"Yeah, *oh*." He had his stoic face on, with maybe just a microscopic spark of humor in those gray eyes. I could not deal with thinking about last night right now. "Millie said you spotted the hat guy and that you were heading up to the ballrooms."

"I saw him in that direction, and then Jesus multiplied the mixologists and that ballroom barfed out a hundred people wearing hats."

He laughed and looked around. "So now what?"

"The pretenders have logos on their hatbands. And I think our guy went that way." I pointed to one end of the lobby, where there was another ballroom entrance and a corridor that curved around toward guest rooms and the back stairs.

In the minute we'd been talking, the crowd had thinned, and we were able to move more quickly, but the One True Hat failed to make an appearance by the time we reached the other end of the second-floor lobby.

"Back stairs?" Neil asked.

"Maybe, but he came up the stairs to here, so I don't know why he'd do that. Unless his room is on this floor."

Bennett jogged up to us. "The hats are pretty much gone, and I didn't see the guy come to the elevator."

"I have a thought before we go banging on every door on the second floor," Neil said, glancing at the ballroom door.

"That's a good thought," I said. He might be in the seminar.

We approached the door—now closed after its exchange of prisoners—and I gingerly opened it. A New York cocktail columnist was on stage, waxing rhapsodic about seventeenth-century punches. And there were about eight people in the room wearing hats.

"I'll wait here in case he does a runner," Bennett whispered.

Neil and I nodded and moved up the center aisle between the rows of tables and chairs, each of us checking the hatted ones. Until I saw a hat that stood out from the vodka crowd. I waved at Neil, and he waved at me as if to say, "Go ahead."

Thanks for nothing. I grimaced. Of course the guy was in the middle of the row. Instead of squeezing behind the chairs at the tables, I waved at him, smiling, gesturing that he come out.

He did have a huge beard, just as the hat-store clerk had suggested. He also had flushed cheeks that indicated he'd already been enjoying all that Cocktailia had to offer this morning. He smiled at me, glanced at my boobs (at least they worked on *some* men), and worked his way out to the aisle.

"What is it?" he whispered as the presenter shot us a dirty look.

"Come outside." I grabbed the guy by the arm and pulled him toward the door. I wasn't getting a murderer vibe off of him. More of an inebriated bearded cherub vibe.

"But I don't want to miss the first drink."

"Shhh." Bennett opened the door, and Neil followed us out to the lobby. I waited until the door closed. "Where were you Thursday night?"

"What the hell is this?" the guy asked, starting to look annoyed.

"Just answer the question," Neil said.

"I was at a Distiller Dinner at La Bonne Vie."

We exchanged glances. "What about after that?" I asked.

"I went drinking with friends."

"Where?" Neil asked.

"Does it matter? Look, I need to get back in there." He blinked. "Hey, aren't you that guy who wrote the cocktail book that won the award? Way to go, man."

"Thanks," Neil said.

I tried a sweeter tone. "Tell me about your hat. It's really nice."

"Isn't it great?" Now he smiled, his lips pink through his Santa-quality brown beard, the dewiness of his buzz shining in his eyes. "I just got it back today. I left it at that damn dinner, but when I went back, they said someone had taken it. I never thought to look in the hotel lost and found before today. Cost me a fortune at Chapeau Brothers."

I nodded and inwardly screamed. This guy was a dead end. Probably.

"Thanks," Neil said. "I'm sorry we disrupted your seminar. Look, if you give me your name and address, I'll send you a copy of my book."

"Really?" The guy fished in his pockets and pulled out a business card. "That's awesome. You can send it here. Great to meet you guys. What are you looking for, anyway?"

"Hats," Bennett said. "Really nice hats."

"Right," the guy said, nodding in that way drunk people do, as if Bennett's statement totally made sense. "Right on."

He slipped back into the ballroom, letting the door shut behind him.

"What do you think?" I asked.

"I think somebody borrowed his hat," Neil said in exasperation, "maybe accidentally leaving it at the cemetery, maybe on purpose."

"Well, I'd better get back to Millie," Bennett said, looking between us, reading the unspoken words. "Call me if you need anything."

"Thanks, man," Neil said. And then, after he left: "We need to talk."

Chapter Twenty-Two

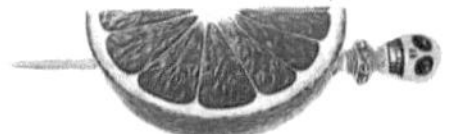

"**R**eally, Neil? Do we really have to talk? Because I don't want to talk about last night. If any occasion called for *not* talking, it was last night."

He shook his head. "I—I'm not ready to talk about last night."

"Why not?"

He quirked up a corner of his mouth. "I thought you didn't want to talk about it?"

I rolled my eyes and let out an overly dramatic sigh. "Fine. Then what?"

"Will you come with me to my book signing? Then we can run errands afterward. I've got the others setting up our station at the Lakefront Airport."

"What?" *Errands?* This man confused the hell out of me. But I couldn't help melting just a little in his confounding presence. "OK."

Ten minutes later, we'd retrieved the rental SUV from the parking garage and were on our way to the bookstore. And I couldn't help poking Neil about our almost-hookup, even if I didn't want to talk about it. The truth was, I didn't want to be rejected again, or worse, told in great detail about why he'd turned me down.

"Tell me again why you turned me down last night." *Yeah, I know.* Glutton for punishment.

Neil, both hands on the wheel, kept his eyes aimed straight ahead. "I didn't turn you down. Not exactly. You were drunk, and it wouldn't have been right."

"I was sober this morning."

"You were sleeping." He paused. "And if you must know, leaving you this morning was one of the hardest things I've ever done."

"You didn't have to leave me."

He shot me an exasperated expression. "I think I did. Getting attached to me is a bad idea, Pepper."

"That's pretty presumptuous. Why do you think I plan on getting attached to you? And what does that have to do with you leaving me alone in bed?"

"Are you saying you need me as just another mark on your bedpost?" he asked in that wry tone that was becoming so familiar.

I rolled my eyes. "Sure, if I can find any more room to make a scratch."

Now he looked a little shocked.

I laughed. "Just kidding, dude."

"Hmph. Well, even if you don't plan on getting attached to me, I'm worried about getting attached to you."

I was stunned into silence. And I wasn't so sure that I wasn't getting attached to him, either. I just didn't want to admit it. I needed to save face somehow after my little performance last night.

I cleared my throat. "Would it be so bad getting attached to someone?" *Not me, of course.*

"People who are close to me don't end up in happy places."

"That's the vaguest and most melodramatic thing I've ever heard."

He laughed. "You're probably right. I'm just no good at taking care of people."

"Presumptuous again and wildly inaccurate. You're always taking care of everyone and everything."

For once, his voice lacked the assurance I'd grown used to. "I try."

So Neil had problems. We all had problems. And I couldn't help liking him even more.

"Listen," I said. "You don't have to take care of me. I've been taking care of myself for a long time. But if you happen to see a homicidal maniac chasing me, I won't argue if you clunk him over the head with the nearest bottle of booze, OK?"

"Not good booze."

"That goes without saying." And I grinned at his joke and maybe, possibly, fell a tiny bit in—

No. Down, girl.

We drove in silence for a couple of minutes, heading through the business district.

I couldn't keep my mouth shut for that long. "So did you see my tattoo?"

He guffawed, and the smile stuck on his face. "Did you see mine?"

"*What?*" I sat up straight. "You have one?"

He glanced at me, the twinkle back in his eyes, then focused on the road. "A man has to have a little mystery."

I huffed, sat back and crossed my arms. "Says the man in the iron mask over here."

Neil laughed again before responding in a low, rough voice that shot right to my lady parts. "I liked the fire."

I started to feel a little warm. "I thought you'd like the cocktail shaker part."

"That's cool, especially how you have it launching like a rocket into the stars—"

"The bartender-astronomer would notice the stars."

"Yeah," he said even more softly, "but the fire from the rocket is lowest on your back. It disappeared into your underwear."

"And?" I was imagining him watching me as I slept, his eyes scanning my body with impunity, and the idea had all of me on fire, not just the tattoo.

He stole a glance at me, then riveted his gaze on the road before replying gruffly, "It gave me ideas."

Oh, my. I already had a lot of ideas about Neil. "You're a tease," I declared.

"Me?" Now he really was shocked.

"Well, it certainly isn't me." It was kinda fun keeping Neil off-kilter. My phone started ringing in my purse with my "Rum and Coca-Cola" ringtone. I dug it out and answered. "Millie?"

"Yeah. I did some quick web research on Tocks. Have a second?"

Damn, she was fast. "Hang on. I'm putting you on speaker so Neil can hear." I hit the button. "OK, you're on."

"Tocks Development Corporation has been around since 1964. Raquel Tocks expanded it considerably from where her father left it when he died. He had, shall we say, a lot of other interests. Served some time for wire fraud, bank fraud and conspiracy in a fake mortgage scheme. He was often under investigation or rumored to be involved in more serious stuff, but none of it ever amounted to anything legally."

"Like what serious stuff?" Neil asked.

"Like Miami mob stuff. Like sometimes he'd lose a crony

on a permanent vacation, or he'd hook up shady characters in real estate deals."

"What about Raquel?" I asked. "Is she clean?"

"Her record is clean, but it's hard to say if that reflects the whole reality," Millie said. "The business looks pretty legit, but her firm is constantly getting slapped with fines and lawsuits for violating environmental laws and stuff like that. And a couple of the guys following her around have records. Her lawyer has some unsavory clients."

"How'd you get that?" I asked in wonder.

"She appeared in photos I found online with one or more of them at society events, and their names were listed in the captions. It was easy to look them up from there. By the way, she had another piece of interesting eye candy at a few galas."

"Who?" Neil asked.

"Travis Reynolds."

"Huh. Well, he *is* pretty hot," I said for Neil's benefit.

"What?" Neil exclaimed, just as Millie started laughing.

"So are they seriously dating?" I asked Millie as I enjoyed Neil's reaction.

"Does Travis do anything seriously? I don't know their level of involvement. I just found a few photos, a couple in Miami and one from an event in Bohemia Beach."

"Maybe she's courting him to try to buy the distillery building for condos since Dash isn't all that enthused," I mused. "Get to Dash through his cousin."

"That's beyond the range of my crystal ball," she said. "I can let you know if I find out anything else."

"Excellent," Neil said. "Great work, Millie."

"Catch you later, girl," I added, disconnecting.

Neil looked at me. "Did you ask her to do that?"

"Yes. Do you mind?"

He shook his head. "Not at all. It was kind of brilliant. I guess the next question is, do you really think Raquel Tocks would go so far to get her hands on Dash's building?"

"If they thought there was enough money in it, sure. Especially if they don't mind getting their hands dirty, which may very well be the case. And if they anticipated the bad whiskey would be discovered, maybe they're just trying to scare Dash, not kill people. Get him to walk away and sell."

"The flying arrows in the cemetery seemed like a legit way to kill people. And there was the guy who attacked you."

Cold zipped through me. "I'll grant you, both of those instances scared the shit out of me, but maybe that's what they were intended to do."

He reached over and grasped my hand briefly, then gripped the wheel again as he found parking on the street. "We're here."

Chapter Twenty-Three

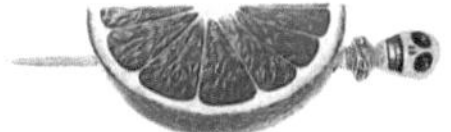

The bookstore was nestled in a mini-mall in a funky two-story building in the Garden District. Inside, the store was as strangely constructed as outside, with multiple levels exploding with tables and shelves stuffed with colorful old and new books basking in the light of tall, street-facing windows. I was itching to check out the mystery and romance, but first I wanted to make sure Neil had what he needed. With the help of an annoyingly adorable clerk who kept fluttering her eyelashes in Neil's direction, he was fully supplied with books, Sharpies and water.

A modest crowd had shown up to see him. He talked for a few minutes about his book and the pleasures of well-made cocktails, and then he sat at a table decked out in a red table-cloth and piles of his books and started signing and chatting with fans.

Wait. I knew one of those guys. *Oh, hell.* He was an ex-boyfriend from my more naive days who'd gone from flunky Bohemia barback to Los Angeles online celebrity mixologist Mr. Mixy. And boy, had he changed. He used to be kind of cute back in the day. I liked him clean-shaven. Now his beard was so big he looked like a Chia Pet. I did *not* want to see him, but I guessed at Cocktailia, I had to see everybody.

That didn't mean he had to see me. I ducked into the

stacks and started browsing. No titles jumped out at me in my usual niches, so I moved on to the case that held the cocktail books.

Ah, *The Savoy Cocktail Book* by Harry Craddock. I needed to replace mine, an old clothbound edition that had been the victim of a devastating Hanky Panky accident at home—a spilled cocktail, not actual hanky panky, unfortunately. The book had been soaked, prompting me to leave it out to dry on the back patio I shared with my aunt at our duplex.

The book then suffered a worse fate, as the Cavapoo I shared with my aunt—a mildly demented sweetheart of a dog named Astra—apparently liked the scent of gin so much, she chewed the spine and corners off before I found her with it.

This time, I picked up a paperback so I would be out less money when it met with the next disaster. Cocktail books tended not to remain pristine for long.

I peered around the end of the row of bookcases and glanced at Neil. The line had dwindled to a half-dozen chatty enthusiasts, who were gathered around him talking. Mr. Mixy was still there.

Neil had about fifteen more minutes anyway, so I meandered, finding myself in the childhood classics. What was it Dash had said about devouring books like these as a kid? C.S. Forester was one of the names he mentioned. I found one and pulled it out. *Ship of the Line*. Seafaring adventures. I loved the idea, even if boating made me resemble one of those science-project volcanoes that overflow when kids mix vinegar with baking soda. It wasn't pretty.

Not a good image when one has a waning hangover.

I put the volume back and looked further. Howard Pyle— that was another one Dash had mentioned. Ooo, they had a pretty purple and gold edition of *The Story of King Arthur and*

His Knights. I'd read this during my first swords and sorcery phase. I fanned through the pages, admiring the illustrations, wondering who would be considered a knight in today's world. Arthur was a tough act to follow. Neil? Could his Excalibur be a cocktail spoon?

Ah, and Pyle's *The Merry Adventures of Robin Hood*—opening it gave me a flashback to going to the library as a girl and getting this book. The language was a little thick for a kid, but that was part of the appeal. It talked about "a whole host of knights, priests, nobles, burghers, yeomen, pages, ladies, lasses, landlords, beggars, peddlers, and what not, all living the merriest of merry lives, and all bound by nothing but a few odd strands of certain old ballads ... which draw these jocund fellows here and there, singing as they go."

They could have been bartenders.

I pushed my glasses up on my forehead so I could look closely at the beautiful illustrations. I was so enraptured that I screamed a little when a hand clasped my shoulder. I spun around.

"Neil!"

"Yeah," he said slowly. "That's me." He smiled. "I'm done. You ready to run our errands?"

I took a deep breath. "OK."

"So those aren't reading glasses?"

"Huh? Oh, yeah." I pulled the glasses back down in front my eyes. "Actually ..."

"What?"

"They aren't really for anything. They're not corrective. I just like the way they look. Plus, they keep juice out of my eyes."

Neil barked out a laugh. "You're kidding, right?"

I shook my head and bit my lip.

His gaze went there. His nostrils flared, and then he caught my eye—my eyes, which were widening behind my fake glasses at the lightning bolt that leapt between us.

"We'd better go." My voice was husky. What the hell was that about? On an impulse, I hung on to *Robin Hood*. I could use a merry man. Serious guys made for too much angst. "I've got to check out."

"So did you sell many books?" I asked as Neil drove us to our next destination, a big restaurant supply store with all the fruit and herbs we needed for tonight. Still a little freaked by that moment with him in the bookstore, I hugged my messenger bag, which was now nice and fat with my two purchases.

"They tell me it was a respectable number for a signing," he said. "About twenty."

"That's awesome!"

"It's kind of cool to think that someone is using it in their bar. Mr. Mixy even bought one."

"Yeah?"

"What?"

"What what?"

"Your tone," Neil said. "What about Mr. Mixy?"

"Formerly known as Stephan Sully. He used to live in Bohemia."

"Oh? I never ran into him there."

"Worked with me briefly." I shot Neil a glance that said a lot more than my words.

He chuckled. "Did you mix it up with Mr. Mixy?"

I rolled my eyes. "I was young and stupid. At least *I'm* smarter now."

"But you're not an Instagram celebrity."

"He's still a loser. Now he's just a famous loser."

Neil looked pleased at this remark. "I saw you got Craddock's book?"

"Yeah, my dog ate mine."

A bubble of laughter popped out of his mouth. "You have a dog?"

"I have joint custody with my aunt. The truth is that Astra owns both of us."

"Astra? Like the dog in the *The Thin Man?*"

"That's *Asta*. This is *Astra*. My aunt named her. "

"Ah, Astra. So she's the 'star' of the house."

"Ha ha! You have no idea."

"I'd like to meet her." He smiled. "Hey, we have a little time. Do you want to stop by and see if your parents are home?"

Talk about a change of subject. Talk about bad ideas. Dread filled me all the way to my eyebrows, but I didn't want Neil to know just how chicken-shit I was.

"Sure," I said.

I directed Neil to the Lakeview neighborhood. A lot had changed since the hurricane. There were nicer houses now, at least for those who rebuilt, but there were scars. All these years later, the roads were still buckled from being drowned when the levee broke and set the 17th Street Canal free. I felt like a time traveler, coming back here. A stranger.

I even got us a little lost on my way to my parents' place, partly because I didn't recognize it when I got there. The old house, a weathered one-story wood-frame affair that my father had inherited, was gone. In its place was a two-story brick home. It wasn't upscale, exactly, but it had a solid, prosperous look about it.

"They're doing OK, aren't they?" Neil commented as he eased up to the curb and stopped.

"So it would seem." Neatly shaped bushes and bright flowers grew on either side of the few steps that led to the green front door. Windows flanked the entrance; there were three windows on the second floor and a steeply pitched roof.

I didn't move when Neil turned the car off.

He sat and watched me. "Pepper?" he asked finally.

"You might not want to come in."

"I want to come in," he said without inflection. Then he got out, came around and opened my door for me.

I couldn't say no to that, could I?

It occurred to me that I was bringing a man home to meet my parents. I mean, they didn't know the deal between us. But that's what it looked like. At least Neil was sharp in another one of his vest and skinny tie combos. I was starting to regret giving my girls so much air time today in my tight T and vest. But what the hell. It wasn't like I could disappoint my folks any *more*.

I surveyed the modest flower garden as I walked up the steps. It was punctuated with statuary, including a couple of cutesy bunnies, a little girl holding a watering can, and a praying garden gnome wearing an insipid expression. I wasn't exactly sure where gnomes figured into my parents' pantheon, but OK.

I rang the doorbell.

The door opened to reveal a strange woman in a pants suit, tidy pinned-up hair dyed black, and meticulous makeup on her seasoned face.

She looked me over with a mix of confusion and denial. "Kayanne?"

Chapter Twenty-Four

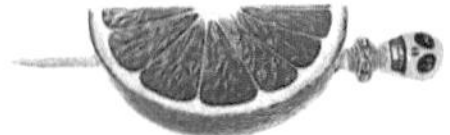

"Oh my—Mom?" It had been a few years since I'd seen her. Not forever. But she'd completed an evolution into someone as shiny and polished as a chrome bumper.

"You should have called first." Then she noticed Neil. "Hello, young man. Would you like to come in?"

I bit my tongue to stop myself from asking if I was allowed in, too. "This is Neil. We work together."

"Nice to meet you, Mrs. Revelle," was all Neil said, and I followed them into the house.

We walked into the ruthlessly beige living room and stood. No offer to sit. Photos on the wall showed my parents in tropical places doing their thing—hugging children. Riding donkeys. A china cabinet was filled with a collection of holy manger snow globes. A carved wooden cross on the wall was big enough to crucify a large teddy bear.

She noticed me looking. "Do you like it? We got it in El Salvador."

"When did you do all this? I mean the house. It's new."

"It's coming up on five years old. Have you really not been here?" my mother asked vaguely. "Oh, yes, the last couple of times we saw you, we went to dinner near your hotel."

That was because my aunt and I were never invited to the house.

"And how is Celestine?" she asked. "It's been a while since we talked. It's so hard to keep track of my little sister."

"I think she feels the same way about you," I said, "since you're always on the move."

A smile crossed my mother's face. "It's the work. Your father was just arranging the next trip to Nicaragua. Kevin!" she called in the general direction of upstairs. "We have visitors!"

Footsteps on the stairs signaled my father's approach. When he entered the living room and saw me, a smile crinkled his eyes. He put a hand on my shoulder. "Kayanne. It's so nice of you to come see us. We got your message about the dinner, but it just didn't fit into our schedule."

At this point, I was pretty sure I'd have to grow wings and a halo to fit into their schedule. "It's OK. This is Neil. He owns the bartender company that made drinks for the dinner. I'm working with the team."

My father shook his hand. "Nice to meet you."

"And you," Neil said. So much for relying on Neil's conversational skills to get me through this.

My mother brightened. "Does that mean you quit working at the bar in Florida?" she asked.

"No. I own half of it now."

She looked as if she'd swallowed a lemon garnish. "And have you found a nice church?"

"It's kind of informal," I said. OK, so my idea of church was long Sunday morning walks on the beach.

"Her Sazerac is a religious experience," Neil said idly.

My father chuckled, and I laughed out loud.

My mother frowned. "Alcohol is forbidden in this house."

The subtext was that I might as well be forbidden, too.

"Well, we have errands to run before a big event tonight," I said with all the bravado I could muster. "I'm sorry we disturbed you."

"Not at all!" my father exclaimed. "Why don't you stay for a cup of tea?"

"They can't," my mother said. "We have to get to the church. The baptism."

"But—" My father's protest was cut off by my mother's steely glare. His look of hope melted like a wax candle, and then he gave me a brief hug and stepped back, letting Mom lead, as he always did.

My mother patted my back as if I were a stray cat, angling me toward the door. "Thank you for stopping by. Please tell my sister I said hello."

"Sure." *Thanks for stopping by?* "Uh, have fun at church."

"I will never know why you are so interested in *fun,*" my mother said, showing us to the door with her bland smile.

When it closed behind us, I stood there for a second looking at the praying garden gnome, and then I stalked toward the car.

Neil called after me. "Pepper?"

"That was the dumbest idea of all dumb ideas."

Neil caught up with me halfway down the walk. "That's my fault. I'm sorry if you're upset," he said as we got into the SUV.

"Maybe I should be, but I know the deal by now." I looked at the house one last time.

Neil started the car and fiddled with the radio for an awkward moment.

"I've never met missionaries before," he finally said.

A corner of my mouth lifted. "My parents are not typical.

As a kid, I knew a lot of folks who do what my parents do. Friendly families who seemed to have fun together, traveled together, whereas my folks left me with friends or my aunt when they did their long summer trips. Honestly, I was jealous. Maybe if our family had been more like the others—but it couldn't be."

"Why? What do you mean?" He settled on a jazz station and looked at me.

"Nothing."

"You can't pull the 'nothing' card with me," Neil declared. "Because then I'll ask about it every five minutes until you tell me the truth or make something up."

I snorted a laugh. I needed that. "OK. I overheard my parents talking once—my mom never told me this herself, but she apparently gave up a baby when she was a teen. That's when she turned to religion. And I think she always hoped that baby would come back to her in some way. When she married my dad and then had me after a bunch of miscarriages, I was her second chance. Last chance, I guess. When I turned out bad, my parents didn't have any backups. My mom treated me as if my wicked ways might be contagious."

"That's ridiculous. You're not wicked." Neil put the car in gear and pulled away from the curb. "So you have a sibling out there somewhere?"

"I suppose I do. I used to imagine a brother or sister tracking my mother down and knocking on our door. They'd have to be fifteen years older than I am, but I always wanted a sibling."

"Yeah." Neil's voice was rough, and I remembered that he'd lost a brother.

"Yeah," I echoed. I turned to him as we bumped along the flood-buckled roads of the neighborhood. "I've thought about this a lot. My mom was probably worried I'd get in trouble the way she did. But once I figured out who I was, that I loved people and the bon vivants and all the fun, glamorous craziness that is this city, when I started sneaking out to see the Mardi Gras parades and finding ways to skip church on Sunday, it was like my mom gave me up, too. Only I was still in the house. I was a bad girl, and they had no idea what to do with me."

"You can't have been that bad."

"I didn't think so until after the storm. When they sent me to my aunt, it seemed reasonable to have me evacuate. The effects of the storm were terrible, schools were closed for a long time, and we knew it would be very difficult to live here. But even then, I figured out what they were doing. I was being sent into exile."

He shook his head. "It's really hard for me to imagine that. I guess I'm lucky."

"I am too. I know that now. I mean, I had to get over the whole rejection thing. But life with my aunt was fun. She was easygoing, and so was Bohemia Beach. I loved it. So when no invitation to come back materialized after New Orleans started to recover, I was almost relieved."

Neil made a small sound of what I thought was sympathy anyway. "What was the hurricane like?"

Not my favorite memory, but it had gotten a little easier to tell it over the years. "We didn't evacuate for the storm. The hurricane really wasn't that horrible for us at first. The winds, I mean. But of course it was the levee breaks that screwed most of us. The water rose really fast. We didn't have a second floor to go to, so we went into the attic. Dad punched a hole in the roof with an ax."

"Scary."

"It was. We climbed up there and were stuck there for

hours, waiting for a rescue, listening to other people calling for help. And then it was dark except for the occasional helicopter searchlight. The car and house alarms were blaring, and when they stopped, all you could hear was the frogs. A boat came through in the middle of the night and got us to shelter."

I pointed outside the car. "See, look at this." We were crossing over the canal. "When you grow up here, you don't even think about the fact that this water is higher than most of the city around it. We just accepted that the walls would keep the water out. We lived under the guillotine for years and never even realized it."

We watched the neighborhoods glide by, dry for now. In a few minutes, we reached the market, went inside and grabbed a buggy. It had a cup holder. Only in New Orleans.

We spun through the aisles, grabbing what we needed, saving the produce section for last. A familiar figure was browsing the citrus, hair leaking out from under his hat. Making a decision, Alastair grabbed large bags of lemons and dropped them in his cart next to gargantuan bottles of honey. When he looked up and saw us, he turned white. Well, as white as an already pale Englishman can get.

"Alastair," Neil said by way of greeting. He gestured to the British bartender's cart. "Bee's Knees?"

"You think you're so bloody brilliant," Alastair said.

"Yes?" Neil replied in an innocent tone. It wasn't exactly a question. I suppressed a laugh as Alastair fumed.

"Why are you so insecure?" I asked him. "You're making drinks for the distillery that won the big medal."

"That's outrageous," he said in that crisp accent. "I'm not insecure."

"Then why did you feel a need to taste Bohemia Distillery's whiskey the other day when no one was around?" I asked.

His jaw set and one eyelid twitched before he regained his composure. *"Someone* was around. That Barnard fellow. I was just being sociable. That's what Cocktailia is all about, isn't it? Tasting. Trying new things. Sharing. Learning. And I learned that your cocktails have to work bloody hard to hide the taste of that awful whiskey."

Anger gripped me in spite of myself, and I wanted to defend Dash, defend the Bohemia Bartenders' work. But that would mean admitting to that bad batch—which Alastair might know about already. Maybe he was fishing.

Maybe I'd go fishing, too. "Ever play around with bows and arrows, Alastair?" I asked him.

He rolled his eyes. "What do you think I am, Robin Hood? They scare me witless. Almost got an arrow in my arse at a country weekend with Mark."

"Fairyland's Mark?" Neil asked.

"Fairman's a fiendish archer, and we were all a bit drunk on a lot of scrummy G&Ts. Don't ask. What a peculiar question. The only weapon I need to demolish you tonight is a good shaker," Alastair shot at Neil, sporting a wild grin as he pushed passed us. "And then again on Sunday. You all might as well go home."

"Do you think he's a couple of olives short of a jar?" I asked as he got out of earshot.

Neil granted me a half-smile, but he had a pensive look in his eyes. "I think he likes attention."

"If Alastair isn't an archer, what about Fairyland's owner? Do you think he was shooting arrows at Dash and us?"

"I don't know," Neil said. "What connection could there be?"

"Dash said a British distiller had made an offer to partner up with him. What if it was Fairyland? Maybe they're trying to get Dash to want to sell out. Maybe they're looking for a bargain."

"We'll have to ask Dash. Maybe it was a legitimate offer. I know Mark Fairman casually. He seems like a pretty good guy. Let's not borrow trouble. I'd rather focus on showing up Alastair tonight, even if he and his sponsor don't *literally* want to kill us."

I put that thought aside so I could function without worrying about crazed statues and arrow-wielding attackers. "Let's do it."

Chapter Twenty-Five

We'd packed the big cooler in the back of the SUV with our ingredients and were making our way to the hotel when I had an inspiration. "Hey, stop here!"

"Why?" Neil asked.

"It's La Bonne Vie. Let's see if Nicki's home."

"I guess we have a few minutes." He miraculously found street parking around the corner. "You know what you want to ask her?"

"I'm going to ask her if she's seen the guy who suggested the boomerangs."

The bar was busier than it had been the other day. Saturday afternoon brought out the drinkers early. Nicki was busy muddling mint. We waited until she finished the mojitos and flagged her down. It took her a second to recognize me.

"Hi, Nicki. Busy day?"

She nodded, glancing from me to Neil and back. "Yeah, and we're working the big party tonight. You?"

"Yep." We both nodded.

She smiled. "Get you something?"

"I just have a quick question. Have you seen the guy who suggested the boomerangs the other night?"

She didn't answer for a second, busying herself with

washing a couple of glasses. "I don't really know why you need to know this, but if it's important—"

I sensed a breakthrough. "It is."

She sighed. "OK. Yes. I saw him that night, actually, after work. We had a late date. The bar we wanted to go to was already closed, and the Carousel Bar was too crowded, so we grabbed a beer on Bourbon Street. And that's all I'm going to tell you."

I was pretty sure I knew what that meant. They had a date, and then they had a night.

"Did he have a beard?" I'd asked the question before, but I wanted to see if she changed her answer.

"No. Not a real beard. Just scruff, you know," she said, distracted as a fellow bartender shouted an order down to her. Not exactly what she'd told me before.

"And he had a hat, you said?" I pushed.

"Yeah, he had a hat. Well, he'd almost forgotten it, but when he came by the bar to pick it up after the dinner, we got to talking. That's when he suggested the boomerangs."

So he'd lost his hat once. And then again—at the cemetery?

"Did he have the hat later?"

She looked at me like I was stupid. "Why this hat obsession?" When I shrugged, she sighed in exasperation. "No, he didn't have it for our date. We didn't spend the whole time talking about *hats.*" She rolled her eyes.

And he didn't have a real beard, so it definitely wasn't the guy who'd recovered the hat from the lost and found.

"We know you're busy, and we hate to pry, but we really need to track him down," Neil said apologetically, his gray eyes shining with sincerity. "Did you happen to get his name?"

She pursed her mouth in exasperation. "He said his name was Tinker. Rob Tinker. He was staying at the Hotel Lebeau. I don't remember which room—" She flushed, realizing how much she'd said. "Anyway, when I called the hotel the next day, they said nobody with that name was staying there. Not the first time a guy gave me a fake name. Men are assholes."

"Some of us are," Neil acknowledged without rancor. "Thanks, Nicki."

He grabbed my elbow and steered me out of the bar.

"So the boomerang guy has to be with Cocktailia," I said excitedly as we got into the SUV. "And he had a hat, or at least took the opportunity to grab a hat after the dinner. But the boomerang guy wasn't the hat guy we found, because the hat guy had a full beard."

"Which we'd surmised already. This is getting us nowhere." Neil started the engine.

"I had to try." Something was bugging me as we wove into heavy Quarter traffic. "Can I ride over to the venue with you?"

"Absolutely. We probably have room for everybody. I'm going to text the group when we get back, OK?"

"Sounds good." The group. I liked the sound of that. I wanted as many people around me as possible right now so I'd feel safer, but it helped a lot that they were my peeps.

NEIL ESCORTED me to my room and hovered in the doorway while I checked for mad killers, then made a hasty exit, muttering something about having to get ready. Which was true, but still, I had no doubt he was avoiding being alone with me.

Something did feel off. It took me a minute to realize there was no tuba honking outside. I kind of missed it.

I took a few minutes to call Jorge, my partner in my bar

back in Bohemia, to make sure everything was running smoothly at Nola. With the exception of an expensive repair bill for one of the ice machines, it was. As an engineer, often he could fix that kind of stuff, but this required a part and an emergency repair. Fortunately, Jorge was pretty cool about emergencies, and we had a little money in the bank. Maybe we could make more once we launched the new restaurant menu, after several months of terror, of course.

I also called Aunt Celestine.

"Well, I wondered when you'd get around to calling me," she said. Soft sounds of tweeting birds and wind suggested she was outside by the little pool behind our duplex. I pictured her in one of her tie-dye coverups, relaxing on a lounge chair, surrounded by palm trees and dozens of pots overflowing with green herbs and flowers.

"Is it warm enough to swim?"

"Not for most Floridians, but you know I'm not like most Floridians. How's the conference?"

Someone's trying to kill our client and maybe me and I want to shag my co-worker. And my mom is still frostier than a frozen margarita.

"Uh, crazy as usual."

There was a beat. "Did you see them?"

I only got about fifty percent of what I was trying to hide past Aunt Celestine. "This afternoon, just for a minute. I stopped by the house."

"And how were they?"

"Busy. On the way to church. The new house is pretty slick."

"That's not what I meant."

I sighed. "Weird. Judgy. Dad was OK, I guess."

"You're a good girl to try."

"Stupid girl."

"We both know that's not true."

She was right. I was a secret brain in high school. I ended up getting an associate's degree at the local culinary college with the idea I'd own a bar someday, but I could've gone down an even nerdier path.

"I'm emotionally stupid, and that's even worse," I said. "How's Astra?"

"She misses you. She keeps running over to your sliding glass door and licking it."

"Gross." Also cute.

"When are you coming back?"

"A couple of days. Give her a hug for me."

"I'm sending you a hug, too," Aunt Celestine said. "Kissy kissy. Call me if you need me."

Chapter Twenty-Six

The theme of the party was Flappers to Fifties, a nod to the fabulous little art-deco airport where it would be held. I hadn't seen Lakefront Airport in years. It had been totally restored since the hurricane, so I was excited to see it again.

Neil had asked our crew to go black and white and gray, but he didn't specify a theme. I'd opted for a poofy black-and-white number, which I donned after wolfing down a room-service hamburger, hoping the dress would still fit afterward.

The fifties-style white frock had peekaboo black pleats in the fluffy skirt—black fabric with white polka dots—and the white was accented at the seams with black buttons. The dark fabric was repeated in a "V" at the va-va-voom bodice. As a bonus, the gown had a pocket just big enough for my badge/hotel key card. But I'd still bring my messenger bag. I had trouble going anywhere without it. If I didn't have it, I was constantly looking for it, like a phantom limb.

I wrapped the black leather cord of my gator-tooth necklace around my wrist as a bracelet, just in case I needed a little luck. I put on the special sparkly rhinestones edition of my cat's-eye glasses and added a black crinoline under the skirt, so I was quite the rustling puffball by the time I emerged from my room. I didn't see Neil, so I headed to the lobby and found the rest of the crew gathered behind a potted palm.

"Damn, girl," I said to Melody. "When's Gatsby coming over?"

She was poured into a slinky silver and black flapper dress. It was sleeveless, and the colorful flowers and musical notes tattooed up her arms seemed to glow in contrast. Her blond hair was wavy tonight and held in place by a sparkling 1920s headband punctuated by black feathers.

"I'm more interested in the band right now." She grinned.

"The brass section?"

"Just the trombone. He's supposed to be playing tonight. That boy has an embouchure!" Melody puckered her lips, and I laughed.

"How can you work in those?" I eyed her strappy heels with suspicion.

"Years of training."

I shook my head in wonder. I'd opted for saddle shoes. They weren't sexy, but they were black and white, and they'd be comfortable for a night of hard work behind the bar.

Luke and Barclay sidled over. They matched in black pants, crisp white shirts rolled up at the sleeves, black suspenders and adorable black porkpie hats. No ties, but they were kind of devastating without them.

Barclay caught me looking, and he flashed me a beautiful, knowing smile that almost made me pass out. He was definitely more friendly since I gave him the rum. That was all it was, right? It was hard to tell. The man threw off enough pheromones to make a girl ovulate. "You look ace, Pepper."

I couldn't help but smile in return. "You two could be runway models," I said, gesturing to Luke as well. "Hey, there *will* be a runway ..."

"I'm not running out in the middle of the fireworks," Luke said. "A plane could land on me. I could be shot as a terrorist. Are you crazy?"

"Ooo, there will be fireworks?" Melody squealed.

"I can give you fireworks, baby," Luke said, and she laughed and batted his arm, only I thought maybe Luke wasn't kidding. "Oh, hey, Neil."

I turned around and almost popped out of my polka dots. Neil wore a tux with *tails!* Slim-fitting, it brought out every line of lean muscle with its charcoal-gray jacket, a light silver-gray vest, dark gray patterned tie, white shirt and pinstripe pants. Instead of a flower in his buttonhole, he wore a Bohemia Bartenders pin on his lapel.

"Omigod," I sputtered, "can I be the Ginger to your Fred?"

He laughed, his cool face on, though I couldn't miss his quick scan of my dress, the dilation of his pupils.

"You're in the wrong decade for me," he joked. "Another time. Everybody ready?"

I shook off his turn-down as I followed the group to the front of the hotel, where Neil tipped a valet to bring the SUV around, then tapped on his phone. In a few minutes, the car pulled up just as Bennett arrived from inside with a cart loaded with cases of Bohemia Beachside Bourbon and Bohemia Rye.

"These are from the general stash?" Neil asked him.

"Guarded 24/7 by hotel and convention security," Bennett confirmed.

"Excellent. Let's load up."

The others had delivered our bar tools to the airport already, so all we had to do was get the whiskey in the car and get rolling as sunset streamed across the bustling city.

Twenty-five minutes later, we arrived at an art-deco fantasyland.

The Lakefront Airport wasn't the city's main airport, but it was the most beautiful. The terminal was a palace of streamlines and symmetry. Built in 1933, it was cloaked in an ugly facade in the 1960s, then trashed by Hurricane Katrina. When the city chose restoration over rebuilding, the glorious art-deco art and architecture were resurrected.

That's what the articles said. In person, it was pure elegance, a magical throwback to a time when air travel was still suffused with romance and not all about people taking off their stinky shoes at the airport and getting nuked by the X-ray machines.

Two big spotlights cut through the twilight, shooting up beams that roved the pink skies, catching the scudding clouds. The facade, with its stylized carved figures, was lit in blue and purple. A round silver overhang thrust over the entrance and the steps that led to it. And above, the word TERMINAL cast shadows in a delicious deco font that made me want to do the Lindy.

The crowd hadn't arrived yet, but bartenders were busy setting up. Several booths lined the drive outside the entrance, populated by different bars and distilleries, themed by era—1920s, Prohibition gangsters, '40s film noir, World War II USO. An ambulance stood by with a crew and a little medical tent, ready to deal with drunk-related injuries.

"Where are we?" I asked.

"Prime spot inside," Neil said. "Is it all set?"

"We didn't have to do much. It's gorgeous." Melody led the way in her teetering heels while the guys wheeled the cooler and a dolly stacked with whiskey into the building.

The airy two-story hall was filled with delicious deco details, from the patterned terrazzo floor with its compass rose to the elaborate coffered ceiling. I'd seen pictures of the fabulous restored murals on the second level, and I hoped I'd get a chance to peruse them. A jazz band was setting up in one corner, and small tables were arrayed around the space in anticipation of guests.

A retro cafe, enclosed behind glass, looked out on the space from the edge of the hall. Its diner counter, lined with art-deco stools, was parsed to two teams: us and a team dressed all in red. We were weirdly complementary, color-wise. It took me a minute to realize we were next to the Fairyland Distillery people, who apparently were pushing their Vexatious Vodka tonight. The red flags behind the bar featured the Soviet hammer and sickle, evoking the Cold War. Leading a team of four glamorous women in tight, low-cut red T-shirts, black shorts, crimson lipstick and silky red scarves, Alastair Markham wore tuxedo pants, a red jacket and a ridiculous red fur hat the size of St. Basil's Cathedral.

"Don't look now, but there's a Muppet eating your head," Luke said.

"Don't say another bloody thing," Alastair snarled as we eyed him.

"It's a shame it hides your beautiful hair," I said, half meaning it. Neil shot me an inscrutable look that I hoped was jealousy.

Alastair, who was building elaborate garnishes, chose to take my comment as a compliment and smiled briefly. "Thank you, darling. I couldn't agree more, but the customer is always right." He grimaced again, then smiled beatifically as his sponsor arrived.

Mark Fairman and a few of his friends swirled into the room in colorful suits like a tornado of autumn leaves.

"Alastair, will you make us something with the Vexatious Vodka, please?" the Fairyland owner called out in his yummy accent. Then he scanned our group. "Neil. Hot Pepper." He winked.

"Hi," was all I could manage. My gaze traveled from his natty wingtip brown and white Oxfords all the way up to his saucy smile and cropped dark red hair. Mark wore an ivory linen suit with a caramel-brown vest and yellow tie. His clingy pants left little to the imagination. And those eyes. Those lips. That rough scruff around his square chin. Dangerous, to be sure.

There was no way he didn't notice my reaction. He slid over to me and leaned close as he had at the awards, murmuring in my ear so only I could hear him.

"Nice dress. It'd be a shame if something happened to it." He barely brushed the skin of my shoulder with one finger, leaving a trail of electric fire, and grinned at my open-mouthed shock as he backed away, grabbed drinks from Alastair and led his party back into the hall.

Did he know something about how my other dress had been ruined by a certain walking statue? Was he complimenting or insulting the dress I wore now?

Or did he just want to take it off?

Heat flushed my body. I avoided Neil's stare and exchanged a glance with Melody, who looked like she was about to burst with excited curiosity. I slid behind the counter with the rest of the bartenders and did my best to focus on the task at hand.

At one end of our bar was a dark barrel emblazoned with the Bohemia Distillery logo, along with marketing brochures for the whiskeys. The room's gleaming art-deco design needed little adornment, but four large, vertical black-and-white banners had been hung behind our section, covering most of the wall. It took me a second to realize they were reproductions of pages from Neil's book, featuring recipes for classic and twisted whiskey cocktails, complete with the adorable black and white sketches he'd commissioned as illustrations.

"Nice promo," I commented.

"It's a little embarrassing, but Dash suggested it," Neil said as we settled in and began our *mise en place.* "He thought we could give each other a boost." Despite his easy reply, I could tell he was ruffled, maybe by Mark Fairman's brash come-on. Hey, Neil was the one who'd put the brakes on whatever it was between us.

"Awesome banners," Luke said. "And they'll look good at the Junction Box when we get home."

"No way that's happening!" Neil said to our chuckles.

"Embrace your fame," Luke said.

"Ha!" Neil shook his head, but he was smiling. Now that the walking inferno of Mark Fairman had left the room, I felt Neil's pull again. And did I mention he looked positively lickable in his tux?

What the hell? I had enough hormones flowing tonight to power a nuclear submarine.

The four banners dictated our menu for the evening: two classics, a Sazerac and a Surburban; and two variations on classics, a Sour Cherry Old Fashioned and a Black Manhattan with a bittersweet amaro instead of vermouth. Needless to say, we had a lot of garnish-building to do with lemon peels, orange peels and cherries. I was glad I had my sparkly fake glasses on to keep the juice out of my eyes.

As I worked, my mind raced, going over the last few days. Something Alastair had said came back to me. The night he delivered Nicki's boomerangs, he'd been drinking at La Bonne Vie with Mark Fairman ...

A bellow yanked me from my reverie.

"The Bohemia Bartenders, as I live and breathe!"

We looked up to see Travis, grinning and flushed, already a drink or two in, I guessed. He wore a black suit, skinny tie and a white shirt and might have escaped from *Reservoir Dogs*. A glamorous blonde in a sparkling, clingy, dangerously short white dress was draped on his arm, sloe-eyed and smiling like the cat who ate the canary.

Raquel Tocks.

Chapter Twenty-Seven

Travis and Raquel, together in the flesh. She had a fancy camera slung over her shoulder and took a moment to take shots of us and Alastair's team.

She and Travis were followed by a couple of those big guys who always seemed to be treading on her shadow. They wore black suits and looked like extras from *The Godfather*. And while we were at the movies, sartorially speaking, Dash might have walked out of Rick's Café Americain with his white dinner jacket and the straw hat he wore on our expedition to Chapeau Brothers.

Dash awkwardly slid between the goons and approached Bohemia's counter, looking nervous. "Are you ready?" he asked.

"Just about." Neil smiled. "Can I make you something?"

Dash visibly relaxed at his confidence. "The Black Manhattan sounds perfect. I'm a rye guy."

"And I'm a bourbon guy. Or vodka!" Travis laughed and elbowed Dash, who scowled.

"I'm definitely a vodka girl," Raquel Tocks said, sliding over to the Fairyland display, tugging Travis along with her. "I'll have one of those." She pointed to a photo of a virulently red cocktail, and Alastair bared his teeth in a semblance of a smile and started making it. "You boys want anything?" Raquel asked over her shoulder.

One goon shook his head. The other said, "I wouldn't say no to a snort."

A snort? What decade was he from again? He sounded like a character from an old movie. Familiar. I couldn't quite remember which.

"Two of those," Raquel told Alastair. "Travis, honey?"

"I'm going with bourbon. Make me something, would you, Pepper?" Travis called over to me. He shot me one of his magnetic roguish smiles, and I couldn't help returning it, even if he was in the company of the scary porcelain doll.

"Coming right up." I got to work on the Sour Cherry Old Fashioned.

"Interesting placement," murmured Dash, looking over at the Fairyland display as Neil and I worked.

"What do you mean?" Neil asked.

Dash shrugged. "Maybe Mark Fairman was anticipating I'd say yes to his offer and requested we be side by side in here."

My eyes snapped up to his. "Fairyland was the distillery that wanted to partner with you?"

"Uh-huh."

Neil and I exchanged a look as the jazz band started up out in the hall. More guests were filtering in. I finished making Travis's drink, topping it with a twist of lemon and a brandy-soaked cherry, and held it out for him.

Travis held it up to the light. "That's a beautiful thing." He took a sip and hooked his free arm around Raquel. "And it's a beautiful night! Come on, baby. Let's check out the band."

The drinking goon shotgunned his red cocktail. "Girl drink," he muttered, then raked me with a predatory gaze. "I'll prolly be back for a shot later."

"Great." I raised an eyebrow at the guy, but my sarcasm was all bravado. He kind of creeped me out.

"Dude, you have that tripod?" the goon said to Alastair.

"Here." Alastair, mumbling something about not being a bloody bellboy, pulled a long black bag from behind the counter and handed it to the goon.

Neil elbowed me as the group left the room, trailed by fifth-wheel Dash. "Play nice."

I shot him a look and elbowed him back, only in slow motion, so I got to lean against his deliciously clad body. "Are you sure you want to play nice?"

He coughed and stepped away, putting a few inches between us.

I shrugged inwardly. "Anyway, it's pointless being nice to a guy like that."

"Maybe he's OK." Neil was making drinks and taking orders from guests even as he talked to me. All of us were. Multitasking was a bartender thing.

"He's not." Mix. Ice. Stir.

"How can you be sure?"

"I can't explain it—" And then I dropped my cocktail spoon.

Neil looked at me sharply. He took the drink I'd been making, garnished it and handed it to a guest, then pulled me back from the fray at the counter.

I barely noticed.

"Pepper? Are you OK?"

"It was him!"

"What do you mean, it was him?"

"The statue guy. The voice. It was him!"

"Are you sure?" Neil looked around, but no one was paying attention to us. Everyone was serving or drinking.

"I—I'm pretty sure. I mean, he looks different. Really different."

"Not being bronze and all."

"Yeah, that." I looked through the glass wall of the cafe at the crowd out in the hall, but I couldn't see the Tocks crew or the Reynoldses. "Maybe I need to hear him again. But—" I started shaking.

"Pepper?" Neil spoke more softly this time, laying a hand on my shoulder, squeezing. "Are you going to be OK?"

"Yes. Yes, I will be OK." *Oh, hell, I hope I'm OK.*

"You need to stay close. Have someone with you at all times tonight, do you hear me? If it's him, we need to keep you safe."

"It's probably not him," I croaked.

"You can't take that chance."

"If it's him, then Raquel Tocks is our problem," I whispered. "Or could it be Alastair? He was holding that bag for him. And what about Dash?"

"Travis won't let anything happen to Dash tonight. And there are hundreds of people here anyway. We'll have to deal with it later. Are you OK to work?"

"Yes, damn it. Sorry," I said, throwing back my shoulders and getting ahold of myself as he raised his eyebrows. "We have a job to do. Let's do it, OK?"

He searched my eyes. "All right." He gave my shoulder one more squeeze, a shot of warmth and courage, and then we dove back into the rush, making cocktails.

Melody gave me a curious look. "Later," I mouthed.

She nodded. "I'm hoping we get a break so I can check out the band. My guy is playing."

"We'll take breaks in shifts once the first wave dies down a little," Neil said. "And they want us to shut down before the fireworks anyway."

It took a while for the first wave to crest and ebb. There

were a lot of happy people who wanted to try every cocktail available to them. Which meant there were a lot of drunk people in fairly short order as they sampled bars at the outdoor booths and the stations set up throughout the terminal building.

The work prevented me from thinking too much, but I couldn't help but wonder why Raquel Tocks would sic her beast onto me or Dash. To scare us, I assumed. Him. To get him to give up his business so she could turn the building into condos? She must be planning on some crazy swanky condos to make all this nastiness worthwhile. Why was Travis with her, anyway? She had to be the light-haired woman he'd taken to his room last night. Hard for a playboy to resist, I supposed, given she looked like the cover of *Vanity Fair.* All she needed was a nude photo shoot with Annie Leibovitz.

Ugh. That was a thought I didn't need cluttering up my brain.

Finally, the traffic slowed to the point where we had a brief lull. "Who needs a break?" Neil asked.

"Me," Luke and Melody said at once. She elbowed me, and I echoed, "Me, too." I wanted to get a look around, see where the goon had gone, maybe get him to talk again so I could be sure.

Neil held me back a moment as Melody grabbed her small purse and she and Luke moved toward the door. "Be careful. Come right back."

This wasn't Cool Neil. He was as intense as I'd ever seen him.

I swallowed, trying not to think about all the things it would be much more pleasant to think about, like having one more try at getting through his wall of ice.

"I'll be back," I promised, grabbing my bag.

Melody was waiting for me at the door, and we headed out into the busy hall, echoing with voices and jazz.

"Where'd Luke go?" I asked.

"Restroom," she said. "Which I want to do, too, and then go check out the band real quick."

"We can't be gone long."

"We won't," she said as we made our way across the thronged floor. "So what was all that about back there?"

"Which part?"

"Well, Mark Fairman was obviously about to eat you up. I mean what were you and Neil whispering about?"

"You know how I was attacked the other night? I thought I might have seen the guy who did it."

"The statue guy is here?" she exclaimed.

"Shhh!" I looked around but didn't see the Tocks entourage. "I'm not sure. I was so freaked by the attack, maybe I'm hallucinating things."

"Trust your feminine intuition," Melody said as we entered the restroom.

A few minutes later, we touched up our lipsticks at the sinks. As she adjusted her flapper headband in the mirror, she turned her blue eyes on me. "Speaking of intuition, mine is telling me something else is going on."

I tucked my lipstick in my bag. "What?"

"What's really up with you and Neil?"

I caught the slight pinking of my cheeks in my reflection in the mirror. "Nothing."

"Really? Nothing?"

I quirked my mouth at her reflection. "Not for lack of trying."

She made a moue as she regarded her gorgeous self in the mirror. "Good. He needs to get laid."

I burst out laughing. "Don't hold your breath."

We reentered the hall and made our way to the band. Melody got as close as she could to the trombonist, who winked at her as they wrapped up their song.

"We're going to take a pause for a worthy cause," the saxophonist who led the group said. "We'll be right back."

"Excuse me," Melody murmured and headed up to the stage to intercept her trombone-playing Romeo.

I looked around, fighting the jitters, then noticed the tuba player.

"It's you! The bard of the Hotel Lebeau!"

"I like that," he said, his dark eyes twinkling, his deep brown skin glowing in the soft light of the hall. "Maybe I'll steal it."

"I didn't know you were in a real band. I mean, between the cab driving and playing on the street."

"Aw, you know. If it's not one gig, then it's another. It's the Gig Economy. I make apps, too. Do you need an app? How about a piece of furniture? I make awesome tables. Or bars! I can make you a bar. I'll do pretty much anything." He pulled a business card out of his pocket and shoved it in my hand. "Hell, the other night I moved a bunch of liquor for one of you convention people. He came right out to me on the street and asked if I wanted to earn some money. It paid better than the tuba."

I blinked at him. "Liquor? What kind of liquor?"

"The boxes said whiskey."

"When was this?"

"Ah, uh, Wednesday. No, Tuesday afternoon. Had to move the stuff out of a suite and down to the front, but he didn't want it to go through the hotel. I had to take the freight elevator and then cart it around the building to the front with the dolly. Seemed kind of stupid to me."

"Do you remember the name of the whiskey? On the box?"

He eyed me closely. "What's it to you?"

"Oh, please," I said. *"Please. It would help me so much if I could know this one thing. And—and I'll tip you really well when I hear you playing outside the hotel. Please."*

His laugh was more musical than his tuba. "You don't have to tip me. You want to know so bad, I'll tell you. It said 'Bohemia' on the side of the boxes. I remember because I got to thinking about a story I read once about a scandal in Bohemia, and—"

"So you took these boxes of whiskey to the front of the hotel?"

"Yeah. And the bellboys had me put them in a storage room, and the guy paid me a hundred bucks."

"What did this guy look like?"

"Oh, I saw him earlier tonight. He was kind of rough look-ing. White guy. How about I tell you if I see him again?"

"He's here? Was he with a blonde?"

"Yeah, he was. Pretty thing. But not my type." He shook his head. "Cold."

Chapter Twenty-Eight

Oh, crap. It *was* the guy. I was right about the voice. The statue guy had hired the tuba player to move Bohemia's whiskey! It didn't arrive late at the hotel. It was there the whole time—being doctored. Poisoned!

"Thank you. Thank you!" I gave him a swift hug. "I've got to get back to our bar. I'm working in there in case you think of anything else." I pointed to the cafe. "Thank you so much."

"Glad to help. You come visit me again at our next intermission, OK? And let me know if you want an app." He winked, and I smiled, wondering if I'd been a little *too* thankful, and then I popped his card in my bag and booked it back to our pop-up bar.

Melody and Luke were already back behind the counter, but there wasn't much traffic. Barclay and Neil were missing, presumably taking a break.

"Find a new friend?" Melody asked.

I shrugged. "I suppose you could say that." I didn't want to tell them what I'd learned, not yet. I wanted Neil to be here at least. And I wanted to warn Dash, even if he was surrounded by people. We needed to figure out how to get the evidence we needed to nail the guy, too. Maybe the hotel had surveillance cameras that would show the goon hiring the tuba player to move the whiskey.

By the time Neil and Barclay got back, we were in the middle of another rush, and there was no time to talk for the next hour. I couldn't see a clock anywhere, and my phone was tucked away. I tapped Barclay's wrist, and he held up his sexy retro watch when he saw my intent.

"Thanks," I murmured, and we exchanged a smile. He gave good smiles.

Neil shot me another funny look, and I returned a *"What?"* expression. I needed to talk to him, damn it, even if he didn't know it.

The late hour meant the fireworks would start soon, and we'd have to shut down. Then I could fill in Neil, and we could go find Dash together.

"Bloody hell!" Alastair's curse—which followed the crash of breaking glass—carried over the buzz of the crowd in our small space. All heads swiveled to him in his giant furry hat. He was clutching one hand, and blood oozed between his fingers. It matched their costumes nicely.

"The garnishes!" one of his model-worthy minions screeched, pushing him back so he wouldn't drip into the tray of olives and carefully cut fruit that represented hours of work.

Leave it to Neil to leap into action. He was there in a flash, wrapping Alastair's bleeding hand in a towel.

"What happened?" Neil asked.

"I tapped the bloody glass with the shaker and it just blew apart," said Alastair, now ghastly pale and wavering.

"Don't faint on me, man. Let's get you to the medics."

"I'll be fine with a little gin."

"Too bad you only have vodka tonight," I noted.

Alastair bared his teeth at me as Neil, who'd shed his jacket and top hat while we were working, tugged him out from behind the counter.

"It's time to wrap up anyway." Neil tossed us instructions as he manhandled Alastair out of the room. "Close it down. Fireworks start in fifteen minutes."

"Shoot," I muttered. If Neil wasn't back in time, I would have to find Dash on my own.

"Any idea where Dash and company went?" I asked my colleagues as we served the last few drinks, broke down, cleaned up and stowed our supplies for pickup after the show.

"Neil and I ran into them when we were out there earlier," Barclay said. "Raquel said she got special permission to watch the fireworks from the observation deck so she could take pictures, so that's where they were going. I guess she's a shutterbug."

"And a sponsor," I noted. So special permission probably wasn't a big deal for her. "Where's the observation deck?"

No one knew. I was going to have to find it myself. As we finished and the others nabbed the cocktails they'd made for themselves, I grabbed my bag and slung it over my head, cross-body, so it wouldn't get in my way.

"If you see Neil, tell him I went to find Dash, OK?" I told Melody.

"Neil will be disappointed," she teased.

"It's not like that!" I said. Dash wasn't my type. Hell, Neil wasn't, either, but there was something about his steady state that drew my chaotic nature. "Anyway, tell him, will you?"

"I'll make a point of finding him and telling him," Melody reassured me. "I wonder if the band is playing?"

She had big long sliding things on her mind.

I hugged my bag for comfort and headed out the door and into the colorful chaos of the terminal.

Chapter Twenty-Nine

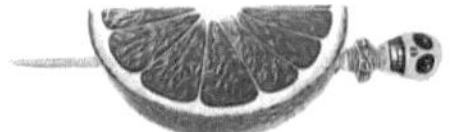

The hall was a mad mishmash of happy drunks. Most were ambulatory, but one or two obliterated ones were helped along by their snazzily dressed friends. Jazz swirled through the wide-open space of the two-story atrium. I could see the upper floor from where I stood, and there were no obvious doors there, only the ones on the lower level leading out to the runway.

A bored-looking security guard loitered at the edge of the room. Big guy. Arms crossed. His beer belly looked thirsty. I approached him with my most charming smile.

"Excuse me, sir? Can you tell me where the observation deck is?"

He scanned me up and down. "You're fluffy, aren't you?"

My smile flattened. "I don't know what you mean." Though my dress *was* pretty fluffy.

He shrugged. "Down that hall and to the right."

"Thanks." I turned away from him.

"But you can't get up there." I turned back to see him smiling at me with mild malevolence. "It's closed tonight. It's set up for a big wedding tomorrow."

"Oh, darn!" I lifted my hand and snapped my fingers sarcastically, if there were such a thing. "Thanks anyway."

"No problem, doll." He winked. "I'd like to fluff that," he muttered as I walked away.

I rolled my eyes and headed down the crowded hall anyway. There was a lot of activity at the end, in the restaurant that overlooked the runway, and I swam through a steady stream of people as I moved down the corridor, looking for a door.

Someone bumped into me. "Did you *find* him?"

I was so focused on my quest that the chirpy, drunken voice almost made me jump out of my shoes. I looked up into the face of Nicki, flanked by a couple of other bartenders from La Bonne Vie, all in their Gatsby best. Nicki's flapper-dress fringes fluttered as she leaned toward me. "I said, did you *find* him?"

I blinked. "Dash?"

"Who? No, Rob Tinker or whatever he's called. My asshole date you wanted to find. He's here."

"The guy who packaged the boomerang?"

"Duh. Yes. He pretended he didn't recognize me. Had some blonde hanging on his arm. But that's OK, isn't it, boys?"

"You're a doll, Nicki. You don't need him," one of the guys flanking her said, kissing her on the cheek.

"We'll take care of you," said the other, slightly more protectively. "Come on. I want to get to the fireworks. They're letting people go out on the runway side."

"Good luck," Nicki said to me with just a hint of sarcasm. "But I wouldn't waste my time with him."

"Yeah. Thanks," I replied absently, renewing my hunt for the door as they staggered off. My thoughts swirled like ice in a blender.

Some blonde hanging on his arm.

Raquel Tocks? Was she fraternizing with the staff?

Rob Tinker or whatever he's called.

A fake name. I clutched my bag, which was weirdly heavy. That's right. The books were still in there. *Robin Hood,* like the Reynolds boys used to read when they were kids, like I used to read.

The Tinker.

"Oh my God." I stopped right there in the hallway, fumbled my bag open and pulled out the book. I flipped through until I saw the chapter about the tinker that Robin hornswoggled. Then the classic movie with Errol Flynn came back to me. In that version, Robin Hood disguised himself as a tinker to win the archery contest.

Rob Tinker! Could it be?

I looked up and around and spotted the dimly lit side corridor. Double doors beckoned at the end. One was subtly propped open, not so it was noticeable, unless you were looking, as I was.

I stuffed the book back into the bag as I sprinted to the exit. I pushed the propped door open and let it close gently behind me so the tiny doorstop would keep it from closing and locking.

A staircase loomed over me. If Dash and Travis and Raquel and the goons were up there, I needed to be careful, especially if my suspicions were true.

I walked out to where the stairs ascended from the tarmac back toward the building and hesitated, taking in the expanse of runway in front of me. It was pretty much dark now, with the palest hint of orange at the horizon to the west. With flights halted for the fireworks display, the runway area, extending outward on a chunk of flat land that thrust into Lake Pontchartrain, was quiet. The only activity was the crowd gathering to my right, where people were spilling out of the center of the terminal building to watch the show in a roped-off area. Far to my left, a couple of shadowy figures at lakeside moved around with flashlights amid a cluster of boxy shapes on the ground. The fireworks, I assumed, ready to go.

As I started up the stairs, I began to hear angry voices. When I turned to take the second flight of steps, I ran into Raquel Tocks, her camera still slung over her shoulder. One of the goons—not the guy who worried me—hovered behind her.

"Oh!" I said with my usual eloquence. "I thought you were taking photos of the fireworks."

"I've given up. Brutus forgot my tripod."

"One of your guys picked up a tripod earlier."

"No, he didn't." She squinted at me, not looking nearly as cool as she did earlier, then looked up toward the sound of men arguing. "Besides, family quarrels bore me. You can have him."

"Who?"

"Either of them," she called over her shoulder as she went down, followed by Goon No. 2, and I went up, taking it slow until I emerged on the end of the observation deck.

The shadowy deck, lit only by the scattered lights of the airport, had a commanding view of the nearly dark runway. Chairs were lined up with an aisle in the center, ready for a wedding. The rows of chairs faced the three men clustered by an arbor at the other end, next to the railing that encircled the space. They were so involved in their argument, they didn't notice my arrival.

Travis was barking in Dash's face as Raquel's lackey looked on. "And when were you going to cut me in, Dash? How long do I have to work for you to be a real partner in the company?"

"This summer!" Dash looked overly warm, even in his light white jacket and matching hat. "The paperwork is almost done. You've proved yourself."

"Proved myself?" Travis laughed. "What did I have to prove? It's been more than *eight years.* We're cousins. You used to say I was the brother you never had."

"After we got out of school, you didn't act like a brother. You avoided coming home and having a real job for years, and I know what you were doing. How could I trust you? How could I just cut you in when—"

"Maybe because our fathers wanted it that way? *I know what you were doing,*" Travis mocked him. "Do you think I had any alternative? I didn't have money for school or to go find myself. I didn't have a dad to buy me a business."

"I—I guess I didn't think of it that way."

"Of course you didn't. You've always had blinders on." Travis shook his head. "Running drugs was easy compared with working for you, especially when you won't take my advice. You push drugs, too, you know. It just so happens that yours are legal."

Dash sighed in exasperation. "We sell alcohol, and maybe it's a drug, but it's also an art."

"It's not about art. It's about money, but you just don't get it. Like your stupid refusal to make vodka."

"Why are you bringing this up now?"

"Because it's over."

"What?" Dash looked stricken. "The partnership? You're important to the company, Travis. Don't leave."

"I'm not leaving. You are." Travis gestured to Goon No. 1, aka Brutus, who handed him the long, black bag. The tripod? "This is going to be fun," Travis said as he unzipped the bag.

Dash spotted me, his eyes catching mine just as Brutus grabbed ahold of his arms.

Travis must have caught Dash's glance, because he whirled to see what his cousin was looking at, tossing the empty black bag aside as he did so. Now he held a bow and a quiver full of arrows, which he slung over his shoulder.

"Damn," I murmured under my breath.

"Pepper," he said with a slithery smile, and the sound of his rough voice sent ice spiking down my spine. The charm was long gone.

"What are you doing, Travis?" I tried to sound cool. "Going to watch the fireworks?"

Just then, the whistle of the first mortar climbing into the sky pierced the night, and a dazzling explosion of light illuminated the runway and terminal, followed by a burst of shouts and applause below. My friends. Too far to help. And it was too loud for them to hear us yell, though Dash tried.

Brutus clapped a hand over Dash's mouth as the slim man struggled. The goon was huge. Dash didn't have a chance.

"Hold on to him," Travis ordered Brutus.

Then Travis advanced toward me.

"Pepper. How fortuitous. You've given me an idea," he said, that grin I'd thought so handsome flashing in what I now saw was a face hardened by anger. "I need some target practice. Got a lime you can put on your head, Pepper? Dash can watch before we convince him to take a flying leap. He'll enjoy watching us, I think. He has a thing for you, you know, but he's too chicken-shit to act on it."

Like I gave a rat's tail at the moment. Dash struggled futilely with Brutus behind Travis, who strolled down the aisle, notching an arrow against the bowstring as I took a step back.

"I thought eliminating you might push him over the edge, make him walk away even when nothing else did, but I just couldn't seem to get to you. You're a stubborn little bitch, aren't you?" He leered at me. "Too bad I don't have a hat you can borrow. I'm good at hitting hats. Dash told me about you two trying to track the one I picked up after the dinner. Hilarious. You two were so easy to confound."

"You shoot Dash, everyone will know it's you," I said, stepping back again, wanting to talk Travis down, somehow knowing I couldn't. The glint in his eye hinted at a well-developed madness—as if the bow and arrows weren't enough of a clue.

"But I'm not going to shoot Dash. I'm going to shoot a bunch of those people down there"—Travis waved casually over the railing at the crowd whooping at the next round of fireworks—"unless he fulfills his destiny and commits a tragic suicide by jumping over the conveniently low railing. Or we throw him over after breaking his neck. It doesn't matter, really. I just thought it would be so *neat,* that first he tries to kill everyone with bad whiskey, and then he takes out a few more with the bow and arrow before committing suicide. This whole week's been building up to this. The breaking of Dash Reynolds." Travis smirked.

"That makes no sense," I protested.

"It's perfect. Dash has proven himself quite breakable, you see. The good guy broken by failure. Mr. Straight Arrow. He always wanted to be King Richard while I was Robin Hood. Always had the fancy friends, never liked the crowd I ran with. Had a dad who gave a shit, even about me. Dash lived a sheltered life. You'd think my little cousin would be happy. But Dash is a depressive sort. There have been plenty of witnesses to that this week."

I swallowed, clutched my bag and backed up another step. "But you could be a partner. What do you get out of—of him—going away now?" I couldn't bring myself to say *dying.*

"Everything," Travis said simply. "That's how the will was written, under the trust created by my uncle. Dash's dad.

Preserving the family business meant everything to him. If my *dear cousin* had just walked away, the distillery would have gone to me, and I could have done with it what I liked. But I'm through waiting. Whether he leaves or dies, the distillery stays in the family. I get it all." He laughed. "I already have all the money."

"But what about Raquel?"

"What about her?"

"Is she helping you?"

"I hired Brutus to help me out. As for Raquel—everyone needs a backup. The distillery fails, it will make a nice condo. Hell, maybe I'll sell it right away. Real work has always bored me."

"No!" Dash managed to eke out before Brutus got him in a chokehold that scared the hell out of me.

"Everyone will know you did this," I told Travis as I backed toward the stairs. "I'll tell them!"

Travis lifted the bow and took aim. "Not if I kill you first."

Chapter Thirty

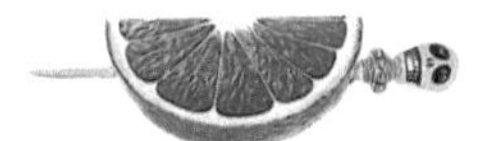

The arrow twanged past my ear as I ducked and ran for the stairs, gasping for air and sanity.

"Don't throw him over until I give you the signal!" Travis shouted to Brutus, giving me a few precious seconds. "I want to see him die!"

As he called out his orders, I practically flew to the bottom of the stairs and ran for the double doors that would get me back into the terminal.

"Fuggleduck," I muttered when I saw they were closed tight. A quick yank confirmed they were locked, and I had a split second to get out of this alcove before I was trapped with crazypants Robin Hood.

I broke into a sprint toward the open runway as Travis hit the pavement behind me. There was no cover, but it was fairly dark—at least until each blossom of sparks and color lit up the night with heart-pounding *booms*. And I probably stood out like a giant marshmallow in my fluffy white dress.

I darted toward the crowd outside the terminal steps, then realized Travis could easily take out a lot more people than me if I went that way. I swerved just as another arrow whizzed past me, then pivoted and ran the other way, toward where the fireworks were going off. There were a couple of buildings over yonder, and I dodged between a few small planes parked on the tarmac as I aimed for whatever cover I could find.

This was a brutal game. I wasn't much of a runner and wasn't exactly dressed for track and field. Every time a firework dazzled the airport, I was lit up like a Japanese lantern in my dress, so I ducked to the left or right to make it harder for Travis to hit me. At least he was hindered by running, though when I glanced back, I sometimes saw him stop and aim, a terrifying sight that made me take even more evasive maneuvers.

As I ran well beyond the cluster of small planes, my knees and feet were already screaming, and my tight bodice wasn't much help, either. Frankly, I was gasping for oxygen like a landed trout. I risked another look back at Travis, who was closing the distance as he left the airplanes behind him. Then I glanced up toward the observation deck and froze.

And screamed.

Two figures struggled there in the semidarkness. In a heart-stopping moment in which time seemed to grind to a halt, one figure tumbled over the edge and hurtled toward the ground.

And didn't move.

Dash. Oh, Dash.

"DAMN IT!" Travis had stopped, too, and shouted up at the deck. "I told you to *wait!*"

But his disappointment did nothing to deter him from resuming his chase. If anything, it egged him on. He roared, and despite his momentary pause, I felt him getting closer as I sprang forward, running flat out. I looked over my shoulder and saw him notching another arrow as he ran. He fired as I tried to pick up speed in my clunky saddle shoes.

"Ouch!" A sting zapped my leg like an angry hornet, prompting a stumble to my knees. I found my feet and took off again, shifting direction more often to make it harder for him. "It can't be that bad," I told myself, though the wound hurt like a lemon in a paper cut. "But if he got blood on this dress, I am going to be *pissed.*"

Maybe my thoughts weren't rational. But at this point, what was?

The fireworks guys seemed oblivious to the little drama approaching them, but I was far from oblivious to their barrage. My eyes hurt with the launch of each brilliant star-burst. My ears ached and my entire body trembled with the blasts as I zigged and zagged closer to their source.

Illuminated by the explosions and light-reflecting smoke, two men in hard hats wielding flares walked around clusters of crates filled with tubes, setting the rockets off.

Another arrow bounced off the pavement next to me. Just how many freaking arrows did Travis have, anyway?

"Hey!" I hollered to the fireworks crew, partly in warning, partly for aid. "Help!"

One of them looked up. And then he stiffened, wavering, gasping in pain.

I clutched my own chest in sympathy. "Oh, no." One of Travis's arrows had found its mark.

The man collapsed backward onto a particularly large cluster of unfired shells. His flare flew out of his hand and clat-tered into the middle of the stack. I could see an arrow sticking out of the man's shoulder—his chest? His neck? Would he live? I already blamed myself as I contemplated whether to keep running to the men or find another shelter.

It took only a split second for my choice to be made for me.

"Arnie!" the other man screamed, dropping his flare and grabbing his friend, pulling him off the pile of fireworks.

But even as his pal hauled Arnie away from the mortar rack, it was too late for anyone to grab the wounded man's flare. There was a sizzle and an initial fountain of sparks, followed by an earth-shaking, unraveling blast of light and noise and smoke. It was as if someone had declared war on Lakefront Airport. The rolling flare set off several fuses at once, and the fireworks set off one another, shattering the fireworks structure and shooting off like Mount Vesuvius on a bad day.

I didn't even have enough breath left to curse. Bits of flaming fireworks shot at me and around me. One burning pea-size chunk hit my glasses so hard it cracked a lens, so I thanked them for their service, tossed them over my shoulder and adopted a new course. Too bad. I really loved those rhinestones.

I veered away from the explosions, exhausted yet fueled by fright. Mortars shot past me, exploding against the pavement, flying toward the building, the runway, the screaming, fleeing spectators. One rocket tore into a small plane, which went up in a blast of fire. Sparks and acrid smoke obscured everything, and I choked on the foul air as I tried to get oriented. Each near miss roasted me with heat; the incessant, air-shaking concussions hammered my ears. Distantly, sirens blared. I almost didn't have a spare thought for Travis and his arrows, until another whizzed by my head.

Amid the din, I had the weird idea that someone much closer was shouting at me. And then, zooming out of the boiling smoke and sparks and flashes and darkness, an open golf cart hurtled toward me, its headlights barely penetrating the smoggy haze. A security woman drove it, and Neil, bless him, was in the passenger seat, leaning out the side, screaming my name.

"Neil!" My voice cracked, but I found a new burst of speed and headed for him as Travis's hysterical laughter cackled in my wake, a high-pitched counter-note to the cannon fire, the raucous swarm of fireworks toppling and exploding all at once.

Neil grabbed my hand and swung me up onto the back-facing seat, and I clung to the cart as it turned hard and wheeled away from the war zone, leaving Travis screaming *"Squirrel-fuckers!"* just behind us.

I held my breath as Travis paused, notched an arrow in the bow, drilled my eyes with his gaze and took aim.

Until a mortar blasted into him and he went up in flames.

Chapter Thirty-One

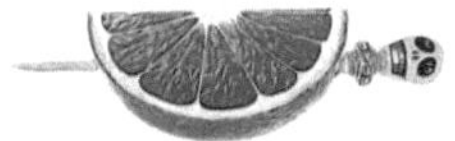

The image wouldn't leave me, though all I saw was darkness.

Travis running in his suit on the tarmac, waving his bow and arrow. Howling. Shouting. Completely mad. Taking aim at me, his eyes full of hatred. Then his body thrown back and incinerated all at once by a giant blast.

My smoke-seared eyes were closed as I lay on a stretcher next to an ambulance in the parking lot in front of the terminal building, chilling, willing my nerves to settle. I was fine, really. They'd patched up the cut on my leg. My throat was a little sore from the smoke. An eyebrow was a little singed.

There was chaos all around as those with injuries were treated and police combed the airport for would-be terrorists. The sounds were muted; my ears felt like they'd been in the front row of a metal concert. Neil had gone to check on our crew, so I'd accepted the offer of the stretcher and was trying to find a calm center again.

I ruminated over the craziness of the past few days. Travis manipulating everyone, playing the long game to scare off Dash. Hijacking the whiskey—probably after bribing the delivery driver to report mechanical trouble to explain the late arrival—and doctoring it and hiring Tuba Guy to "deliver" it again. Leaving Snaiquiri to go back to La Bonne Vie, lucking into the lost hat and arranging the boomerangs. "Losing" the hat at the cemetery to throw us off when he attacked with the arrows, later meeting Nicki for their date. Then hooking up with another fair-haired damsel the next night—Raquel, no doubt. Draining the distillery bank account. Hiring the goon to intimidate me. And if the goon gave the "tripod"/bow and arrows to Alastair to bring in before the event tonight, the bag wouldn't have gone through security.

I flexed the wrist wrapped in the makeshift shark-tooth bracelet, feeling weirdly lucky.

"I need a drink," I croaked to no one in particular.

A low chuckle greeted me, and I opened my eyes to see Neil hovering over me. He took my hand.

He mumbled something. Or at least it sounded like mumbling.

"What?"

He grinned. "You're a sight for sore eyes," he said, more loudly this time.

I looked down at my dress, ripped and soot-stained and speckled with a dash of crimson near my injured leg. "More like a sore sight for eyes."

"Do your eyes hurt? I can see them better now."

"They feel weird without the glasses."

He bent closer, soaking in my gaze. "They're kind of a misty green, aren't they?"

"Lichen," I eked out.

"I like them too." Was he teasing me?

He squeezed my hand. His gray eyes—shining a little—invited me for a swim in his deep thoughts. He barely looked ruffled in his formal wear. More to the point, he exuded a steady tranquility I couldn't help but envy.

I smiled. And then I frowned. "The bartenders?"

"They're good. There were no significant injuries outside of the ones you know about. Even the man shot with the arrow should pull through. Everyone's fine, more or less. Or will be."

I reluctantly released his hand and sat up, running fingers through my hair, brushing out ashes. "Except the Reynolds cousins."

"Dash is pretty shaken up, that's true."

"Dash?" I gazed at Neil in disbelief.

"He's the one who called 9-1-1. I happened to be out here with Alastair and the ambulance, and the radios all lit up. Just as they were issuing the dispatch, Dash called me. I grabbed security, and we came out to find you just as the real explosions started."

"And here I am." Dazed only began to describe my state at the moment. "Is he really OK?"

"Dash? I'll let him tell you."

And then there he was, Dash, walking up to us, rumpled and pale, his fair hair limp and half-falling into his eyes. A couple of cops stood nearby, keeping an eye on him. I had a feeling his night wasn't over.

I slipped off the cot, stood and gave him a hug. He held on tight. I could swear a tremble went through him.

"How—?" I asked after I'd released him.

"Brutus got sick of me struggling, I guess. He slammed me to the deck to take the fight out of me. My hat popped off, and while I was on my hands and knees, I had a second to pull out the knife."

"The *what?*" Neil's eyebrows were at full height.

"Pepper's knife. She lent it to me, stuck it in my hat. I never thought I'd use it." Dash looked at me. "Sorry. The police took it along with the hat. The knife was still in Brutus's chest when he toppled over the railing."

"You carry a *knife?*" Neil asked at the same time I said, "Holy shit." My campaign to tamp down my cursing was not going so well.

"A cocktail knife," I explained to Neil. "And that's fine," I told Dash. "I really don't want it back. And I'm sorry you had to use it."

Dash swallowed. "Travis ..."

"I know." I rubbed his arm. "You have a lot to straighten out now, don't you?"

"Yeah. The money he stole, for one thing. It'll probably be hung up in court for a while. And the police will wonder why your fingerprints are on the knife and why you gave it to me in the first place." He looked over at the cops, and one in plainclothes with a badge started walking toward us. Dash lowered his voice, and I leaned in to hear. "It's time for me to tell my story. And they very much want to talk to you, too. Tell the truth. Tell them about the cemetery. But if they don't ask about the whiskey, they don't need to know, do they?"

I pursed my lips and turned to Neil, who nodded at me almost imperceptibly. I wasn't sure why I felt like I had to get Neil's approval, but what Dash asked wasn't unreasonable. Travis was dead. The crime was done.

"I'll make sure Barnie's OK," Dash said, anticipating my next question. "He'll always have a job if he wants one. And I'll cover his medical expenses. I owe him that."

"Mr. Reynolds? We'd like you to come with us now," the detective said.

"Questions," Dash reassured me. "Nothing to worry about."

"Ms. Revelle?" The detective had turned to me. "Would you like to give your statement now or in the morning?"

"Now, I think."

"We'll take you downtown," the detective said.

Great.

"Here." Neil held up my fat gray canvas messenger bag. It had an arrow sticking out of it. "You might want this."

TURNS out *The Merry Adventures of Robin Hood* saved me from being punctured like a balloon. The detectives took the book, more out of curiosity than anything, but let me keep my bag. *The Savoy Cocktail Book* was unharmed.

That night, I told them what I knew, describing the cemetery attack, the threatening note, how I gave Dash the knife, Travis's final rant, and the statue guy who was really Brutus—who was definitely dead, though whether the knife or the fall had killed him wasn't clear yet. They never asked about the whiskey, which meant they hadn't heard the rumors. At least not yet. I figured they had more than enough wackiness to handle and ample motive and evidence to explain the deaths they were investigating.

From what I gathered from their questions and the little they would tell me, Raquel Tocks told the cops she knew the cousins casually and had only pursued the purchase of the distillery because Travis had suggested it was for sale. She knew nothing of Brutus's involvement.

Or so she said. She was a sly one, and I wanted nothing to do with her. But with her interests in Bohemia, I had no doubt we'd see her again.

By the time I'd taken a cab from the police station back to

the hotel, I was as flat as a club soda that'd been left out for three days. But at least I could hear a little better.

It was two thirty in the morning, and the hotel lobby was still buzzing with Cocktailians, no doubt excited about their wild night.

Me, not so much, though I was relieved that I didn't have to worry about a killer in my room. Probably. I had no doubt I'd be checking my closets for a while.

I hesitated a moment there amid the revelers, letting them swirl around me. A few glanced at me askance. OK, so I looked like I'd been shredded in a blender with bad tequila. I wasn't exactly fit for the bar, but I wondered if I should get a nightcap to help me sleep. As exhausted as I was, I dreaded the nightmares I was likely to have. That's if I got to sleep at all. And Tuba Guy, who'd had a full night playing with the band at the party, wasn't even honking outside. Weirdly, I would've welcomed that familiar lullaby tonight.

There was a buzzing in my bag, and I dug around until I found my phone.

A text from Neil: "You back yet? You still want that drink?"

"You read my mind," I texted back. "Bar?"

"Come up to my room. I've got the good stuff."

Oh, yeah. He had the good stuff. Only *he* was talking about liquor.

"Give me ten minutes," I replied. I stopped by my room first and doffed the ruined dress. I unwound the gator-tooth necklace from my wrist and set it on the bathroom counter, silently thanking it for whatever luck it had given me. Then I took a lightning-fast shower to wash off the grit and smoke, did a quick blow-dry and fluffed my hair.

A few minutes later, clad in pink jammy pants with martinis printed all over them and a soft black Nola T-shirt from my bar back home, I stepped across the hall and knocked on Neil's door. I guess I felt pretty comfortable with him if I was letting him see me in my comfy jammies, no makeup and no glasses, again. Being in danger tended to accelerate a friendship.

"Mmm, you smell good," he said as he let me in. He'd changed out of his formal wear, too, and wore gray pajama pants with white stripes and a white T-shirt.

"If I no longer smell like a firecracker, that's a good thing."

"But you're still a firecracker." He smiled and gestured to the end of the bed, which was made, of course. All very innocent.

Fine. I sat on the edge of the mattress, too tired for shenanigans, lacking the energy to throw myself at him. Although there was something about the way his T-shirt clung to him that perked up parts of me that should have been asleep. I swallowed and remembered I was thirsty. "What are you making?"

"I thought you could do with a French 75."

"Oh my gosh!" I clapped a hand over my mouth for a second. "You still haven't gotten there, have you?"

"Maybe we'll have time at the end of the day tomorrow," he said, measuring the ice, a very nice gin, simple syrup and lemon juice into a shaker as he spoke. "After the competition. Are you up for it?"

"The contest? I'll be there to cheer you on."

"No, I want you to do it with me. The competition, I mean," he added.

"Really?" I smiled at his clarification while he tucked the smaller tin upside-down into the larger one to form a seal and shook vigorously. "What about the rest of the team?"

He stopped shaking and gently unstuck the tins. "I've

agreed to lend the boys to Alastair since he hurt his hand. I texted Dash as a courtesy to make sure he didn't mind, and he texted back a few minutes ago that it would be OK."

"Is Dash done with the police, then?"

Holding the two tins together to control the flow, Neil poured the mixture from the shaker into two champagne flutes, filling them partway. "He said they would probably talk with him again, but they let him go for now."

"He must be heartbroken."

Neil nodded thoughtfully as he peeled the foil off a bottle of champagne and twisted the muselet to free the cork. "The little he told me earlier suggested he had regrets."

"What did he say?"

He held a towel over the cork as he worked it out of the bottle to prevent an explosion. Careful and professional, as always. There was a pleasant *pop*. "He wasn't sure whether he should have brought Travis fully into the company earlier or maybe somehow seen that he needed help, headed off the crisis."

"He shouldn't blame himself."

"I agree. Still, with what happened to Barnie and the harm Travis has done, he can't help feeling guilty. Guilt is something I understand."

"Oh?"

Neil only smiled and topped off the flutes with the champagne, then added lemon twists to each glass. He handed me a sparkling cocktail. "You still haven't told me whether you'd help me out in the competition tomorrow."

"Melody won't mind?" I didn't want to get on the wrong side of any of the bartenders. I liked this team too much.

"She thinks competitions are dumb. Plus she's trying to get out of her job at the hotel, and she doesn't want to bring glory to a bar program that thinks hot-pink frozen drinks are the height of mixology."

I laughed. "Then I'd love to."

"Great." Neil sat in the desk chair and raised his glass. "To surviving Cocktailia."

"Yeah. Had no idea how hard that would be." We gently clinked our glasses. I took a deep sip and closed my eyes as the fresh, bright lemon, the floral gin and the tangy-sweet champagne bubbles played over my tongue. The potion seeped into every cell at once, relaxing me as nothing had yet this evening. Except maybe being here with Neil.

Did I nod off there for a second?

When I opened my eyes, he caught them with a penetrating gaze. "Do you like it?" he asked softly.

"A lot." My voice came out almost as a whisper. He was working that magic over me again whether he knew it or not. I took another gulp to avoid saying more.

We drank silently for a couple of minutes, avoiding each other's eyes, as something like tension filled the room. Sexual tension. At least it was a welcome change from the tension of thinking about crazed killers and cops and ...

"Pepper?" Neil had finished his drink and sat next to me on the bed.

Deja vu. I shivered as he took my empty glass and set it next to his on the desk. He slipped a hand behind my head, pulled me close and kissed my neck.

Oh my gawd. The sizzle that shot across my skin was a hundred and eighty proof, and I swayed drunkenly as he wrapped his other arm around me, trailing kisses up to my jaw. Then he pressed his warm mouth against mine.

Ahhh. Heat and champagne and lemon. And intent. So much more than before. As his lips tasted me, he slid one hand up my back, under my shirt. He let out a soft moan when he felt nothing but smooth skin. I mean, heck, I wasn't going to wear a bra under my sleep shirt, was I?

I broke the kiss, and he looked at me in surprise. Then I scooched backward up the bed and beckoned to him. He crawled after me, and as I fell against the pillows, he nestled his hard body against my soft one, running one hand up my leg and hip and slipping it just under my shirt, caressing my belly, dangerously close to my breasts. Then he crushed his mouth against mine.

This was what I'd wanted. I floated on a cloud of citrus and champagne and desire and that intangible thing that was Neil. I didn't know why I was so crazy for him, but I couldn't deny it as I hooked one leg over his and opened my mouth to his tongue.

His body was so hard. The pillows were so soft. This was a really good bed. And I was *so* tired. I closed my eyes and drifted.

Kisses. Pillows. Was this just a dream?

"Pepper?" Neil's voice sounded far away. "Pepper? Poor little Pepper." Suddenly his arms weren't there, and I missed them, but the pillows welcomed me, and the blanket he tucked around me was so nice.

His chuckle followed me into darkness.

Chapter Thirty-Two

Sun hit my face. Warm. Strange.

I eased up on my elbows, blinking, completely disoriented.

Sunlight poured through the hotel window. I was still in bed. Neil's bed.

Neil stood by the desk, dressing. He already wore sharp gray pants and a crisp white shirt. He was donning a light gray vest, whose pocket sported a silky sapphire-blue handkerchief that matched his bow tie. The pop of color picked up the blue that rimmed his gray irises, and the morning light burnished his rusty hair with gold.

I might have let out a little whimper worthy of Astra the dog.

I hastily covered it with a question. "What time is it?"

He looked up from his vest-buttoning and smiled. "It's ten. I was about to wake you. The competition starts at noon. I want to be there by eleven to get everything ready. Want to meet me in a half hour for breakfast?"

He was all business.

And I was still in my jammies and didn't—well, I could tell I hadn't been out of them.

"What the hell happened?"

His eyes twinkled in amusement. "Last night? You fell asleep."

"I *what?* You *let* me fall asleep?"

Neil sighed and finished buttoning his vest. "It's not like I wanted you to. I've always been accused of being boring."

"Trust me, I was not bored." My face heated. "Oh, hell, I'm sorry."

He shook his head. He looked yummy again, and his smile didn't hurt. "You were exhausted. I was presumptuous."

"You were hot."

Now it was his turn to look embarrassed. "Maybe this isn't meant to be, Pepper."

I looked around for the nightstand clock and double-checked the time, trying to wake up. "I disagree, but we don't have time for this conversation now. Or for breakfast, now that I think about it."

"They have a buffet Sunday brunch today," he said. "It'll be quick."

"Oh."

He rolled up his sleeves to his elbows, revealing those sinewy arms. "Look, no pressure, OK? I have to check in with everyone, and if you feel like it, meet me for breakfast at ten thirty. And if not, then meet me in the ballroom at eleven."

His voice was even, and that cool demeanor was firmly back in place. Once again, I'd messed up my chances.

I managed a nod. He gifted me with a tiny wink, scooped up his wallet and phone and badge, and left the room.

"Poopsicles," I muttered, and I flew across the hall to get ready.

When I reached the hotel restaurant thirty-five minutes later wearing gray jeans, a scoopy white T-shirt, the leather necklace with the gator tooth, my black cat's-eye glasses and a gray pinstripe vest, there was no Neil to be found. Odd. I didn't think I'd ticked him off. It just wasn't like him not to be there. And I was starting to count on him being there.

I waited a few more minutes before rushing through the buffet. Restored by a pile of eggs and bacon and pancakes and two hastily downed cups of coffee, I made my way to the ballroom, absently rubbing the puncture in my messenger bag left by the arrow. I'd have to do something about that.

This was one of the smaller ballrooms, long and relatively narrow, lined with tall windows that faced the street. Mixologists were already setting up their ingredients behind a string of ten rectangular tables on one side of the room. Each was decorated with a white tablecloth, a bamboo cutting board, a full set of sponsor-branded bar tools, several glasses in whatever shape each bartender had requested, and a stack of tiny plastic cups bearing the Cocktailia logo. A banner hung from each table touting that team's featured liquor.

At the far end, a judges' table was set up with a white tablecloth, more flowers, and pitchers of water and glasses. Hydration was key at Cocktailia.

Bohemia Distillery's table was almost in the middle, two tables down from the Fairyland table, which featured Frilly Fairy Gin. There, Luke and Barclay were shooting each other arch glances as they took orders from Alastair, who was using his puffy bandaged hand to jab them whenever he was displeased.

Spectators had begun to wander in, filling the few rows of chairs that faced the bartenders. Melody waved at me as she slipped into the back row with a rumpled-looking but undeniably cute guy—the trombone player. And Mark Fairman and a few of his friends came in, too. This time, he only smiled at me.

A table behind the audience held a tiered display of bottles of the featured liquors. The booze nestled among lush floral arrangements and bowls filled with a bright assortment of oranges, limes and lemons. Smaller bowls featured other fruits and spices. There was also an array of small bottles of various bitters provided by another sponsor.

I strolled over to the boys. "Have you seen Neil?"

Barclay put down a lemon and a knife and shook his head. "No. I thought he'd be here a half hour ago. Hey, are you OK?" The soft warmth in his luminous, amber-flecked green eyes was almost more than I could take. I'd repressed the horrors of the previous evening, and sympathy only brought the bad memories out of hiding.

"I'm fine," I said brightly. At Barclay's questioning look, I added, "Or I will be. Neil wanted me to help him today, but I don't know where he went."

"Please, *gentlemen,*" Alastair interrupted in his crisp accent, which was almost as posh as his suit. He puffed to get his floppy boy-band bangs out of his eyes. "We have chopping to do."

"We've got this," Luke said, unperturbed. Then to me: "Neil left a recipe over there, I think. Holler if you need us."

"You are *mine* today," Alastair told him with a glower.

"You wish," Barclay muttered under his breath, and Luke and I laughed. But I took the hint, moved behind the tables to Bohemia's spot and set down my bag.

As promised, there was an index card face-down on the table behind the bottles of Bohemia Rye. I turned it over to find a recipe written out in small, neat capitals. It was from Neil's book, a variation on a recipe created by a Portland bartender, the Blonde Redhead. Neil credited that one in his book for inspiration but called his the Hot Blonde.

I looked it over, then went to the table to pick up a few oranges and, in a moment of inspiration, a cup of cloves and a bottle of chocolate bitters.

It was almost show time. Where was Neil? I checked the broken screen of my phone. No calls. The only text was from Melody from earlier this morning: "Girl, what the hell do you get up to when I'm not looking? See you at the competition."

I scanned the audience. Melody was making out with her guy. Great. I was somewhat surprised to see Dash slip into the back of the room. He gave me a wan smile and waved, but there was a question in his eyes when he didn't see our fearless leader.

I texted Neil. "Getting ready. Where are you?"

But he didn't answer, and he didn't appear. I was getting really worried, perhaps because of recent events, when a convention official appeared to start the competition—a tall, authoritative woman with a glistening afro and a purple pants suit that hugged her curves. She had a silver bell in her hand.

"Cocktailians, we have a special treat for you today," she announced. "Some of our best mixologists are competing to see who can make the best cocktail from our amazing sponsors' spirits. They have just thirty minutes to produce their cocktails. Now let me introduce the judges!"

To my dismay, the judges were not mixologists, bloggers, restaurateurs or enthusiasts. They consisted of a pretty entertainment reporter for a local TV station, a big guy who owned several car dealerships, a bigger football player, a semi-famous author (at least *he* probably knew how to drink), a bored-looking barely legal fashion magazine correspondent who would fit inside one of my pants legs, and the ubiquitous Raquel Tocks, who gave me an icy look before proceeding to ignore me.

Neil still hadn't arrived, so I sucked in a deep breath and steeled myself to mix my ass off.

"And go!" our hostess said, ringing her bell, and we were cutting and clinking and pouring and mixing and rattling shakers.

I opened a couple of bottles of the Bohemia Rye straight off, just to be sure I had enough. The Italian liqueur followed, the bittersweet Barolo Chinato, along with a really nice vermouth. Then I worked on the garnishes. In a few minutes, I'd created pretty orange-peel spirals studded with cloves that smelled fantastic.

I was just getting into the mixology, measuring enough to make two cocktails at a time, when I remembered what I forgot.

"Oh, crap. The ice!" I muttered. I looked around. No cooler. No fridge. When the competition started, hotel staff had brought out a big, clear bowl that was now filled with what we inelegantly called shit ice—sad ice machine cubes that been sitting around melting for a while. It mocked me from the table with the liquor. Not good enough, but unless I borrowed from someone else, it would have to do.

Just when I was about to hyperventilate, or worse, ask Alastair for help, Neil walked into the room carrying a cooler. I could have kissed him right there. Well, anywhere, really, but I controlled myself.

Right behind him was someone I never expected. My dad. Still dressed in his Sunday church suit, he nodded at me and smiled, then sat awkwardly in the back of the room.

I tried to speak as Neil came around to the table, but not much came out. "I—that's—"

"Your dad. I know. I ran into him in the lobby when I went to get the ice, and he insisted on buying me a cup of coffee around the corner. He wanted to know all about you, how you were doing. He felt bad about the other day. Then I realized I was running late, so I invited him up. How's it going?"

"Um, OK." I struggled to get over my shock. "I—thank you?"

"Least I could do after I railroaded you into seeing them," Neil said.

"No, you didn't." Well, he had, but that was OK. I shot my dad an answering smile, then dove into the work.

I caught Neil up, and between us, we used pretty faceted mixing glasses to stir together the ingredients, more than enough for six cocktails. Neil placed large, glistening ice cubes in seven sparkling rocks glasses, and in tandem, which made for a very pretty shot for the event photographer roaming the room, we poured the potion into the glasses. Synchronized mixology.

As Neil brushed the rims of the glasses with the insides of orange peels, setting free wonderful aromatics, I fingered the bottle of chocolate bitters, wondering if I should say anything. Finally I worked up the courage.

"Listen, I know this isn't in your original recipe—"

Neil discarded the orange peel pieces and quirked his mouth at me. "Yes?"

"But I was thinking these bitters might be a nice touch."

"I concur."

"You sure?"

"Of course!" he said. "I saw you had those and wished I'd thought of it myself. All recipes are works in progress, and I want our team to come up with twists, as it were. Makes us all better."

I smiled. I was part of the team. "We should test it first, though."

"That's why I made an extra." Neil pointed to the seventh glass. "Have at it."

I carefully used the eyedropper to add a few drops of the bitters to the glass. Then I gently placed one of the clove-studded garnishes in the glass. Normally we'd test a drink with a straw, but to get the full impact of the aromatics and the bitters, we needed to taste the complete cocktail.

Neil sipped first. His eyes rolled back, and his low moan made my lady parts want to do the rhumba.

I tried the drink next. "Yessss," I hissed, once I found words after my mouthgasm.

It was bittersweet. Complex. And I knew it would get better as the hunks of ice melted a bit. We exchanged a grin, and our eyes connected for a hot moment. Then the moment was gone as the noise of the crowd and the shout of "Five minutes!" popped our bubble.

We got back to work, garnishing the remaining six glasses and setting them on the edge of our table.

Despite some colorful English-flavored cursing from the Fairyland table, Barclay and Luke also were setting out their cocktails. That is, Alastair's cocktails. So were the rest of the teams as our hostess rang her bell.

"Time's up, and what a fabulous-looking lineup we have for you!" She waved at the chef-jacketed helpers, who swept by the tables with their trays to pick up and deliver the glasses to the judges' table at the end of the room.

The judges wore broad smiles now as they took in the array of liquid jewels before them, and then they started sipping.

"Now we have to make another batch," Neil said.

"What?"

"It was in the memo I got." He gestured to the plastic cups. "We have to put out a few samples for the crowd."

As the judges worked, so did we, whipping up enough of the mixture to fill a couple dozen of the small cups. We stirred the batch with ice first, since we couldn't put fat cubes in the little cups, and we twisted orange peels over them to add some of the aromatics the judges were getting through our more elaborate presentation. Miniaturizing cocktails for the hoi polloi was one of those things mixologists hated about cocktail competitions.

When we were done, we set the cups on the edge of the table and eyed the judges, who were nearly through their beverage bonbons.

"What do you think?" I asked Neil.

"I think it's always better to be first or last. You're either the first impression, or they're drunk."

I laughed. "Raquel didn't like ours."

"You saw that? What a face."

"I'm starting to think she never smiles."

"Maybe she's in mourning." Neil was always so understanding. For a moment I'd allowed myself to forget the horrors of the previous evening.

Our hostess rang her bell again.

"We need just a few minutes to tally the scores. I'd like to invite you all to come up and help yourself to a sample while we do the math!"

The crowd wasn't large, but when everyone rushed to the tables at once, it was a little overwhelming. Melody, who looked half-drunk from her makeout session at the back of the room, managed to slink her way to the front to pick up one of our Hot Blondes. Given her bedroom eyes, the drink could've been named for her.

"Where's your guy?" I asked, noticing the distinct lack of a trombonist on her arm.

"He had a gig. *C'est la vie.* Just two ships passing … blah blah blah." She took a sip. "Oh, *damn,* this is good. It will never win."

We laughed.

I noticed my dad didn't come up. He just sat at the back of the room, looking a little dazed.

The bell rang again, and the spectators shuffled back to their seats, cups in hand, as our hostess began the announcements.

"In third place, representing Bohemia Distillery's Bohemia Rye, the Bohemia Bartenders with the Hot Blonde!"

Neil and I looked at each other and laughed again. Melody was so right. But third wasn't bad. We gladly went up front to accept our medals—one each for us, and one to give to Dash.

We stood to the side as Fairyland Distillery won second place for its Frilly Fairy Gin concoction, a variation on a Bee's Knees. Alastair waved off Luke and Barclay and went up front to accept the award. They just shrugged, smiled and sipped their cocktails.

"I told you I'd beat you," Alastair purred as he took his place next to us.

"Revenge is a drink best served cold," Neil murmured back, and Alastair's eyes grew wide. So did mine. The retort was so unlike Neil, I had to chuckle.

The winner, unsurprisingly, was a bright blue vodka drink.

While Melody went to help Luke and Barclay clean up the Fairyland table, Neil and I began to pack up the Bohemia gear.

With a goon following her, Raquel Tocks shot us a sharp look on her way out, curling her lip in an expression of distaste.

Her teeth were blue.

Dash came over and shook hands with both of us, then

took his medal from Neil. "I don't know what I would have done without you this week. All of you." He touched the raised surface of the medal, and his brow wrinkled. "Or if I would have survived the week at all."

"Oh, Dash," I said. "I hope it all works out."

"We'll be happy to work with you anytime," Neil added. "How's Barnie?"

"Much better, though ..."

We knew what he meant. But Barnie seemed like the solid kind of guy who would transcend his new disability, especially with Dash's help.

"Anyway," Dash said, "thanks again. I'll take you all out for drinks tonight for a change, OK?"

"French 75 bar?" Neil and I both said at once.

A genuine smile lit up Dash's face. "Done. I'll text you later."

Neil's phone buzzed. "Excuse me," he said as he fished it from his pocket and stepped away from the table.

My father approached, his eyes bright. "This is quite the production. I really had no idea this is what you did," he said. "It's actually kind of neat."

I almost laughed at his astonishment.

"I'm sorry I didn't try your drink," he added.

He never was a drinker. But it almost felt like his apology wasn't just about the cocktail. I nodded. "It was nice—I mean, thank you for coming."

"I think I needed to, Kayanne." He held my gaze for a moment, then looked around at everyone loading up to leave. "Well, I'd better get back to your mother. We'll talk soon?"

I nodded, fighting an awkward impulse to cry. "Uh-huh," I managed. We exchanged a brief hug, and he left.

Getting ahold of myself, I resumed packing up our gear,

and members of the audience snatched what was left of the branded cocktail kits out from under our noses. I snuck looks at Neil, who was still on the phone. He ended the call just as I finished closing the last box, but he didn't move. Just stared out a window.

I went over to him. "You OK?"

He startled, then looked at me. "Um, fine. No. Maybe. Actually, I'm not sure."

"What was that about?"

"I got a phone call from my dad."

"Oh, no. Is everything OK at home?"

"It's hard to say, since we don't know all the details yet."

I raised an eyebrow. "Meaning?"

"Remember I told you about my grandfather?"

"The treasure hunter with a potential secret fortune and the antique dildo collection?"

A hint of a smile cracked Neil's serious mien for a moment, but only for a moment. "He's missing."

Acknowledgments

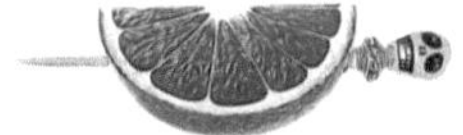

Risky Whiskey is entirely fictional, as is the Cocktailia cocktail convention. That said, the convention was partly inspired by Tales of the Cocktail, a signature New Orleans event I've attended as an aficionado and as a member of the media. The Hotel LeBeau is also fictional, as is La Bonne Vie and some of the novel's other venues. But there are a few real places in my book, including Latitude 29, famous for its fabulous tiki drinks. And don't miss the Hotel Monteleone's Carousel Bar or the French 75 Bar at Arnaud's if you visit the city.

Thanks so much to Eula Huffman for answering my random phone call and filling in the blanks in my knowledge of the layout of New Orleans's beautiful Lakefront Airport. That said, any inaccuracies (or, shall we say, liberties with reality) are entirely mine. The airport is an art deco masterpiece and is open to the public; I recommend a visit.

Thanks also to Jeanne Vidrine for clearing up a detail or two about the city and for the tour on our last visit. I've been to the city several times, including not long after Hurricane Katrina, when I interviewed survivors of the storm for a newspaper project. I came away with a huge respect and tender heart for the people of New Orleans. Even now, the streets bear the scars of the storm.

I really appreciate the support and friendship of my fellow

writers, especially Maria Geraci, Alethea Kontis, Naomi Bellina and Karen Ann Dell. Maria's early read of the book was immensely helpful.

Mahalo to George Jenkins of the Straw Hat Barmen for the bartender reality check. I also offer a toast to the savvy Holly Martin for her editing acumen and for a particularly good pun.

I wrote *Risky Whiskey* before the pandemic, and I was halfway through the second book when it took hold, changing our lives indefinitely. But, I hope, not forever. All of a sudden, I was writing a series about a time that seemed like science fiction, when people got together in large groups and had fun without a second thought. I had some real moments of doubt about continuing. But after some anguish, I decided we could all use an amusing escape from the harsh realities of the world. And in the Bohemia timeline, these books easily could take place in the before time ... or what I hope is the happier, "normal" after time. Let's all drink to that idea, shall we?

My final thanks go to you for reading *Risky Whiskey*. It's definitely a departure from my previous books, or at least the steamy romances of the Bohemia Beach Series, of which this book is a spinoff (in that series, Neil is a minor character, and Pepper appears briefly, though she isn't named). I have written mystery before—the standalone *Desire on Deadline* is, at its heart, a mystery.

I thought about launching this mystery series under a pen name, since it's so different from the romances, but I'm confident readers are smart enough to know what they like and figure out which books fit their tastes. If you love hot romance, then you might like the earlier series. If you prefer mysteries, stay tuned. *Wrecked by Rum* is on its way!

Lucy Lakestone

Cocktail Recipe

SAZERAC

There's no more quintessential New Orleans cocktail than the Sazerac. Sure, I think of the Vieux Carré, Pimm's Cup, Milk Punch (brandy or bourbon), French 75, Café Brulot. But this is my favorite. And it's quite simple to make once you have the ingredients.

INGREDIENTS

    1 sugar cube
    2 ounces rye whiskey
    1/2 ounce absinthe
    4 dashes Peychaud's Bitters
    piece of lemon peel

DIRECTIONS

First, you need a way to get your old-fashioned glass cold—stick it in the freezer for a bit, or pack it with ice and set it aside. And/or do as I prefer and prepare to serve this drink over one big ice sphere or cube.

In another old-fashioned glass, add the bitters to the sugar cube and muddle them together until the sugar cube is crushed. Add the rye whiskey (or bourbon, if you prefer) to this glass and stir until the sugar is dissolved.

Dump the packed ice from the first glass (if that's how you chilled it) and pour in the absinthe, rolling the glass around until the insides are coated. Discard what's left. Add a big ice cube or sphere (if you wish) and pour in the whiskey mixture. Twist your strip of lemon peel over the cocktail and drop it in. Serve and enjoy!

Next in the Bohemia Bartenders Mysteries...

WRECKED BY RUM

When rum collectors collide ...

When mixologist Pepper Revelle joins the Bohemia Bartenders for what promises to be an entertaining, rum-soaked tiki convention in sultry South Florida, she expects divine ukuleles, sublime swizzles and a chance to know chief bartender Neil a little better. What she gets is chaos — the death of a high-profile rum collector, a cast of sneaky suspects and ten thousand limes to squeeze.

With one of their own under suspicion, Pepper and Neil set out to find the real killer. But behind the aloha shirts and cocktail parasols is a blender full of secrets. The centerpiece of the convention is a high-dollar tasting of rums that survived a shipwreck and other disasters, and when a precious bottle vanishes from the crime scene, everyone with a ticket is a suspect.

As Pepper tries to keep the insatiable crowd inebriated and her gregarious dog Astra sober, she finds peril under every palm tree. It seems like everybody's guilty of something. But who's guilty of murder? And can she and Neil find the culprit before they're smacked like the mint in a Mai Tai?

Wrecked by Rum is the second book in the Bohemia

Bartenders Mysteries, funny whodunits with a dash of romance set in a convivial collective of cocktail lovers, eccentrics and mixologists. These cozy culinary comedies contain a hint of heat, a splash of cursing and shots of laughter, served over hand-carved ice.

GET A FREE BOHEMIA BARTENDERS STORY

Thanks for reading *Risky Whiskey!* Want a free story set in the Bohemia Bartenders world? In "Baffled by Bitters," Pepper, Neil and Astra the dog set out to learn the secret behind a discovery they've unearthed behind Pepper's bar. (Timewise, the story is set after *Risky Whiskey* and before *Wrecked by Rum,* but there are no spoilers!)

Sign up for my newsletter at LucyLakestone.com/signup to get the story, along with fun original content, giveaways, news and cocktail recipes.

I also have a Facebook group where readers can hang out and chat about books and life — please join us in Lucy's Lounge.

And you can always find me at LucyLakestone.com.

Books by Lucy Lakestone

BOHEMIA BARTENDERS MYSTERIES

These funny mysteries star Pepper Revelle and a team of mixologists who travel to colorful events where life is a cocktail of fun — until it's shaken into madcap mayhem ... and murder.

RISKY WHISKEY

BAFFLED BY BITTERS - *story free to subscribers*

WRECKED BY RUM

VEXED BY VODKA

JIGGERED BY GIN

BEGUILED BY BOURBON

SHOCKED BY CHAMPAGNE

WHY OH RYE?

SMOKED BY SCOTCH

BOHEMIA BARTENDERS COCKTAIL COLORING BOOK

COMET COVE MYSTERIES

SCOOP AND SCANDAL

PEN AND PERIL

The **BOHEMIA BEACH** Series

Award-winning hot contemporary romance

In a beautiful small city on Florida's east coast, artists meet, create, laugh and love. Where restless hearts are fueled by secrets and imagination, romance is impossible to resist. Welcome to the seductive tropical escape that's home to drama, humor and lots of heat – Bohemia Beach.

BOHEMIA BEACH

BOHEMIA LIGHT

BOHEMIA BLUES

BOHEMIA HEAT

BOHEMIA NIGHTS

BACK TO BOHEMIA - *story free to subscribers*

BOHEMIA BELLS

BOHEMIA CHILLS

Bohemia Beach Series Boxed Sets:

Books 1-3 | Books 4-7

The **STORM SEEKERS SERIES**

Writing as Chris Kridler

FUNNEL VISION

TORNADO PINBALL

ZAP BANG

Storm Seekers Series Boxed Set: Books 1-3

About the Author

Lucy Lakestone writes books that offer fun escapes, whether they're humorous mysteries, hot romances or storm-chasing adventures (as Chris Kridler). She loves sipping a classic cocktail and chasing tornadoes, but not at the same time. An award-winning author and photographer, she's also told stories as a journalist and video producer. She lives with her husband and two crazy dogs on Florida's Space Coast, which inspires many of the colorful settings in her books.

Learn more at LucyLakestone.com

facebook.com/lucylakestone

instagram.com/mslucylakestone

amazon.com/Lucy-Lakestone

bookbub.com/authors/lucy-lakestone

goodreads.com/lucylakestone

pinterest.com/lucylakestone

youtube.com/@lucylakestone

threads.com/@mslucylakestone

www.ingramcontent.com/pod-product-compliance
Lightning Source LLC
Chambersburg PA
CBHW060917190726
48286CB00002B/539